THE DEN OF THE BASILISK

A novel by Richard Parsons

Published by

MELROSE BOOKS

An Imprint of Melrose Press Limited
St Thomas Place, Ely
Cambridgeshire
CB7 4GG, UK
www.melrosebooks.co.uk

FIRST EDITION

Cover designed by Jeremy Kay

ISBN 978-1-907732-93-5

Printed and bound in Great Britain by:
TJ International Ltd, Padstow, Cornwall

MIX
Paper from
responsible sources
FSC® C013056

"The calf and the lion and the sheep shall abide together; and a little child shall lead them ...
And the weaned child shall thrust his hand into the den of the basilisk. They shall not hurt,
nor shall they kill in all my holy mountain."

Isaiah, Chapter 11

Basilisk: a fabulous reptile
Basilisk glance: the evil eye

1

"What does chef recommend today?" asked my host, as the maitre d'hotel hovered above us, flapping like a penguin.

"It is all good, Mr Molnar."

"Should be, at your price. But surely, Pierre, you can offer something specially delicious for my guest." Ludovic Molnar, I could see, was the type of successful business tycoon who enjoyed throwing his weight around. He would bully waiters unmercifully in that loud, confident voice.

"The rillettes de Tours are excellent."

"I'll have some of that then. What about you, Mr Bellingham? Pork pâté, you know."

As an experienced diplomat, I hardly needed coaching in French gastronomic terms. I might not have been born in Budapest like Molnar, but I had eaten my way across the Continent for the best part of half a century. However, I meekly accepted the implied suggestion. I was in no position to deploy the lofty hauteur which I reserve for rebuking the over forward. I needed this man at least as much as he needed me.

"And then the baked lamb with coriander," proclaimed Molnar. "Don't forget the redcurrant jelly."

"I'll take that too," I said. It was no moment to fuss about the menu. I was all agog to find out the reason for this mysterious invitation.

"We'll have a bottle of the Château Sauman 98, as usual," boomed Molnar. The Maitre d'hôtel bowed low as he withdrew. My host was obviously a regular luncher at this hugely prestigious restaurant where ordinary people thought themselves lucky to secure the little dark table under the stairs. We had a splendid place by the window, with a view over the gardens and the river. Two tables away, an American female film star was pecking moodily at raw carrots washed down with mineral water.

In my long years in the British Foreign Service, I had become used to eating at elegant restaurants and hobnobbing with grand people. But now I was sorely out of practice. Diplomacy was like show business. You left by the stage door. For the last three years, Susan and I had been living in rustic retirement in one of the remoter villages of East Anglia. Then suddenly, quite out of the blue, I had received this mysterious invitation to lunch in London with Ludovic Molnar, the well-known tycoon, much featured in the tabloid press.

"Why you?" asked Susan in her usual direct way. "Perhaps he's got the wrong man."

"The wrong man?!" I snapped. "Are you implying, my dear, that I am a lowly person unworthy of attention?"

"Well, nobody does bother about us much these days, do they?" It was only too true. Unlike so many of my more assertive colleagues, I had not received the accolade of knighthood. After nearly forty years of service, some of it in most unattractive spots, my dear wife and I had been compelled to retire as a plain Mister and Mrs. That carried a negative message in a still semi-feudal area like north Norfolk. I was not deemed locally to have been a worldly success.

I thought how we had all started out with high hopes in the Foreign Service so many years ago. And some of those hopes had been realised. Toby had ended in Washington, Launcelot in Paris. Whereas my final post had been Felicidad.

"Where on earth is that?" people would ask, rather rudely.

"It is the capital of the small, but strategically important, state of Concordia in Central America," I would counter coldly.

It was not quite the glittering career my dear mother and aunt had prophesied for me. This did not matter greatly to Susan, whose main interest had always been gardening. She had never cared much for Abroad, disliking the extravagant gestures and exaggerated shrieking of so many foreigners. I could not help wondering privately whether I might not have risen higher if she had put more energy into our entertaining and imparted a more international flavour to our menus. Tomato soup and mutton chops had not been quite the thing for Rome. But I did my best to dismiss such thoughts. I still loved Susan, her soft skin at fifty-two, her blue eyes and wistful smile – an English lady to her fingertips. She had settled placidly into the care of our herbaceous borders at the Old Rectory, Little Bigney. My own more vivacious mental powers had felt distinctly underused in this placid rural environment. I longed to cut my teeth again on issues larger than those presented by the parish council and the Amateur Dramatic Society.

So I had accepted Ludovic Molnar's unexpected invitation like a shot, travelling up to London in the last of my Savile Row suits and a rather smart blue silk tie picked up in the bazaar on a package holiday to Istanbul. And here I was, munching pâté, rolling claret round my taste buds and eyeing expectantly a host who gobbled his food as if he had not eaten for days. In the flesh, he was smaller than I had expected. But there was the stamp of authority in those dark eyes, that high forehead and those virile blue jowls which looked as if they needed shaving three times a day.

I could see he was appraising me, wondering perhaps if I had retained my vigour. So many of my colleagues had not. It was a great shock to the system to be cut off duty-free alcohol and an official driver. I saw some of them occasionally at memorial services and they looked a pretty seedy bunch, often needing a good haircut. Surely that could not be said about me, still in my early sixties and raring to go.

"I'll come straight to the point, Mr Bellingham," said Molnar. "You were Ambassador in Felicidad, weren't you?"

"Yes."

"And you know the ruling clique? President-Generalissimo Ignacio Raro and his wife Elvira?"

"Certainly. I used to play bridge with the President. And my wife was on Señora Raro's Ladies Committee for the Friends of the Botanical Gardens. They took it in turns to host the coffee mornings."

"Splendid. What about the chief of security, General Tiberio Golosina?"

"My regular golfing partner."

"Better still. I gather he had a reputation for using … shall we say … somewhat ruthless methods."

"Oh, indeed. He used to carry spare balls, so as to find them in the rough. He needed to. His swing could be erratic, especially after lunch."

"I mean … prisoners vanished from his cells, didn't they? And sometimes reappeared years later, rather the worse for wear. If they were lucky."

"It's Latin America, Mr Molnar. You can't use kid gloves if you're trying to keep a place like Concordia together."

Molnar nodded approvingly. I could see that I had struck the right note.

"I gather that the country is in turmoil," he said.

"It's always been like that," I replied. "Ever since the Spanish left in the nineteenth century. You've got the Tozudo minority in the interior, and the Nevera rebels along the coast."

"You probably know that, in recent months, efforts have been made to unite the illegal opposition. They have this charismatic leader holed up in the hills, Victor Fernandez."

"A pity he has taken up politics," I murmured. "In my time he was the only decent dentist in Felicidad."

"Do you keep in touch with Concordian affairs?" Molnar asked doubtfully. He certainly seemed to know more about current developments than I did.

"We get invited to their embassy in London from time to time," I replied defensively. "Hector Garcia, the Ambassador, is quite civilised, from an old Spanish colonial background, he claims. He's done a lot for that big residence in Belgrave Square. It's paid for with American aid money."

"Did you know, Mr Bellingham, that the Americans are having a rethink about Concordia?"

"I can't say I did. They used to bankroll the regime as a bulwark against communism. And also as a source of secret information in the fight against the drugs trade between Bogota and the States. The Raro Regime are helpful to American Intelligence."

"My friends in Washington are confused at the moment. They're starting to suspect that the Felicidad leg of the drugs trade is actually run by the Raro family. You seem surprised."

"My wife and I became rather fond of the Raros," I said. "She was always so beautifully dressed. And he was so generous with his hospitality. The most delicious Chilean wines."

"And this guy Golosina?"

"A thoroughly amusing companion. Though with a slightly grim sense of humour."

"I realise that it was your job as Ambassador to cultivate the powers-that-be. What about your old associates in the Foreign Office, here in London? I suppose they'll tag along with the Americans, as usual?"

"I'm too busy to keep in touch with the Foreign Office," I retorted. In fact I had not been invited to go near the place since my departure. Rather woundingly, Her Majesty's Government, though paying me a modest pension, had taken no steps to avail themselves of my expertise.

"Busy?" questioned my host, raising his eyebrows. "What with?"

"Local affairs," I countered enigmatically. The great thing about retirement is never to admit, even to yourself, that you are doing nothing.

"Then I'll tell you what they say about the Latin American side of the Foreign Office today," said Molnar. The fellow seemed a regular know-all. "It's in the grip of this woman Minister of State, Dame Rosy Clumber. A human rights fanatic. Greatly influenced by her husband, Trevor Pilkington QC, the high-profile crusader for the poor and the downtrodden all over the world. He's made a fortune out of free legal aid paid for by the British taxpayers. Mansions in Hampstead and Provence. Dame Rosy wants to abandon our traditional support for the Raro regime, and get rid of them damn quick."

"You seem to know a lot about it."

"I make it my business to find things out," riposted Molnar smugly. "You have to, if you're going to beat the competition."

"But why are you bothering to tell me?"

"You'll see. Now listen. This is a bad time for the Raros. They don't want to go the way of the Ceaucescus. There are no more cosy bolt-holes for failed tyrants. Poor old Ignacio would settle peacefully for a retirement home in Florida near a golf course, but his wife is determined to hang on in Concordia. She has expensive tastes, as you may remember, and needs access to … shall we say, official funds. Tiberio Golosina, of course, could never give up. He has too many enemies. Without his bodyguards, he'd be a dead man, anywhere in the world. So, between the two of them, Raro is under pressure to keep his regime going. That's not easy. They're facing these internal enemies. And an increasingly hostile attitude in Washington and the EU capitals."

"Very interesting, Mr Molnar, but I can't see what it has to do with me."

"You are an essential element in the equation, Mr Bellingham."

"Me?"

"Yes. As one of the few people in Britain with any love for Concordia. You do love Concordia, don't you?"

"Up to a point." I loved the blue hills, the highly coloured cockatoos, gin and tonics on the veranda in the dusk. I detested the mosquitoes, the snakes and the climate, and I was not too keen on the people.

"President Raro, your old friend, is in need of you."

"Maybe he is." It seemed most unlikely. "But I'm busy." I was not going to get involved in some do-gooding adventure at my time of life. My aim was to live a long time and draw my Foreign pension peacefully over the twilight years.

"It would be well worthwhile," said Molnar, smiling sardonically. "I'm making you a commercial offer."

A commercial offer! That was more like it. Come to think of it, a dubious figure like Molnar, from the mysterious world of high finance, was unlikely to involve himself in any form of human activity unrelated to money. This was a high priest of Mammon. I felt better already.

"Just tell me what you want me to do," I said, with one of my urbane smiles so often deployed in the past for charming the upper echelons.

"I am engaged on a project which will be of great value to the unhappy people of Concordia," said Molnar, unctuously wiping his big lips with a huge linen napkin. "It involves strengthening the armed forces of the country and especially the police. They are badly in need of fresh equipment."

"Arms?"

"We prefer not to use that word, Mr Bellingham. It has distinctly negative overtones. The expression currently used is 'defence equipment'. Concordia is hardly in a position to take up arms against anyone. Her enemies are all internal. What their government badly needs is material to control angry mobs, assassins, guerrillas fighters, that kind of scum. That's what I mean by helping the people. Law and order would be a splendid gift to them after all the chaos they have endured."

It was all clear now. Ludovic Molnar's interest in the unhappy land of Concordia was in the lucrative trade of arms dealing.

"Delicious claret, isn't it?" added the merchant of death. "98 was such a wonderful year for the Côtes de Bourg." He darted me a benevolent smile, giving him the demeanour of a basking crocodile.

"I have been working for a year on an extensive deal with the Government of Concordia," continued Molnar. "My English associates up in Lancashire – Wedmore and Bassenthwaite – have taken trouble to fulfil a complicated order for what one might call restraint items. We thought we had it in the bag, in spite of fierce competition from our unscrupulous French and American competitors. But now we have struck a tiresome snag. We have to apply for an export permit. That, as you know, is required for all transactions in this particular field. With it would go an exports credit guarantee, providing the financial backing of the British Government. But that wretched woman Dame Rosy Clumber is threatening to reject our application."

"How exceedingly tiresome."

"Tiresome, Mr Bellingham?! I should call that a distinct under-statement. If this Jezebel gets her way, the British Government will feel able to bask in the glow of righteous self-approval. But the contract will go to the perfidious French, thousands of jobs will be destroyed in Greyburn, and..."

"You will lose a large commission," I prompted.

"That too," admitted Molnar. "But we cannot allow that to happen. So all agree that we must take desperate steps. We wish to engage you as a consultant to our consortium. To manage relations with the governments involved and the whole public relations side. We want people, all over the world, to know about the positive aspects of the Raro regime."

"That won't be easy."

"You seem the ideal man for the assignment, Mr Bellingham. A professional diplomat of long experience, deeply versed in handling both the British Foreign Office and the people of Concordia, a personal friend of the Raro family and their cronies ... I mean, their entourage. Of course the remuneration will be in proportion to the stakes involved. It can be paid, for tax reasons, if you wish, into a numbered account in the Cayman Islands."

He mentioned a very considerable sum. And a generous expenses ceiling. Could I really be worth that to anyone? Over the years, the Personnel Department of the Foreign Office had done their best to lower my self-esteem, informing me that recent reports on my performance had been disquieting, that I was hard to place in another post, and that perhaps I might care to seek early retirement. In the end, it had been made abundantly clear that I was fortunate to receive, as my final assignment, the very modest position of Ambassador to Concordia – not exactly one of the plums of the service. And now this marvellously perceptive man, scooping up the remnants of his redcurrant jelly like a greedy child, was treating me as a jewel of rare price, to be coaxed and indulged because of my infinite expertise. I felt a delicious glow of satisfaction, not wholly caused by a conspicuous consumption of expensive claret. My heart warmed towards Ludovic Molnar – not perhaps a beautiful man but one with a generous soul.

"Will you take it on?" he asked simply. "There will be work for you here at first. And then you will need to go back to Felicidad to make sure that the Raros are still on course."

A tempting prospect. It would mean escaping from the windy Norfolk skies of Little Bigney with its parochial atmosphere and constant backbiting. I would be back in the great world of affairs, which I should never have had to leave. There would be a fresh spring in my walk, more lead in my pencil. And I should have a lot more money.

"Yes," I said, "I'll take it on." Little did I know!

Molnar leaned over the table and patted my hand in a rather un-English way. "Good man," he barked. "And now for the pudding. I do love puddings. Here they do the most delicious chocolate éclairs with far too much fresh cream."

I am partial to chocolate éclairs. God was in his Heaven; all was right with the world.

***

My euphoria slightly evaporated on the prolonged train journey back to King's Lynn – one of the most tedious in the Kingdom. As usual, there seemed to be an unexplained delay as men tapped the wheels near Cambridge. My stomach was beginning to rebel against our gargantuan, alcoholic luncheon. Susan's spartan fare was less taxing on the digestion. I was out of training for the finer things of life.

Ludovic Molnar had been devilishly persuasive. There was something mesmeric about those bushy eyebrows and that commanding stare. Had I been unwise to become involved in his dubious project? Did I really want to go back to that flyblown tropical backwater where the ungrateful Foreign Office had doomed me to spend the culminating years of my inglorious career? And what sort of welcome would I receive there? The Raros had been civil enough to us. But then people are usually polite to you when you are an ambassador, with access to British aid money. Would they bother about me now that I was a retired nonentity? At least I might still be addressed in Felicidad as 'Your Excellency', or, in the American style, as 'Mr Ambassador'. That was hardly the case in north Norfolk, where I had once heard the impertinent youth at the garage describing me to his rustic paramour as a boring old fart.

That was the one thing I missed about Concordia: the sheer dignity of representing a great nation. It might be a small pond – in fact one of the smallest in the world – but at least there I had been a big fish. That word had not sunk through to Little Bigney, where you were a county family or you were nothing. There had been several wounding episodes. We were not invited to the Lord Lieutenant's annual ball.

Since retirement I had turned to literature and had written a couple of plays on the Ibsen model about the horrors of domestic life. I had offered these to Admiral and Lady Harrison Bedford, the self-appointed big cheeses of our amateur dramatic society. My efforts had been returned with a brief note saying that something more modern and with more humour was required. But, if I wanted to perform, they might be able to cast me as the Widow Twankey in their Christmas production of *Aladdin*. I had not replied. After shaking hands with His Royal Highness the Duke of Edinburgh, who once refuelled in Felicidad at three o'clock on a Sunday morning, one does not appear as a pantomime dame. One got quite enough low life from the vulgar caterwauling of the O'Callaghans and their brood – a large semi-criminal family who unfortunately occupied the other half of our inadequately soundproofed Old Rectory.

On reflection, it would be decidedly agreeable to escape from Little Bigney. Would Susan be willing to accompany me to Felicidad? That was far from certain. We would presumably be able to stay at the 'residence'. Our successors, Gerald and Monica Haverstock-Jones, a colourless couple, could hardly refuse to put us up. I naturally hoped that Susan would come. I was used to her, and I needed her in all sorts of small ways. She was the one to take care of the tickets, the passports and the house keys.

On the other hand, I could not help thinking with a certain frisson what it would be like to wander around Felicidad at night, solitary and incognito. There were certain notorious waterfront bars which no ambassador could ever be seen to enter. It would be a different matter if one was a private person, almost a tourist. And why not? There was life in me yet, and I might as well enjoy my last declining years before becoming banged up in sheltered accommodation. These thoughts occupied my mind as we pottered through the dreary fenland between Ely and Downham Market. I had a momentary vision of the great surf rollers crashing on the beaches of the blue Caribbean; the graceful royal palms in the elegant garden of the British Ambassador; and the cheerful, smiling faces of the country girls as they brought their sun-kissed melons to market. And then there was always the money.

Susan met me at the station. She is a good wife but she does have the tiresome habit of thinking that her activities are more important than mine. I always have to hear about her day first before she is willing to listen to my report.

"Bad news," she cried, executing a somewhat frisky turn as we swept out of the station car park. Susan was trained at her convent school to take everything on the chin, so she sounded quite upbeat about the bad news.

"The O'Callaghans are giving a party?" I suggested.

"Not that. But I'm afraid Lady Moggeridge is being rather silly about the church fête. She's desperately anxious to make it high profile this year. They need money so badly for repairing the church roof."

"I've already told the woman," I snapped, "I'm willing to open the function."

"That's the point, Dear. She's got someone else."

"Someone else?"

"A girl called Tracy Snodgrass."

"Never heard of her."

"Apparently she plays the kid sister in one of those soaps on the telly. They have an audience of ten million viewers."

"So I am turned down," I commented ominously, "for a junior Miss."

"It's not like that, Darling. But as Lady Moggeridge pointed out, the village have heard all your jokes before. Several times. And this time they want a real celebrity to attract the crowds."

"Some chit of a girl one has never heard of."

"Everyone else has, Dear. Lady Moggeridge says they will be running special buses from Norwich and King's Lynn. It's quite a coup for the committee."

"I am the Duchess of Malfi still," I announced. Susan did not appear to understand the literary allusion, so I relapsed into the dignified silence which Susan unjustly describes as my massive capacity for sulking. My patience was sometimes near the snapping point these days. I needed scope, variety, challenge, something to live for. In short, an adventure.

Later, over our nightly drink, I told Susan about the incredible offer I had received. She took it with her customary sangfroid.

"That's nice, Dear," she said calmly.

"Nice?! It's a fantastic breakthrough!"

"I'm glad you're pleased."

"We shall be based in London for a time. And then off again to dear old Felicidad."

"You mean I'm invited too?"

"I couldn't manage without you, Darling."

"It's good to hear that, Ambrose. But you know I can't leave the garden at this time of year. There's too much work with the dahlias. Besides, I must be available for Neville."

"Neville! The boy was thirty-six in February."

"He still needs me, Dear. They always do. And we were abroad for so long. That may be why he has turned out ... the way he has."

Neville, our only child, was the apple of his mother's eye. But not of mine. Since Susan is a Roman Catholic, I had been persuaded by her mother, a brigadier's widow of commanding presence, to send him to a fashionable Catholic boarding school in the north of England. I had hoped that the Benedictine monks of Calderbeck would instill in him respect for traditional values. The reverse had happened. Neville had developed into a professional activist. He was against nuclear power, the class system, private medicine, field sports and, above all, the British Foreign Service. One never saw a picture of a rioting mob these days without looking out for the familiar features of our beloved son. He had never held down a proper job and consequently lived in considerable squalor in a squat in Stoke Newington, propped up by the occasional surreptitious dole from his doting female parent. We had hoped that things would improve when he took up with a sluttish young woman called Sharon. But not at all. Her interests apparently revolved around the re-greening of the planet, her speciality being to ensconce herself in tall trees to prevent the construction of much-needed bypasses through areas of remote woodland.

When they are feeling unusually destitute, Neville and Sharon tend to pay us unannounced and lengthy visits. These are only moderately enjoyable for either side, since the opportunities for friction are numerous. They give pointedly disapproving glances when I light up my pipe. They snigger when I happen to mention our more distinguished friends. And Sharon leaves unspeakable things in the bathroom. I could not think why anyone should want to remain in England in order to be near Neville. Rather the contrary.

"Very well, Susan. Stay here if you must. But I'll have to go alone if necessary. There's a lot of money at stake."

"It will be nice to have money," replied Susan pensively. "I should so love a nice big greenhouse for the winter bedding."

"I shall miss you, Darling."

"Of course you will, Ambrose. You're a great booby and quite unable to do anything for yourself."

***

I had proposed to Molnar that for the opening phase of my assignment I should position myself, at his expense, in some respectable hotel like Claridges or the Ritz. This would give me ready access to the opinion moulders I was seeking to influence: cabinet ministers, minor royals, tabloid editors – the highest in the land. But Molnar did not seem at all keen.

"As you advance further in the defence procurement business, my dear Ambrose – I may call you that, may I not? – you will find that we practitioners have to be very careful. There is much prejudice against our useful and necessary trade. In public estimation, we rank somewhere between professional burglars and house agents. So one has to watch one's lifestyle. No conspicuous flaunting of the expense account, please. Do you not have some discreet gentlemen's club where you could stay in London?"

I had indeed been a member, for years, of the dear old Voyagers in Pall Mall – an excellent spot for nobbling the members of the Senior Promotions Board in the Foreign Office and reminding them of my continued existence. But now the place was infested with former spies masquerading as retired diplomats, all with elaborate cover stories to explain why they had never become an ambassador. Moreover, I had no great desire to encounter my more fortunate contemporaries, oozing with the distinction of their knighthoods, their great embassies and, since retirement, their lucrative non-executive directorships.

"What are you up to now, Ambrose?" they would enquire dismissively, not staying for the answer, as if I were some low creature brought in by the cat from the garden. Susan says I have a chip on my shoulder. No wonder! I have been cold-shouldered so often.

I had intended to transfer to the Sheridan Club in the West End – a more jovial institution altogether, haunted by boozy television commentators and retired actors of the old school who had married money. I had been seven years on the waiting list for the Sheridan but, for some reason, my name had not yet come up. I had therefore not yet been able to sever my links with the Voyagers, in which I now divided my time between a small attic bedroom and the basement bar beloved by the more loquacious of the secret agents.

Although Molnar advised against spectacular consumption, this did not seem to impinge on his own affluent mode of living. Molnar House might be situated in a small cul-de-sac in Saint-James's, with only a discreet polished plate on the front door, but there were two floors of beautifully furnished offices and a large penthouse on the top overlooking Green Park, where Molnar himself resided with a small harem of resident mistresses and, some alleged, the odd boy.

We were seated in his office now – four men with a common purpose, though unlike each other in appearance. Ludovic, as I was now encouraged to call him, sat behind his vast desk, munching a succulent cream bun and intermittently picking his nose when he thought we were not looking. On his home ground he looked inexplicably larger – a sort of miniature Mussolini. I myself am generously proportioned with the features, though not the vocal chords, of a Wagnerian tenor; and a distinguished mane of grey hair, which I get cut in town at Humpers.

Selby Tritton, the MP, was tall and thin with a throbbing Adam's apple when excited, as television viewers will remember. He was a favourite on the less exacting kind of political discussion programme. Like many other politicians, he had developed the sincere, innocent manner of the inherently corrupt. The Concordian Ambassador, Hector Garcia, was a tiny man with the elfin looks and mischievous eyes of a slightly demented gnome.

"I am grateful to you all for sparing me some of your valuable time, gentlemen," began Ludo, with his usual central European courtesy. "I have been fortunate to assemble here such a wealth of talent and knowledge. We have one thing in common. We are all friends of the beautiful but unhappy country of Concordia. You, Mr Ambassador, are a valued member of the Diplomatic Corps in London, and expert exponent of the great historical traditions of your country. I refer of course to its fine Spanish and European heritage." One could but admire Ludo's skill at playing on that delicate and universal instrument: human vanity and capacity for self-delusion. Hector claimed to descend from a noble Spanish family located in the sixteenth century in the old city of Caceres in Estremadura. Like other members of the upper class in Concordia, he liked to think of himself as wholly European, with no admixture of Indian or African blood. I suspected that he fooled nobody other than himself. The Spanish conquistadors like Cortes and Pizarro were mostly cowherds at the start.

"In my dear friend Selby Tritton," continued Ludovic with a benevolent smile, "we have the chairman of the recently formed Anglo-Concordian parliamentary group, and one of the great stars of the present parliament. It can only be a question of time before he attains ministerial office." I doubted that. Tritton had only been in the House for three years but he was already looking like one of nature's permanent backbenchers despite the proddings of his ambitious and silly wife, whom I had also met at the Concordian Embassy. I strongly suspected that Selby was on Ludovic's payroll and I doubted whether he had declared this publicly, as MPs were now supposed to do. He might have the upright manner of an unworldly archdeacon, but rumour placed him at the sleazier end of British politics.

"Finally," added Ludo, "we have been lucky enough to recruit His Excellency Mr Ambrose Bellingham, whom we all know as Her Britannic Majesty's highly successful Ambassador Extraordinary and Plenipotentiary in Felicidad, marking the apogee of his distinguished career in the British Diplomatic Service." It seemed right to give a little bow, and indeed I did feel an inner glow. The whole procedure seemed laboured and un-English, but one had to remember that Ludo had been born in a remote village on the shores of Lake Balaton. At least he knew how to address a senior diplomat.

He went on to summarise what he had already told me: the desperate need to sustain the Raro regime and prevent the whole area relapsing into chaos; and hence the immense importance of removing all obstacles to the early conclusion of the advantageous defence equipment deal offered by the fine old British firm of Wedmore and Bassenthwaite. We knew that there was now some opposition to that in Western government circles. This had to be overcome by showing European and North American public opinion the positive aspects of the present democratic and Christian government in Concordia. Selby had already started this process in an eloquent speech in a foreign affairs debate and a couple of sharp questions to the Foreign Secretary. The vital point was to rebut the allegation that Concordia was a brutal dictatorship, liable to use any equipment supplied to suppress its innocent people. This absurd misconception, fostered by the human rights lobby, was best removed by encouraging citizens of developed countries to see for themselves the problems encountered by President Raro and his dedicated team. Ludovic sat back, took another bite of bun, and waved his hand encouragingly towards the rest of the little meeting.

"I'm making good progress," said Selby Tritton, "with the plans for a goodwill visit to Felicidad fairly soon by my parliamentary group. The Whips have already sanctioned the expenditure from public funds. We had a bit of trouble at first getting volunteers. Members were nervous about how it might look in their constituencies. Long ago, fellows used to get into trouble for sucking up to Hitler and Stalin. But once old Buffy Templeton signed on there was quite a rush to get onto the bandwagon. Now we've mobilised all the usual suspects. People like Valery Ship-Godwin will go anywhere for a freebie."

"These are important politicians, I hope?" asked Ludo rather doubtfully. "Opinion moulders, movers and shakers?"

Selby gave a cynical grin. "Of course," he said simply.

"I have been in touch with the Foreign Ministry in Felicidad," interposed the Ambassador, "about the programme for the parliamentary group. It will be at the highest level. They will take tea with the President himself. His wife will accompany them in person on a visit to the Motherless Babies Home. There will be a special demonstration of folk dancing and Tozudo drumming. We are also arranging excursions to the new cement factory, the anthracite mines, and the yellow fever treatment facility."

"If I know my fellow members," said Selby, "they will also need plenty of swimming, free cocktails, nightclubs, dancing girls and all that."

"Naturally," said Hector gravely. "That goes without saying. Those diversions are included under the heading of optional recreations. In Concordia we want everyone to be happy. The right kind of person, I mean."

"What about General Golosina?" asked Ludovic. "Is he going to be let loose on our British MPs?"

"We have thought carefully about that," replied Hector imperturbably. "I suppose they ought to meet him. After all, his forces will be using the new British equipment. But he does have a rather … shall we say … rugged appearance. And, after lunch, he can de decidedly frank about our penal system. On balance, I have recommended that he should somehow be called away to the interior at the time of the visit."

"Very prudent," agreed Selby Tritton. "My colleagues should be given a simple, clear impression, with nothing to confuse their tiny minds."

"I also hear," added Hector, "that Connoisseur Travel are planning a visit to Concordia to study ancient Nevera sites. It's a specialised firm. They appeal to highly cultivated cognoscenti."

"This all sounds most promising," commented our host, "but we must also have an exchange of elites in the opposite direction. We in Britain are eager to enjoy whatever Concordia has to offer."

"That presents certain problems," said the Ambassador evasively. "Our athletes were all disqualified at the last Olympics for taking drugs. And one of our best poets is under restraint at the moment for publishing offensive verses about the President's mother-in-law. But we do have the Felicidad Opera Company. I am trying to arrange for them to give a short season at Sadler's Wells."

"Oh, good," I said. "What will they be performing?"

"*Carmen*, and *Madam Butterfly*."

"Those are quite well known here already," I pointed out.

"They are the only pieces in their repertoire," replied Hector. "We could, of course, offer the Concordia State Folklore Troupe. But three hours or more of non-stop drumming, harping and conchblowing can be monotonous. And I do want to get away from the image of my country as a primitive backwater inhabited by quaint natives."

"What we really need," opined Ludovic, "is a state visit by President Raro and his lady."

"Those are planned years in advance," said Selby sadly, "though I suppose they could make an official visit, which is the same thing but without the trimmings. That could be highly effective, so long as we got the police to lock up potential demonstrators, as they did for the Chinese. President Raro hardly looks like a cruel tyrant, as portrayed by the human rights industry. And his lady absolutely oozes charm. She's terribly good at orphanages and the whole Princess Diana circuit."

"I've tried all that," said the Ambassador mournfully. "We so badly need television coverage. That's all people care about these days. But the British Foreign Office won't hear of a visit by the Raros. The Foreign Secretary isn't at all interested in our poor little country. So he leaves the decisions about us to that awful woman Dame Rosy Clumber. As we all realise, she has completely swallowed those wretched allegations by our enemies."

"Rosy Clumber is known in political circles as a bear of little brain," commented Selby Tritton. "Her QC husband is the driving force behind that gruesome twosome. She only got into the House on one of those all-female shortlists set up by the party. Political correctness run mad."

"But, my dear Selby," said Ludovic with the freedom of a paymaster, "I thought you were elected to parliament on a highly restricted shortlist yourself." Selby had the grace to blush.

"It was an all-disabled list," he admitted reluctantly. "There was a strong feeling that we innocent victims of the divine caprice were under-represented in Parliament."

"But you aren't disabled, Selby," protested Ludo unmercifully. "You look as fit as a flea."

"I suffer from acute tinnitus," said Selby. "A horrible ringing in my left ear. That means I can't bear silence. When I'm at home, my wife has to keep talking the whole time. Except when I am playing my Wagner tapes at high decibel."

I shuddered. The home life of the Trittons sounded unspeakable. And that of their neighbours too.

"I am not prepared to be foiled by this woman," said Ludovic menacingly. "We must find some way to bypass her. Now come on, dear Ambassador, I'm sure you have some secret weapon."

"As a matter of fact I do," replied Hector with an impish grin. "Young Raro himself. Thirteen year old Dominic, the only child of President and Señora Raro. His father's pride and the apple of his mother's eye. They want to send the lad to school in England. For security reasons. He wouldn't be safe in Concordia or the States. The Nevera rebels, you know, and their diabolical suicide squads."

"That's a good idea," said Selby. "Once the little fellow is installed here, it will be a perfect opportunity for his loving parents to visit him at half-term."

"It must be a Roman Catholic school though," added the Ambassador. "Señora Raro is very religious, in a rather old-fashioned way, and has a horror of her precious boy falling into heretical hands."

"I know the very thing," I interjected. "There is a fine school at Calderbeck Abbey in the north-west of England, kept by kindly and learned Discalced Benedictine monks. My own son has been there."

"And that was a success?" asked Ludovic.

"He has developed," I countered enigmatically, "into a remark-able young man. The headmaster, Father Manfred, is an old friend of mine. I should be happy to supply a personal introduction."

"That sounds most helpful," said Hector. "We must certainly follow up your excellent idea with some urgency."

I had a dim memory of the dictator's son. In my time in Felicidad, he had been a lumpish pre-pubescent child, given to simple pleas-ures like spearing beetles with hot needles and pulling the wings off butterflies. But no doubt he had evolved. The Benedictines had centuries of experience in coping with wayward youths.

"You'd better get up there quickly, Ambrose," said Ludo deci-sively. "Soften up that old monk with a dose of your devastating charm. That has always been my method."

"Discalced Benedictines, you say," interjected Selby. "That sounds very painful."

"It only means they go barefoot. Nowadays they wear sandals."

When the Ambassador and the Member of Parliament – busy people – got up to leave, Ludovic detained me almost peremptorily. I was beginning to discover that once you appeared on his payroll, he considered that he had bought you, body and soul. Well, I suppose he had.

"Listen to this, Ambrose," he said, waving a plump paw to indicate that I should be seated again. He started reading from a typed paper he had before him. "You have been selected as one of the lucky people qualified to win a prize of up to a million pounds, which will be awarded following our forthcoming prize draw. Hearty congratulations! In order to join the list of eligible contestants, all you have to do is to sign the attached form and write in your credit card number so that the necessary sum of thirty-nine pounds ninety-nine may be deducted to cover administrative expenses. Do not delay. Winning a prize could bring you a couple of free tickets to travel to Concordia (Jacquaranda class from Miami on Concordian Airlines) with seven nights at the Waving Palms Hotel in Felicidad and a personal interview with President Raro, the famous Concordian statesman. Send your forms now to me, Ludovic Molnar, European representative of the Felicidad Bank of the Holy Spirit." Ludo gasped for air.

"It sounds as if you were giving away money."

"Exactly, my dear Ambrose. You've got it in one. But kindly note the qualifications. I've had my lawyers run through the text with a fine toothcomb. You may be qualified to win a prize. But it doesn't follow that you will. Up to one million pounds means that you won't win more than that. You might win a great deal less. Following, the draw doesn't say when. Then, winning a prize could bring you a free holiday. But then again, it might not. Meanwhile, they cough up their forty pounds. We need to build up a war chest."

"When you explain it like that," I said with dignity, "it seems to be sharp practice."

"Don't become censorious, Ambrose. We're not cushioned by the British taxpayers now, you know. Welcome to the jungle of the private sector, the cut and thrust of the market."

He gave a self-satisfied chuckle. I felt he had informed me of his shady methods on purpose, in order to make me an accomplice and shake me out of my Foreign Office complacency. Had I been entirely wise to become involved in activities of such doubtful propriety? But it was too late to withdraw now.

"I'm sending you up to Greyburn this week," he continued. "I want you to observe Wedmore and Bassenthwaite in action. It's essential for you to see for yourself the high quality of their workmanship. And also how much it means for employment in their entire locality. You'll enjoy meeting their Mr Atkinson: a genuine, down-to-earth Lancastrian. He's got his head well screwed on."

That has always seemed to me a singularly ridiculous phrase. Has one ever met anyone who didn't have their head firmly screwed on? Heads do not just drop off for no reason. However, in my new role as a thrusting business operator, I simply indicated assent.

"I could go on from there to Calderbeck Abbey," I suggested. "It's not far away."

"Good idea, Ambrose. I can see we've got a winner in you. Don't worry about my rough ways. I'm doing all this to give stability to the poor people of Concordia, and employment to the poor people of Britain. I'm a man of the people myself, and I desperately want to help them. You do realise that, don't you?"

"Of course, Ludovic," I replied with my customary urbanity. I tried not to flinch when he patted me on the knee.

***

Greyburn turned out to be a rather grim one-company town, dominated by the industrial works of Wedmore and Bassenthwaite. I gained an impression of wide, windy streets flanked by redbrick Victorian buildings of great solidity, and statues of local worthies.

The managing director, Greg Atkinson, met me at the station and gave me a warm, indeed an anxious, welcome. He had clearly been briefed about my significance in the scheme of things. After all my petty humiliations in the dreary hinterland of East Anglia, it was gratifying to be treated as a person of consequence once again. I warmed rapidly towards Mr Atkinson – a jovial northerner with a no-nonsense manner. A merchant of death perhaps, but also a kindly family man.

"Which would you prefer, Mr Bellingham?" he asked. "A tour of the works or a stiff gin and tonic followed by a slap-up lunch in our senior management entertainment facility."

"Since you ask me," I replied decisively, "I should prefer the gin and tonic followed by the slap-up lunch." After all, there were only so many lunches in a lifetime.

The meal was certainly solid, consisting of pea soup, beef and Yorkshire pudding, and what Mr Atkinson described as plum duff, washed down by an immensely heavy Rioja. Northern hospitality might be genuine but it was certainly a strain on the digestion. My years in Felicidad and then in retirement had accustomed me to that admirable Hispanic habit: the afternoon siesta. I felt decidedly woozy as my host and his senior colleagues treated me to a prolonged account of the history of their famous firm. It was a sad one, typical of Britain's industrial decline.

Once they had made magnificent guns for the Royal Navy, efficient mortars and grenades for the crack regiments of the British Army, and helpful bombs for the Royal Air Force. They had been an essential element in our rough island story. With products from Wedmore and Bassenthwaite, Wellington had thrashed the French in the Peninsular, the Light Brigade had charged on the doomed field of Balaclava, and dissident tribesmen had been taught a grim lesson on the North-West Frontier. Wedmore and Bassenthwaite had also played their part in curbing the proud Maoris of New Zealand, the obstinate Zulus, and the rebellious sepoys of Lucknow. There had been a fine export business too. The Belgians had bought guns for the Congo, the Dutch for the East Indies, and the Austrians to quell the uppity Serbs. Colonial peace and order had been largely preserved with the beautifully engineered products of Wedmore and Bassenthwaite.

But times had changed. The original founders had left degenerate families. The patriarch of the Wedmores now worked for Greenpeace and lived in Chelsea. The surviving Bassenthwaite was in the rag trade and had not married. It had been left to men like Greg Atkinson to keep the show on the road, in the teeth of extraordinary difficulties. The British Ministry of Defence now put out only a few orders for new equipment. Sometimes they even bought unpatriotically from abroad, from hated rivals in the States or on the Continent. Exports had become much more difficult. Guns and bombs could be made now more cheaply in Taiwan or Korea, where the workers were content with a lower wage. And what orders did become available were often frustrated by the mealy-mouthed attitude of Whitehall, where export licences were frequently refused on the specious grounds of international morality.

"They want it both ways, these bloody politicians," said Greg Atkinson. "They're scared stiff of unemployment rising, but at the same time they keep kowtowing to the human rights fuckers." He had drunk quite a lot of the Rioja. "So that's why we're so keen to get this order for Concordia," he added frankly. "And we need you to help us, Mr Bellingham. I've been there myself. Can't say I should like to live there. All those gun-toting police and the poisonous caterpillars. But they seem a decent enough lot, Golosina and his team. Gave me a very nice time."

"He's a great golfing enthusiast," I commented cautiously. "With a powerful, if inaccurate, drive."

"I always warm to a man who enjoys outdoor sports," said Grey heartily. He gave me a frank, manly glance. I caught his eye. Just for a moment, I wondered whether this was all bluff. Perhaps he was a lot more artful than he seemed at first sight. Was this breezy northern manner assumed as a mask to conceal the reality that, as he knew full well, he was sailing pretty close to the wind? To sup with General Tiberio Golosina, you needed a long spoon.

After lunch, we adjourned to a showroom, where Greg explained in detail the main exhibits in his company's formidable arsenal of lethal weapons. There was an attractive air of professional pride as he pointed out what sensational effects his guns, his mortars and his bombs could have on the human body. I was clearly being groomed as a high-profile salesman for Wedmore and Bassenthwaite. We then had a little tea party, attended by some senior shop stewards, who had obviously been instructed to tell me how desperately the company needed more orders, and consequently how keen they were to export to a friendly country like Concordia.

"The whole town is solidly behind us, Mr Bellingham," they chorused. "It means jobs, mortgage repayments, washing machines and holidays on the Costa." I did not doubt the unanimity. The human rights industry would not get far in Greyburn. The sparsely attended churches would be served by morally robust clergy who had acted as chaplains in the Air Force and were accustomed to blessing bomber crews without demur.

"Mr Molnar is doing a great job," said Grey. "They're a smart bunch, those Hungarians. They say they can enter a swing door after you and come out first. But he needs all the help he can get. That's why I'm so glad he took you on. Have another piece of currant cake."

"He didn't exactly take me on," I countered, slightly nettled. "I have simply offered to share my expertise."

"Sorry, Arthur ..."

"Ambrose."

"Sorry, Ambrose. You did say I might call you that, didn't you? You must forgive us for our rough northern ways. We tend to call a spade a bloody shovel in this neck of the woods." I was not so sure of that. More than ever, I was convinced now that Greg was a much wilier operator than he wished to admit.

"There is just one question I would like to ask," I said, with what I intended as deceptive urbanity.

"Fire away," invited Greg heartily.

"I'm not clear what use your splendid equipment is actually

going to be to President Raro and General Golosina. It all seems to be designed to fight a war against some foreign country. But Concordia doesn't have any external enemies, so far as I know. Surely the Raro regime aren't planning to shoot their own people and bomb their own cities?"

"A good question, Albert."

"Ambrose."

"A good question, Ambrose." I could see he was doing his best to choke down a mood of sudden petulance. Not much escapes the glance of an experienced professional diplomatist like myself. "Domestic peacekeeping is a tricky business," he explained, "especially in central America, where they have a long tradition of violence and skulduggery. Golosina requires a wide spread of weapons, so that he can keep order with the minimum of force. And remember, if he couldn't buy from us, he'd get it from someone else – unscrupulous people like the French or the Czechs, who don't have our fundamental sense of British decency."

"You mean his soldiers might have to shoot into crowds or throw grenades or perhaps bomb them from the air?"

"Well, why not? Don't forget, the poor man is having to fight two undeclared internal wars. The Tozudo leadership will stick at nothing, and they've got most of the interior. And the Nevera rebels specialise in assassinations in the coastal towns."

"But he isn't fighting everybody," I persisted. "He must be doing police work too. Interrogating suspects, staffing his prisons."

"Oh, yes," agreed Greg with relish. "Golosina is an enthusiast for police activity."

"So he needs equipment for all that," I pressed. "Isn't he going to buy it from you too?" Ludovic had talked vaguely about restraint items.

"Indeed," said Greg, "we have a fine line in technology for control, discipline and … er …"

"Interrogation?"

"That too," he admitted.

"I should like to see some of that material," I said. One does not easily pull wool over the cynical old eyes of Ambrose Bellingham. I wanted to know the worst. I felt sure now that there must be a darker side to the activities of Wedmore and Bassenthwaite. They probably had warehouses full of handcuffs, whips, tear gas canisters and electrical cattle prods for poking into unspeakable places. That would be the less acceptable side of their business. In their sentimental way, the great British public might connive at the sale of honest traditional weapons like bombs and grenades, while drawing the line at cattle prods.

"I should love to show you some of our restraint equipment," replied Greg cordially. "It's a specialised area, where we have made giant strides in recent years. There is quite a domestic market for … er … disciplinary items."

"I thought they had abandoned all that in schools these days," I said.

"It's not exactly for schools. We also have a very good trade with friendly governments in Africa and South-East Asia. But the technicians have gone home now. If you like, we could put you up for the night and you could have a session tomorrow."

"That will unfortunately not be possible," I said. "I'm expected at Calderbeck Abbey soon for cocktails and vespers. Some other time, perhaps."

On reflection, it might be wise not to see too much. As Bluebeard's wife had discovered to her cost, some doors are best left shut.

***

Father Manfred gave me a kindly smile through his thick spectacles as he sipped the malt whisky I had brought specially for him. He was a cheerful-looking man, beaming with the benevolence and hospitality which the good Benedictines like to associate with their pedagogic activities. My son Neville, who had been in Father Manfred's house when he was still a housemaster, assured me that he could be a veritable Caligula, but I had always taken this to be poetic licence. Anyone who could put up with our boy for four years had earned my admiration and gratitude.

"How is Neville these days?" asked the headmaster cautiously.

"He is much the same," I replied carefully.

"Has he some profession, some means of gainful employment?"

"Not exactly. He is doing a little of ... this and that."

"A late starter, perhaps," said Father Manfred generously. "Well, Captain Cook was not commissioned in the Navy until he was over forty. And he discovered New Zealand."

"Neville can hardly discover New Zealand. That's already been done," I pointed out. To some extent, I blamed the monks for turning Neville into an unworldly dreamer. How much more satisfactory to be the father of a young merchant banker, or even an adequately remunerated pest-and-vermin-control operative.

"I remember Neville quite well," said the monk thoughtfully. "One forgets most boys in time. But Neville somehow ... stayed in the mind. It was not so much his pranks. Many high-spirited boys indulge in pranks, and we have ways of coping with that. But Neville was against everything we stand for here: showers, rugger, the Immaculate Conception. He was built from the authentic stuff of the great heretics. A Martin Luther in the making, I always thought, with a dash of the young Copernicus."

"He has not changed," I said sadly.

"Well, I wish him well," said Father Manfred blandly. "And now, my dear Ambrose, what brings you here?"

I told him how I had been able to do the Abbey a valuable service by drawing their school to the attention of the ruling Raro family in Concordia through the medium of their ambassador. With any luck, the monks would shortly be offered the custody, if that was quite the right word, of President Raro's much-loved son Dominic. I wanted to brief the headmaster in advance, so that he would be suitably receptive when the embassy made an approach. It could be a very useful new opportunity for the school, which was actively seeking pupils from abroad. Now that British doctors and lawyers were finding it hard to pay the fees, you could not fill an expensive public school entirely with the children of upwardly mobile property developers and asset managers.

"That is very thoughtful of you," replied Father Manfred. "But isn't Concordia the appalling place where you had the misfortune to be stationed as your last diplomatic post?"

"You could say that," I countered, rather coldly.

"And I always thought the Raro regime was one of unparalleled brutality?"

"They have domestic difficulties," I admitted, "and have been obliged to use firm methods in suppressing disorder. But you mustn't believe all you hear from their enemies on the Left. The boy's mother is a devout Catholic."

"Some awful things have been done by devout Catholics," opined Father Manfred with a slight twinkle. "What about the boy? Do you know him?"

"I have met him," I replied cautiously, "a few years ago. He is like other boys."

"I doubt that," said the headmaster. "In my experience, no boy is quite like other boys. We can manage most of them, even the unruly. I draw the line only at the child who seeks to burn down the Abbey church in the middle of the night."

"I doubt whether he is a potential arsonist. The presidential palace in Felicidad, where the family reside, is still standing, so far as I know: a fine example of the late colonial baroque."

"I still do not understand," said Father Manfred, "why they should want to send this boy to a school so far away from home. Is there something unusually wrong with him?"

"They think he will be safer here," I explained. "In Felicidad people keep trying to murder him. Even in the States he would not be entirely out of danger. Here you have a quiet sanctuary."

"A quiet sanctuary?! What a quaint idea you must have of the modern schoolboy. Well, it is an intriguing prospect. I am grateful for your efforts, Ambrose, though I do not entirely understand your motive."

"My motive! To help you, of course. The Raros are immensely rich. They will be extremely grateful if you take this lad off their hands."

"You keep talking as if he were some kind of … liability."

"Grateful for keeping him safe, I meant. In this tranquil country spot." I gazed briefly through the window at the incomparable view of the river estuary, with the stark mountain top behind.

"I detect your drift, Ambrose. You think I might be able to capitalise on their gratitude?"

"The thought had certainly crossed my mind," I answered brightly. "They might well wish to become benefactors of the school in some concrete way."

"I shall give it serious thought," said the headmaster sagely. "But you seem awfully interested in the welfare of the Raros. I thought you had completely retired."

"I have been brought back as a consultant," I explained cautiously.

"Some business deal?"

"You could call it that."

"Nothing that the Church would disapprove of, I hope?"

"Of course not. I am simply assisting an export contract." The headmaster looked at me quizzically. "All right," I blurted out. "Since you are so obviously concerned, it is a negotiation for the sale of certain kinds of defence equipment. Purely for peacekeeping purposes."

"So you're selling arms, Ambrose."

"No harm in that, is there? The Church Militant has always approved of the concept of a just war. You can't have a war without arms."

"That sounds a slippery slope. But I am not your confessor. I only pressed the point because we Benedictines can never accept money from a tainted source."

"Don't worry, Manfred. I was not planning to offer you any of *my* hard-earned gains. But just think what the Raros could do for the school. Don't you need a computer centre? Or it could be a fresh playing field or a new theatre. The possibilities are simply mouthwatering."

"You make an excellent tempter, my dear Ambrose. But what

about the Raro millions? Where do they come from?"

"I feel sure you can trust the boy's mother. She has spent a lot of time on her knees."

***

I disliked Dame Rosy Clumber on sight. A large, blowsy woman with thin greying hair, she combined the tendency to generalise of the under-educated with the bold self-confidence of the upper middle class. Nor did she seem to take to me, as she motioned me peremptorily to a chair in her stately quarters in the Foreign and Commonwealth Office. It was the fine room, overlooking St James's Park, once occupied by the Secretary of State for India in the old India Office. It had two doors of equal dignity, specially constructed so that two status-conscious Maharajas could enter at the same time without losing face. There might be a shortage of Maharajas today but Dame Rosy, with her commanding manner, seemed determined to fill the gap.

"I was recommended to give you a little of my time, Mr Bellingham," she began, without obvious enthusiasm. "Why was that? I wonder. Are you interested in contributing to party funds?"

"Not in the least."

"Oh, yes. Concordia. You are a specialist in that unhappy country."

"I served as Her Britannic Majesty's Ambassador in Felicidad," I stated with cool dignity. The reason for my summons was yet to be made clear. I suspected that Ludovic Molnar had played a part behind the scenes. He seemed to have his sticky fingers in every pie.

"Oh, yes. It says it all here in the brief. Such a lot of paperwork in the Foreign Office, you know. We never bothered with that on the Islington Council."

"I have often thought that foreign affairs would be great fun," I opined, "if it wasn't for the foreigners."

Dame Rosy looked at me strangely. I suspected that sense of humour was not her strong suit. "I find the professional diplomats here somewhat flippant," she snapped. "Are you flippant too, Mr

Bellingham?"

"I have become less so," I replied, "with the horrors of retirement."

"Brought you down to earth with a bang, I suppose," she suggested, rather maliciously.

"I had never entirely left it, Minister."

"Well, I'll come straight to the point. I am worried about Concordia. It is in my bailiwick, you know. The human rights situation there appears to be quite appalling. Have you seen the last Amnesty report? They have this horrible dictator who is murdering the freedom fighters. He is cutting down the rain forests and replacing them with plants for growing cocaine. He has also nationalised the emerald mines without compensation, to the fury of our British investors. And, to top it all, I am being pressed to agree to a large arms deal for Concordia by a British manufacturer. What have you to say to that, Mr Bellingham?"

"These reports have been greatly exaggerated, Minister," I replied urbanely. "Admittedly, President Raro does run an authoritarian regime. His methods of maintaining domestic order are … robust. But he is coping with appalling problems, in a gallant attempt to keep his country together. Raro is an old-fashioned patriot. Like Nelson or Churchill. And his wife is a dedicated Christian who has founded numerous orphanages and homes for unmarried mothers. She has a special devotion to Saint Teresa. Not the formidable Spanish lady, but the Little Flower of Lisieux. The Raros say the rosary together after dinner."

"Indeed! It will take much more than that, Mr Bellingham, to convince me that the Raro regime is worthy of our support. It sounds more like the sort of country we should be bombing." A glint came into her eyes. I had encountered this strange type of mentality before. As we had seen in the Kosovo war and over Iraq, there is nothing so belligerent as a reformed pacifist in public office.

"I think you should go there and see for yourself, Minister," I suggested hastily. "It's not enough to derive your information from the *Guardian* and the *New Statesman*."

"There are precious few other sources," admitted the Minister.

"My private secretary had been checking the files here. There had been very little serious reporting from our embassy in Felicidad for the last three years. In fact the Treasury are pressing us to close the establishment down for that very reason."

I was not surprised. My successor, Gerald Haverstock-Jones, was well known to have gone native after his trying series of postings in the Arab world. A fracas in the Soukh in Damascus had led to his punishment posting to Felicidad, which he and his wife had gravely resented, as they made clear to all and sundry. No doubt he was now coasting effortlessly down towards retirement.

"I am a great believer in sniffing out the truth," continued the minister. "Long years in local government have taught me that there is something nasty underneath nearly every stone. Maybe there is merit in your idea, Mr Bellingham. I could manage a lightning trip."

"The Raros would be enchanted to welcome you."

"They won't be so happy when they see my report," snapped Dame Rosy. "I shall be looking for arguments to turn down that arms order. But I could only fit it in during the parliamentary recess. It might have to be combined with a short annual holiday for my husband and myself. Would that be feasible?"

I knew what she had in mind. Transatlantic fares to be paid by the taxpayer.

"You would have to fly to Miami," I said. "There is a lot to see in Florida: Disneyland; those alligators in the Everglades. From there you have only one airline flying to Felicidad."

"Why is that?"

"British Airways found that the fuel was being watered down there. And Air France couldn't find the right food for their lunch packets. But you would be quite happy with Concordia Airways. Their Jacquaranda class is advertised as the epitome of luxury. You might well be met on arrival by the Felicidad Girls Choir singing a selection of native melodies."

"I am not interested in outward frills, Mr Bellingham. I should be too busy inspecting prisons, concentration camps, ethnic cleansing facilities – the whole appalling apparatus of dictatorship. I shall probably take a television team with me. But my husband must be entertained if it is to be his annual holiday. Poor lamb. He does work so hard. He's got a huge case on now, about a woman who was badly victimised at work. Would there be ocean swimming? He misses his swimming at the Inner Temple."

"Lots of swimming," I replied confidently. "There is a great deal of ocean." I felt no need to mention the sharks. They would be no match for Trevor Pilkington QC.

"There is a huge casino too," I added helpfully.

"Probably a centre for organised crime," commented the minister severely. "What accommodation would be available for us?"

"I feel sure the Ambassador would be honoured to put you up at his residence."

"I avoid those, if possible. British diplomats try so hard to pull the wool over one's eyes."

"No doubt the Government would offer you hospitality in the State Guest House."

"Do you recommend that, Mr Bellingham?"

"The place has been richly decorated, Minister, in what one might describe as Palm Beach Rococo. You and your husband could be made comfortable there. There is, however, one drawback."

"Drawback? Snakes under the bed?"

"Rather worse, I'm afraid. The State Guest House, though situated on an isolated promontory, is just next door to the Harbour Police Station. That can get noisy."

"I don't mind vagrants and high-spirited young people returning late at night. We had them in Gibson Square before we moved to Hampstead."

"It's not quite that, Minister. The inmates of the Harbour Police Station could hardly be described as high spirited. Certainly not by the time they emerge. If they do emerge."

"What on earth do you mean?"

"The place is used by General Golosina for the purposes of … er … interrogation."

"How very unsavoury. We would not wish to be disturbed by

nocturnal screaming."

"I think you'd be far better off," I advised firmly, "at the Waving Palms Hotel, recently built to house American luxury tourism. They have an Olympic size swimming pool, I am told, and a health facility where you can have yourself entirely encased in warm mud. They say that can be most soothing."

"I am not flying all the way to Felicidad to get myself encased in warm mud," announced Dame Rosy Clumber with a certain asperity. "This will be a serious fact-finding mission. You advised me to go, and I'm taking your advice. I will be quite frank with you, Mr Bellingham. My gorge rises at the prospect of conniving at the trade in arms. But one has to live in the real world. Politics is, after all, the art of the possible. If I am to give the Government realistic advice about the human rights situation in Concordia, then I must have seen the situation for myself on the ground. One cannot rely on professional diplomats, with all respect to your former colleagues. They are far too keen to ingratiate themselves with foreigners. I am not against foreigners, but, never forget, higher standards are expected from a great nation like Britain. We have to teach them that in Central America. And everywhere else."

"Concordia was a Spanish colony once," I pointed out, "but that was a long time ago. We ought to treat them now as a fully independent country."

"I am, of course, strongly opposed to colonialism," said the minister, "but some of these nasty little places would do much better under the United Nations."

She would have made an imposing governor, perhaps even a viceroy. Hampstead and Islington were still breeding such figures these days. Under the guise of showing tender care for the rights of downtrodden natives, they were just as imperialist as the old products of the Victorian public schools and the Indian civil service: never so happy as when bombing the impertinent Serbs or boxing above their weight in Sierra Leone. To the Dame Rosies of this world, foreigners were divided between Goodies and Baddies. They could not stand idly by – a favourite phrase – while the Baddies were beating up the Goodies; and semi-hysterical reporters on television encouraged viewers to applaud such national adventures. At heart, Dame Rosy thought that Britain was still ruling the world, though now in the noble cause of freedom and peace.

"You're scowling, Mr Bellingham," snapped the minister.

"Not at all, Minister," I countered hastily. "Just a spasm of indigestion."

"I'm afraid I must let you go now," she said. "My private secretary has just buzzed to indicate that my husband has arrived. We're dining this evening with Selby and Lucretia Tritton. The Member for Porchester, you know. Such a charming man and also very knowledgeable about your beloved Concordia. I expect you have met him."

"Indeed," I agreed cautiously. This must be another of Ludovic's little ploys. I could not help admiring the way he was masterminding our campaign.

The door opened and only one Maharajah substitute appeared. This proved to be none other than the redoubtable Trevor Pilkington QC, the much-feared doyen of the Human Rights Bar. His hawklike features and finely chiselled profile were familiar from the popular press and television. We were briefly introduced. I was amused to see how Dame Rosy's commanding manner faded suddenly in her husband's presence, leaving her as just another solicitous middle-aged wife.

"Have you had a good day, Darling?" she twittered.

"Extremely tiring," he replied. "It's a very shocking case. This poor schoolteacher has been badly discriminated against. They kept refusing to allow her to teach her favourite subject."

"What was that?" we chorused.

"Rugby football. Simply because the unfortunate woman is partially sighted, sixty-two years old and of Afro-Caribbean origin. Damnable racism, sexism and ageism all rolled into one. We are demanding two million in compensation."

"Who from?" I asked drily.

"The British taxpayer, of course."

"Trevor is so marvellous," remarked Dame Rosy with a happy smile. "He fights injustice wherever he finds it, without counting the cost. And so, Mr Bellingham, do I."

***

"I hear from Selby Tritton that you made quite an impression on Dame Rosy," said Ludovic Molnar, as we sat down in the fine long dining room at the Voyagers. Today it was my treat.

"That is always my intention," I retorted.

"She described you as a typical British diplomat."

"How nice."

"I don't think she cares for British diplomats. Nor they for her!"

"I disliked her intensely. Though of course I have long experience in concealing such emotions."

"Do you dislike me, Ambrose?"

"Certainly not, Ludovic. You are my benefactor."

"I only asked out of curiosity. It does not matter to me in the least, either way. You do seem to have pleased Dame Rosy in one respect. She has taken, like a duck to water, to your inspired notion that she should visit Concordia in person, so as to inspect the natives."

"There's a lot be said for playing on female vanity," I remarked airily.

"I suspect that you're a terrible male chauvinist at heart, my dear Ambrose. And a dreadful old cynic to boot."

"I do believe, with Sir Robert Walpole, that every man has his price. But it may be something less tangible than money. The carrot and the stick: those are the weapons of the trained diplomatist."

"With that realistic approach, I am surprised you did not attain a grander position in the Foreign Service."

"So am I," I countered curtly. "I was denied my fair share of the plums." It was a topic on which I had often ruminated. One could not put all the blame on my dear Susan's eccentric catering. There had been certain unfortunate episodes. Mislaying those secret papers in Washington; shutting the fingers of the Foreign Secretary's right hand in the door of the Rolls in Rome; that over-jovial party in Buenos Aires, when we had tossed the British Council representative into the muddy waters of the River Plate. It had been an eventful career, for I never stayed long in any one post until my last. But it had given the Personnel Department the regrettable impression that I was not a safe pair of hands.

"You have scored a hit, Ambrose. It is an excellent plan to lure that silly woman to Felicidad. God only knows what might happen to her there. Her husband too will be a bonus. I gather from my sources that he can be an unguided missile. A poor head for alcohol, they say." There was a gleam in the eye of this truly wicked man.

"Her visit will need careful preparation," I pointed out. "One needs to soften up the Raros, and pack General Golosina safely out of the way."

"Indeed. You must go out there next week. We are all relying on your expertise."

"All right. I'll get the Foreign Office to send a telegram today to the Haverstock-Joneses."

"Don't forget to brief the Raros about that lovely school for their little boy. He should start there at once – if his parents can bear to part with the young fellow."

"I rather think," I answered drily, "that they will be quite ready to make that sacrifice. Just one small administrative point: I suppose I shall be flying first class to Miami?"

"Naturally. I shall send a stretch limousine with darkened windows to take you to the airport. Thank you for a satisfactory lunch, my dear Ambrose. These farmhouse clarets can be surprisingly drinkable."

***

"I'm flying to Felicidad next week," I told Susan on the telephone. "First class."

"How lovely for you, Dear."

"It's not lovely at all," I replied testily. "I am travelling entirely on business. And it's the hot, rainy season in Concordia."

"It's always the hot rainy season there, from what I remember."

"Are you sure you won't change your mind and come with me, Dear?"

"Quite sure, thank you, Darling. Far too much on my plate here. The O'Callaghans have asked me to look after their two Irish wolfhounds."

"Why? Are they going to prison at last?"

"No. Only a week in Ibiza."

"I'll come down this weekend, if the wolfhounds haven't arrived yet."

"No, you're safe, Darling, till next week. It will be lovely to see you. But we do have visitors. Guess who."

"The Archbishop of Canterbury."

"No, silly. Neville and Sharon."

I could hardly wait.

"You'll have to put them into the two spare bedrooms," I said. At least the Old Rectory is spacious, in an unpleasantly drafty kind of way.

"Don't be silly, Dear," riposted Susan. "They've been cohabiting for months."

Sometimes I think that my delicately reared wife has moved more effortlessly than I into this bewildering modern world.

***

"Stop waving your arms about, Neville," I said with a faint hint of well-justified asperity.

"I'm not a child any longer, Dad," riposted our son. Indeed that was sadly true. With his greasy, unkempt locks and lean, unshaved jaw, I could see that our once pretty little boy was now trembling on the verge of under-funded middle age. Strangely enough, he still had the capacity to tug at my heart-strings.

"There was, as usual, a reason for my request," I continued with dignity. "You are in danger of knocking off the mantelpiece one of our Spode figurines. A family heirloom since Grandfather won that money on the Derby in the Coronation year."

"I have never liked them," said Neville ungraciously. Sharon gave a supporting snigger.

"You will like them well enough, my boy, when you come to inherit them and can sell them for a good price at Sotheby's."

"Stop winding your father up," said Susan calmly.

He always obeyed his doting mother. Now he relapsed into gloomy silence. Sharon, a sluttish female with an expression of unrelenting hostility, selected this moment to put her feet up on one of our best Chippendale-style chairs. I was tempted to remonstrate but the pacific Susan darted me a look indicating caution. The evening had not gone well so far, but at least we had avoided a complete breakdown. Susan had provided one of her anaemic meat stews, which Sharon had insisted on hotting up in what she claimed to be the Mexican style. Its aroma still seemed to be lingering around my digestive tract. It was Saturday evening in the Old Rectory, Little Bigney. Through the wall of our drawing room I could hear quite distinctly next door the noise of demonic caterwauling from the hi-fi arsenal deployed by the odious O'Callaghan tribe. With those bongo drums, they might have been boiling a missionary.

"Shall I bang on the wall?" I enquired from Susan.

"No," she replied firmly. "You remember what happened last time."

"Cool it, Dad," chipped in Neville. "No need to get so uptight about everything."

"Sure thing," whined Sharon, in her adenoidal accent. I had come to tolerate her morals, but I still found it hard to bear her vowels.

"I am not uptight about everything, as you curiously put it, Neville. Call me old fashioned, if you like, but one does have certain standards: courtesy to elders, writing letters of thanks, not putting one's feet on the chairs – that sort of thing."

"We know about your old-world courtesy, Dad. Like that time at the golf club when you called Lady Moggeridge a malicious old bitch."

The allusion was to one of the rare occasions when I had lost my temper with our village *grande dame* and emitted some wounding, though entirely justified, comments on her appearance and behaviour. The episode had caused Neville immense delight at the time, and he had never forgotten it. Young people have these curiously selective memories.

"I delivered a well-deserved rebuke," I said coldly. "One has sometimes to make it clear that one has not entirely lost one's cutting edge."

"If you'd been nicer to Lady Moggeridge, Dad, she might have let you open her church fête."

"There is something in that," murmured Susan disloyally. I darted her a quick glance of disapproval, but it took quite a lot to disconcert Susan, who had developed well-bred placidity into a fine art.

"How did you know about the church fête, Neville?"

"They were all laughing about it in the pub," chimed in Sharon. "I think it's perfectly fab about Tracy Snodgrass. Nev and me are great fans of hers."

"I suppose that fills in your time," I said nastily. "You must have a good deal of that to occupy." I could imagine the long, drug-fumed days and nights in their north London squat, when they were not out terrorising respectable citizens like the builders of greatly needed bypasses.

"Me and Nev have a lot on our hands," countered Sharon darkly, "fighting the forces of international capitalism."

"What are the prime targets of your rage at the moment?" I asked casually, just as once one used to ask people whether they would be taking their summer holiday in Scotland or on the Côte d'Azur.

"We are going to fight the Swaffham bypass," said Neville, "and the International Monetary Fund."

"Good luck to you then," I said sardonically. Neville favoured me with one of his horrible scowls, which made him look like an enraged bull on the verge of charging.

"Let's go out to the pub, Dad," he suggested suddenly, implying that he could no longer endure the tense atmosphere of the Old Rectory.

"I'm quite happy here," I replied.

"You know you like it in the snuggery at the Moggeridge Arms, Dear," said Susan pacifically.

"Not any more," I snapped. It was a favourable resort of Admiral and Lady Harrison Bedford. I had once thought that the bluff old sea dog might develop into a kindred soul. But this hope had been rudely shattered by their joint rejection of my literary offering for the amateur dramatic society. They had earlier appeared to cultivate me, saying I would make an ideal Malvolio, or even a Falstaff, but now I had written them both off as dead losses.

"I'll bring in some more coffee," said Susan hastily.

"I hear you're leaving Mum to manage for herself," said Neville provocatively.

"Not exactly," I retorted. He had this extraordinary idea that Susan was a long-suffering spouse, tied to a perfect brute of a husband. "I am going back to Felicidad for a short visit."

"You'll be staying at the embassy residence, I suppose?"

"That is certainly my intention." Curiously enough, I had not yet received a reply to my telegram from the Haverstock-Joneses. Perhaps they were up-country on a safari to the interior, though that would present certain hazards.

"Congratulations, Dad," said Neville cynically. "You always did enjoy the diplomatic life. Duty-free drink, tasty dinners ..."

"Well, why not? Remember what Leo the Tenth said. Since God has given us the papacy, let us enjoy it. Of course he was a Medici pope." I have tried to bring Neville up to be cultured.

"We could stay here with Susan while we mastermind the campaign against the bypass," suggested Sharon hopefully.

"Certainly not," I ruled robustly. "I'm not having the local atmosphere poisoned for the whole family. Mother and I are pillars of the community. Besides, she's too busy to do your washing this time." Sharon's vividly coloured undergarments had run in the machine, ruining two of my best white shirts.

"Don't imagine this is a holiday for me," I continued. "As you will remember, Neville, Felicidad is not exactly an earthly paradise, except in name. I am travelling on business."

"Some money-making project, Dad?"

"You could call it that."

"Lots of lolly?"

"We shall see," I replied evasively. One had to be careful with the young hyena.

"Neville doesn't see the point of having diplomats at all," opined Sharon snidely. "All that eating and drinking and shaking hands."

"He was perfectly content to live off my modest salary and allowances for a great many years."

"Didn't have much choice, Dad, did I?"

"Surely all the work is done these days," suggested Sharon, "by ministers flying out from capitals." I found this heresy particularly annoying.

"You still need resident embassies," I explained wearily, as if to the mentally stunted, "to cultivate good relations with the local government and report on what is happening."

"But you didn't know the opposition in Concordia. Or anyone else except old Raro and his cronies."

"That was scarcely my fault, Neville. Your dear mother and I were living in a tightly ordered society. It's hardly a Westminster-type democracy. I was not encouraged to meet the opposition, as you well know. They were all dead, in prison, or in hiding."

"I don't know how you could bear to shake the hands of those bloodstained oligarchs."

"It's wonderful what you can do," I replied with dignity, "when your livelihood depends on it."

Sharon emitted a low, but distinct, snort. I fixed her with one of my steely glances and she did have the grace, at last, to remove her legs from the chair cover. The effect was somehow spoiled by her choosing this moment to take off her shoes, revealing a pair of greyish socks – one with a large hole in the heel. One of my distinguished old chiefs, like Sir Gregory Capulet in Brussels, would have collapsed on the spot.

"I'll go and help your mum with the coffee," she said pointedly. "A spot of girls' gossip, perhaps."

"How very unfeminist," I commented. She turned at the door and darted me a look of undiluted malice.

"You ought to be nicer to Sharon," protested Neville. "She's pure gold, that girl."

"No doubt she has charms," I conceded drily, "but they have not so far become apparent to me."

"She's terribly worried at the moment, Dad."

"Pregnant, you mean?"

"No. About the Ziggurat."

"What's that got to do with her?"

"She's frightened it's going to be a god-awful flop. Like the Dome."

The Government had recently decided to build a huge Ziggurat on wasteland behind King's Cross. It would be a stepped pyramid of brick, faced with tiles and surmounted by a shrine, on the model of ancient Babylonia and Assyria. The idea was to dispel the unhappy memory of the disastrous Dome and to show that Britain could still produce a vast construction of great beauty. It had been agreed that the shrine must contain a figure, but acute controversy now raged as to what that should be. Suggestions violently advanced had ranged from Jesus Christ and Buddha to Winston Churchill and Karl Marx.

"If it is a flop, nobody is going to blame Sharon."

"I know, Dad. But she can't accept that. She takes everything so personally, poor darling. Global warming. Nuclear weapons. The future of the baboon. She's so caring, you see."

"Sounds perfectly barmy to me," I said unsympathetically. "Human beings have always lived in terror. Until quite recently, it used to be hellfire. Your girl needs to grow a thicker skin."

"To become a happy pachyderm, like you?"

"There are worse ways to live. Shall I give her a little pep talk?"

"No, thank you, Dad."

"Then I'll offer a word of advice to you, my boy. Remember, you're the custodian of the family genes. Never breed from the mentally defective."

He wasn't too keen on that.

***

"Are you sure you've got everything?" asked Susan, on the Monday morning, with her usual solicitude.

"I'm not in the habit of packing with insufficient care," I snapped, though the truth is that I rather like a bit of wifely attention.

"Dad's always been a regular old fusspot," commented Neville.

"So I see," put in Sharon rather nastily. I am not sure she likes me.

"Better to be a fusspot, as you put it," I said with dignity, "than discover at the airport that you've forgotten your passport." On this occasion, the sartorial requirements in Felicidad could prove taxing, and I had fully prepared for them. The well-trained diplomatist, as I have often reminded my staff, should be equipped for every occasion: hot weather, cold weather, intermediate weather, formal attire for state occasions, tasteful clothing for informal groupings. I had filled two substantial suitcases, knowing that Ludovic would pick up the tab for any excess charges on the plane.

"The Duchess of Windsor used to travel like that across the Atlantic," commented Susan. "With mountains of luggage. Why not take a cabin trunk?" The young people chortled.

"Very droll," I snapped. I do not mind a little gentle teasing from my affectionate family but I draw the line at outright mockery. "There will be plenty of room in the large limousine picking me up at the Voyagers."

"Can you spare a moment before you leave, Dad?" asked Neville. He clearly wanted us to be alone together.

"Certainly," I said. I have never begrudged the boy my time. After all, the young can learn a lot from us experienced seniors. I motioned the women away.

"What is it, Neville?" I felt a little emotional. We might never meet again. The physical hazards of Felicidad were far from negligible: the poison-squirting tarantulas, the trigger-happy gunmen lurking in the orange groves. I imagined the boy sobbing as he heard the tragic news of his dad's demise.

"I'm sorry it hasn't gone too well this weekend, Dad," said Neville. "My fault, I'm afraid. Being carted around the world when I was small by you and Mum must have given me a horror of the Foreign Office and all it stands for. I feel angry sometimes when I see you and think of all I missed for the sake of your career. And that makes me want to lash out. It's silly, I know. I ought to grow up."

"That's all right," I said gruffly, touched by the young man's semi-repentance.

"You've done your best for me, Dad. I know I've been a bit of a disappointment to you. But I'll try to do better from now on." It was a moving moment. I felt tempted to give the boy a hug but perhaps he was a shade too old for that now.

"Glad to hear it," I said simply. "What are your immediate plans?"

"Sharon's staying around here. But I've got to go off on an emergency mission."

"Really. Where?"

"I can't say, Dad. It's top secret."

"Don't do anything silly then." I really meant: we love you, we care about you, come back safely.

"There's just one thing I want to ask you, Dad."

"Certainly. What is that?" I would be happy to offer my professional expertise.

"Well, Dad … er …"

"Speak up, Neville." Surely he no longer needed information on the facts of life.

"I don't like to ask. But I have to. Could you lend me five hundred pounds?"

***

The little aircraft had made its ascent from the airport in Miami and was snaking its way across the blue waters of the Caribbean, in the direction of Central America. The transatlantic flight had been pleasant, with me enjoying all the food and drink dispensed to us first-class passengers, well away from the hoi polloi in tourist. Concordia Airways filled me with less enthusiasm. But at least in Jacquaranda class we were spared the close proximity of cut-price British backpackers and other riff-raff. The space provided in the seats, however, was not all that generous. That was important to me, as I am hardly a sylph. I was sorry to find that the space next to mine was occupied by the overflowing form of another corpulent middle-aged man. I prefer to sit next to slim young women. My unattractive neighbour had firmly plonked his large elbows across both armrests, giving me no opportunity to do the same.

I gave him one of my frosty looks. He did not take the hint. Worse was to come. We were served an exotic meal, during the consumption of which my ungainly neighbour managed to spill a good deal of his red wine over my natty white suit – the pride of my tropical wardrobe.

"Look what you've done," I cried in fury, starting vainly to mop up the odious scarlet fluid.

"It's your fault, man," riposted the offender, in a blue-collar American accent. "You shouldn't have jogged my elbow."

"So you're not going to apologise?" I almost shrieked, feeling the air rage in my gullet.

"Apologise to you?!" The man gave an offensive laugh. "Not on your life, limey."

I could see his knuckles stiffening, so I judged it prudent to moderate my stance. Though fat, the fellow looked muscular and horribly virile.

"I shall remember you," I said with dignity.

"And I shall sure remember you too, Buster." We relapsed into a chilly silence, while exchanging glances of mutual loathing.

And now we were circling over Felicidad. I could begin to detect the main features: the distant hills across the bay, the contours of the harbour, the spire of the cathedral. As we descended, I picked out other well-remembered sights: the slaughterhouse where the vultures circled; the central prison on its eerie promontory; even the fish market, always lined with beggars. This was the gruesome little capital where I had been obliged to spend the culminating years of my career.

A driver was waiting for me at the airport, somewhat to my relief, as I had still not heard from the Ambassador. The man had a knowing face, sparkling with low cunning, as I soon discovered.

"You are old ambassador, Sir?" he asked in tolerable English.

"I am indeed the former ambassador," I corrected.

"I am Potiphar, Sir."

"You weren't here in my time."

"No, Sir. Mr Haverstock-Jones brought me from Cairo."

"What happened to Gabriel then? He used to work for me."

"Very sad, Sir. Gabriel drive over old lady. Too much drink. Had to run away to bush."

A huge black car was drawn up near ours, with three large men in dark spectacles standing beside it. My offensive companion from the flight was being obsequiously escorted towards it.

"Who is that man, Potiphar?" I asked.

"That is Mr Marsala from United States. He works here but each week he flies back to Miami for a day."

"What does he do here?"

"He is adviser to General Golosina. Very important man, they say."

My heart almost skipped a beat. A big-shot crony of the dreaded Chief of Police! And he had promised to remember me.

"How do you know all this?" I asked.

"Potiphar knows many things," said my driver darkly, as we screeched out of the airport perimeter along the well-remembered dusty road with perambulating donkeys and ragged urchins attempting to sell purloined trinkets and the telephone number of their older sisters.

Had I started off on the wrong foot?

2

"You may wonder," said Gerald Haverstock-Jones, "why we never sent a reply to your telegram." He was a short, neat man with a languid, defeated-sounding voice. Monica, his consort, was tall and solidly constructed, with a number of strategic bulges. Together they presented a curious spectacle.

"I was rather surprised not to hear from you," I said, in a tone of mild asperity.

"We thought some junior official in the Office must have got it wrong. We couldn't believe that you would return to your old post only three years after retirement."

"Why not?"

"As you know perfectly well, Ambrose, the convention in the Service is that one doesn't behave like that, for fear of embarrassing or outploying one's successor. It's not considered good form."

"Oh, come off it, Gerald," I protested. "That may be all very well for Paris. I know they had trouble persuading Lady Diana Cooper to leave the Faubourg Saint-Honoré, but Felicidad is hardly some delicious plum that one is longing to suck dry. I'm sure you're doing a wonderful job, and I certainly don't want to compete with you."

"Well, now you're here," said Gerald ungraciously, "you'd better stay."

"Thank you," I replied with a touch of sarcasm. "If you prefer, I could move to the Waving Palms."

"I don't recommend that," put in Monica. "Their bedbugs are notorious. And an American woman novelist was throttled in her sleep there only last week."

"You can't be throttled in your sleep," I pointed out. "You would be bound to wake up."

"I meant she was sleeping when the attack started. I see you haven't changed a bit, Ambrose." The pause that followed had a slight chill.

"At least it was kind of you to send your driver for me," I said in a propitiatory tone.

"That was Monica's idea," said Gerald. "Just in case you actually did arrive."

"I didn't like to think of your wandering around in the heat and trying to hail a taxi," said Monica. "They are known to hold up their passengers at knife-point. It's got worse since you left."

"You don't seem to think much of Felicidad," I said.

"We hate the place," said Gerald simply. "We were dragged here by *force majeure*. I told the wretched Foreign Office that we wanted another Middle Eastern posting."

"We were so happy in Damascus," moaned Monica. "All those lovely mosques. And the Arabs are such gentlemen."

"But the Office offered me a stark choice: Felicidad for our last posting, or Bournemouth straight away."

"Gerald protested. He was very firm. He said that Felicidad was the sort of awful little embassy they only kept to hide away the complete duds …"

"I wouldn't put it quite like that," I commented coldly. "If you felt that way, perhaps you should have taken premature retirement."

"We couldn't face that," said Monica. "Gerald has such an active brain. He needs something to get his teeth into." I couldn't quite swallow that either; Gerald was one of the idlest men I had ever encountered. "Besides," continued his embattled consort, "we couldn't afford to." That was more like it. They would be salting away the allowances and skimping on the entertainment, to provide a financial cushion against the horrors of retirement in an English watering place.

Gerald and I went back a long way. I could read him like a book. Once, long ago, when we were young and still keen, we had been resident clerks together – one of the small elite group of junior officials who lived in a flat at the top of the Foreign Office in order to take care of the place after hours, and deal with emergencies. We had chatted insouciantly with prime ministers and foreign secretaries, shielding ourselves with the comforting thought that they were only at the end of a telephone and did not know how to get at us physically. I remembered Gerald only too well. He had been adept at wriggling out of duties on the long weekends like Christmas and Easter when everyone wanted to get away, leaving poor mugs like me to hold the fort.

Nor had I forgotten Monica, in those days an overforward young woman who worked in the News Department, chatting up the journalists while they waited to see someone more important.

We were sitting on the familiar terrace, with its sensational view as the sun set blood-red over the municipal abattoir. I knew from unpleasant experience that the midges would soon come out and start biting our ankles. In our own day, Susan had been a help in decoying them away involuntarily to attack her own succulent flesh rather than mine. But I had a nasty feeling that the muscular shanks of the present Ambassadress would furnish less of a counter-attraction.

"I suppose you want a drink?" enquired Monica, without enthusiasm. Susan and I had plied our official guests generously with duty-free alcohol, in order to keep them sweet. But I could see that this would not be the way with the current parsimonious pair.

"Yes, please," I replied firmly. "A nice big gin and tonic." It was the happy hour when one relaxes in diplomatic circles.

Monica rang the bell, and a familiar figure appeared. It was Felipe, the doddery old butler who had been with the Embassy ever since Marcus Hardcastle had to be withdrawn in a hurry after that naval visit all those years ago. It was indiscreet of him to borrow one of his sister's evening dresses and ply for trade at a waterfront bar. With his penchant for flowing robes and all-male company, Marcus had subsequently been a huge success at the Vatican.

On spotting me, the aged retainer burst into a flood of welcoming Spanish, to which I did my best to respond graciously. I'm not the world's greatest linguist. After three years of rustication in north Norfolk, it would take a few hours to restore my Spanish to its former flow. I gathered, however, that I was being received civilly enough and that Teresita, another venerable domestic, was also keenly looking forward to seeing me again. I felt slightly bad about this, as I had instructed Susan to leave only modest tips for the servants when we left, believing we should never see them again.

"Isn't Teresita the mad washerwoman?" I enquired of my hosts. "She had an absolute mania for taking everything away to be cleaned."

"She still does," warned Monica. "In fact, she's battier than ever." Embassy life may seem easy, but does actually present numerous hazards not easily apparent to the untutored eye.

"I see you had to change your driver," I said. "Just as well, perhaps. We used to find Gabriel quite terrifying."

"He had to leave," said Gerald hastily.

"You should never have made him go so fast, in the wrong direction, down a one-way street," snapped Monica.

"We solved the problem easily enough," said Gerald, "by importing Potiphar. We had known him since I was Counsellor in Cairo."

"Quite a family friend," said Monica with an enigmatic smile. She exchanged a rapid glance with her husband which, I suspect, I was not intended to see. I found that mysterious. Did the sprightly Potiphar have some other, more arcane function besides his duties behind the steering wheel?

"We're rather on our own here," continued Monica, "with the children so far away in Europe."

"They're not exactly children any more," protested her husband.

"What are they doing now?" I felt obliged to ask. When one has produced a son like Neville, one does not exactly revel in this type of exchange.

"Alexander is a partner in Sacheverell and Bulstrode," said Gerald with satisfaction, mentioning the name of a well-known merchant bank. "And Cressida has just been shortlisted for the Booker Prize. What about your boy? Mowbray, isn't it?"

"Neville is a man of many parts," I said evasively. "He does his own thing."

"How nice for him," said Monica politely. "Our children have always been so driven, so ambitious. Do you need another drink, Ambrose? We've still got a few minutes before we have to go up and dress for dinner."

"We always dress for dinner," explained Gerald, "even when we're alone. It's a habit we picked up in the Sudan. Somehow it helps to keep up standards."

People have accused me of being stuffy and old-fashioned, but this couple had become positively mediaeval.

"So you want another gin and tonic?" pursued Monica, with uncharacteristic generosity.

"No, thank you," I said hastily. There had been something rather nasty about the last one. I suspected that Gerald, for the sake of economy, had brought out the ingredients from home and was manufacturing his own tonic water – a not uncommon, but noxious habit in up-country stations. The gin also had seemed a bit iffy.

"What on earth brings you back here, Ambrose?" asked Gerald sharply. "Not for a holiday, I presume."

"Didn't the Office explain?"

"There was some farrago of nonsense about you working for an arms trader, but I thought they must have got it wrong."

"I am indeed involved in the export business," I said with dignity. "A large, secret contract for defence equipment from Wedmore and Bassenthwaite."

"I've heard about that project, of course," said Gerald. "My French and American colleagues are competing tooth and nail. But I can't think why they brought you in." His astonished stare carried offensive implications. I decided not to take Gerald fully into my confidence. The man was a frivolous butterfly, made cynical and perhaps malicious by disappointment. In particular, I would not reveal my connection with Ludovic Molnar, my mysterious paymaster.

"I do have one asset to offer," I pointed out. "When we were serving here, Susan and I became quite close friends of the Raros and their social set."

"So I have heard," said Gerald coldly. "I gather you used to give riotous parties for their cronies. Monica and I prefer to target our efforts more rigorously."

I could well believe that. Not for the Haverstock-Joneses would be our masked balls, our guitar recitals and frolicsome little suppers. They would offer coffee and buns once a month. As a result, by the cruel irony of fate, they must have built up capital and would consequently enjoy a more prosperous retirement in Bournemouth than we in Little Bigney. On return, I would drop a discreet hint to this effect when I attended a debriefing in the Foreign Office. This would only be at a junior level but these things have a habit of percolating upwards, the Foreign Office having an almost insatiable appetite for damaging gossip. I am not an unkindly person myself, but I do think that the interests of the British taxpayer should be watched.

"The Raros are on their last legs," continued Gerald. "As you know, Fernandez is brigading the opposition together. It is only a question of time before he sweeps down from the hills. The end should be positively Wagnerian."

I had never thought much of Gerald's political judgement, and I did not do so now.

"Nevertheless, I shall pay a call on Ignacio Raro and Elvira. They will remember me, I think."

"Of course they will, Ambrose," said Monica ambiguously. "You are very well remembered here."

"The real ruler now is General Golosina," said Gerald. "A most sinister person, as you will recall. Like a huge poisonous jellyfish. He sends shivers down my spine every time I see him."

"Mine too," chimed in Monica. "I find that quite exciting."

"I gather from your well-informed Potiphar," I said casually, "that Golosina has an adviser called Marsala. He was on the same plane with me."

"Keep well clear of that one," advised Gerald. "Sylvester Marsala is a thorn in the side of my well-meaning American colleague, Homer

Fairchild. Marsala is a former heavyweight boxer. He operates out of Miami and is a much-dreaded Mafia boss, with the reputation for never forgetting an unfriendly face. They say he handles the regime's link with organised crime in the States."

"I gather he flies to and from Miami every week," I said, in as calm a tone as I could manage in the distressing circumstance.

"That's his regular run as a drugs courier," answered Gerald.

"Can't the Americans pick him up?" I asked.

"The CIA have forbidden that so far. It would probably bring down The Raro regime. They're frightened what might come after that, if Fernandez turned into another Castro."

"Always keep a hold of nurse," I quoted, "for fear of meeting something worse."

"Very apposite, Ambrose. But now there's another perfectly bloody development. That tiresome woman Rosy Clumber is coming out here with her sanctimonious husband. We shall have to give a dinner party for them."

"It will be an opportunity," pointed out Monica, "to use up some of those tins of ham we bought on leave in Palm Beach."

"There was talk of their staying in the government guest-house, but they have heard nasty stories about the noises there at night. So we're stuck with them here. Some perfect fool she meet in the Foreign Office seems to have put her up to the whole thing." I met Gerald's accusatory stare with one of my steady glances. At that moment, one of the horrible flying insects scored a direct hit on my right ankle.

"Are they biting?" enquired Monica, with aunt-like concern. "They always go for fresh flesh."

"A midge, I suppose?"

"More likely one of our giant mosquitos," said Gerald. "You did remember, I hope, to start your anti-malaria tablets again. Most tropical countries have either malaria or yellow fever. As you will recall, we offer both."

"Perhaps we should go inside," suggested Monica. "It's time to change, anyhow. You could enjoy a nice bath, Ambrose."

I had been lodged in the small room overlooking the scullery. The best bedroom had presumably been kept for Dame Rosy and her husband. My suitcase had been unpacked by the over-zealous Teresita, and all the shirts and underclothes had been removed. Although perfectly clean, she must have considered them to be candidates for the washtub. That was tiresome, since I should be unable to change after my long journey. But I could enjoy a good scrub.

The water was an unpleasant brown colour. I supposed that the room had not been used for some time, my hosts being unwilling to invite house guests. But at least I came back into the bedroom feeling clean and refreshed.

Teresita must have struck again. The clothes I had just been wearing had now also been removed. I had nothing to put on at all. A lesser man would have felt distinctly low. I had to dine that night in Gerald's second-best dressing-gown. Was my mission to be dogged with disaster?

***

"You are happy here, Potiphar?" I asked, as the embassy chauffeur conveyed me to the presidential palace through thin, but ill-disciplined traffic. As I have often impressed on diplomatic juniors, it is wise to chat affably to unimportant persons. There are several reasons for this. First, they may not, in reality, be unimportant at all. Secondly, you may need their help in an emergency, such as a temporary problem with the cashflow. Thirdly, you may be able to extract significant information from them, harassed world leaders being notably indiscreet in front of small fry such as drivers and waiters. Potiphar struck me as just the type of latter-day Figaro to secrete a veritable treasure house of damaging detail.

"Potiphar is always happy," replied the Egyptian, with a grin. "That is his duty."

"Quite right, Potiphar. Everyone likes a cheerful soul." Gerald had kindly made the driver available to convey me to this high-level interview. He had suggested that he should come too, appointments with the now-secretive President being hard to come by. But he had taken the point when I indicated that he might find it prudent not to become too closely informed about my commercial activities. Ambassadors are well advised to drift well above the sordid details of export activity in the so-called developing world.

"You wish to know something, Your Excellency?" asked Potiphar, with beguiling candour.

"Well, yes. It's about President Raro. Is he popular?"

There was a pause. "Nobody speaks against General Raro," replied the driver cautiously. I knew what he meant.

"What happens if they do?" I asked.

"They disappear."

"It can't be a very cheerful country now, then."

"People in Concordia have hot blood," said Potiphar. "They are children. They laugh, they joke, they give babies to their girls. They do not have anything to do with politics."

"Very sensible. What about the President's lady?"

"She is very beautiful, Mr Ambassador. You will remember that. Beautiful clothes, beautiful handbags, beautiful shoes. The people are glad for that."

"Doesn't it make them jealous?"

"Oh no, Sir. They are pleased for her. They cannot have nice things themselves, but they know the *señora* wears hers for them. She is much loved throughout the land."

I was not unfamiliar with this type of female icon – a long line of high-profile bimbos descending from Eva Peron, living in the lap of luxury but still charming the people with their ostentatious displays of mink and pearls.

"Does she still kiss babies?" I asked, a shade cynically.

"Indeed, Your Excellency. War veterans too, and deformed people, and even the totally mad." There would always be a TV crew behind her, of course. As she stooped over the cots of the suffering, she would invariably have one eye on the lens. Madame Raro had omitted only one detail: the requirement to die young and leave the nation mourning.

"She visits hospitals in the middle of the night," continued Potiphar, "to sit at the bedside of the desperately sick." It would add a new horror to death.

"And General Golosina?"

"I know nothing about him," replied Potiphar, with a slight shudder which spoke louder than words about the reputation of the dreaded Chief of Police. It would be vital to avoid encountering again his adviser, the sinister Mr Marsala, with his unfortunate memory for faces.

"How nice that you could join Mr and Mrs Haverstock-Jones again," I continued blandly, as we swept down the massive *avenida* of huge palm trees leading to the presidential palace. "They are very glad about that."

"Potiphar glad too. Mr Haverstock-Jones is lovely English gentleman."

"And Mrs Haverstock-Jones?"

"She is lovely too," replied Potiphar.

I found that hard to swallow, even allowing for foreign exaggeration. Monica had never been lovely, and she was even less so now. But sexual satisfaction often warped the judgement. Was Potiphar the lover of the British Ambassadress, compensating for the fact that poor old Gerald was no longer in his first youth? Even more bizarrely, could he have some covert connection with Gerald himself, who had never struck me as robustly heterosexual? Perhaps they were romping together, three in a bed. That seemed absurd. It would not be in the highest traditions of the British Diplomatic Service. But at least it would help to explain, apart from parsimony, why they did not appear to welcome house guests. Susan says I have an impure imagination. But at least it has given me such harmless pleasure.

Potiphar would be a tough nut to crack – that much was obvious. The cunning of the pharaohs ran in his veins. I sank back in the diplomatic limousine as we drew up at a huge pillared portico. I entered, to find myself striding between two lines of the presidential guard, all with drawn swords, as a bugle blew and a word of command was snapped out in stentorian tones. It reminded of the historic occasion six years ago when I had presented my credentials from the Queen of England to President Raro, then in his first months in office. I had then been wearing my full diplomatic tropical uniform, with gold braid on the shoulder, and carrying my sword. A splendid photograph of this memorable sight stood on our piano in Little Bigney, where it periodically attracted wounding comments from Neville and his iconoclastic paramour. Now I was more conventionally attired in one of my white linen suits, but still retained, I hoped, a certain air of old-world distinction.

The surrounding flunkeys were courteously urging me forward. I stepped into the vast marbled hall, more appropriate perhaps for a great power than an insignificant state like Concordia. A small figure stood up to greet me at the other end. It was President Raro. I suddenly remembered how shamelessly he had cheated as a bridge partner, giving me little kicks under the table when he had a strong hand of trumps. He had aged, I could see, in the last three years. It was hard to believe that this little old man, with his gentle smile, was the same General Raro who had defenestrated the whole Liberal Democratic leadership from the bell tower in the Cathedral of Divine Compassion and later ordered the ghastly Massacre of the Bridge at San Luis Obispo. The history of Concordia is gruesome in the extreme, and not recommended for the faint-hearted.

The President motioned me to sit beside him, and pressed me to drink a cup of horribly strong coffee – the sort where the spoon stands up of its own accord. He greeted me cordially, with the usual Hispanic flowery speeches, and encouraged me to reveal the reason for my visit. I did so with alacrity, explaining that I had it in my power to give his regime an enormous boost by delivering defence equipment of the highest quality. His lined old face, which might have been that of a saintly philosopher, remained impassive.

"Most interesting, my dear friend," said the President in his faint, squeaky voice which I remembered distinctly. "How gracious of you to call on me. I trust that you continue to flourish."

"Indeed. And I hope you are well too, Excellency," I replied with a gracious bow.

"I am far declined into the vale of years," said Ignacio Raro, "but I shall rule this unhappy country for some time yet." Concordian Spanish is never easy to follow, being descended from the bastard-ised dialect of provincial Castilian spoken by sixteenth-century cowherds. "Since you left, our difficulties have increased. The wicked terrorists have found a vigorous leader in the unspeakable Victor Fernandez. And we have lost the only half-decent dentist in Felicidad."

"I never actually met him," I said. "He did not circulate socially, and I used to get my teeth seen to in London."

"You were fortunate to avoid him," said the President. "I employed the wretched man to do a series of complicated root fillings on my lower molars. He offered me a total anaesthetic but I declined, fearing that, when unconscious, I might betray the secrets of state. Then he caused me atrocious pain. To induce him to stop, I had to bite his fingers rather too strongly. The man let out a scream and cursed me, as my bodyguards rushed in and taught him a lesson in politeness to the head of state. That night he left for the hills. On such small things, Mr Bessemer, do the fortunes of great nations depend."

"Bellingham, Mr President. My name is Bellingham."

"I know that perfectly well," said the President with quiet dignity. "Are you happy in England? You have a family mansion, I presume, and a country estate?"

"More or less," I replied equivocally.

"You are in the House of Lords, I suppose."

"At some future date, perhaps," I replied evasively. "May I know the answer to my proposal?"

"What proposal, Mr Ambassador?" I could see that he was beginning to nod off.

"We want to supply you with defence equipment. As I have explained."

"Very generous. It will be for free?"

"Not exactly."

"I have asked the Americans for free arms. And the French."

"If I may ask, what was their reply?"

"They all want to be paid," said the President sadly. "A lot of money too. There is no generosity nowadays among friendly nations."

"You will find, Sir, that ours is by far the best offer."

"You English were always good at killing things," commented the President reflectively. "But I cannot go into details now. I am far too old. I am concentrating on my place in history. And the salvation of my soul. You must discuss these matters with Tiberio. Remember him?"

Indeed I did. One did not lightly forget General Tiberio Golosina, his huge laugh, his flabby but bear-like grip, his enormous thirst.

"I will do as you say, Mr President. I will trouble you no longer now."

"My wife wishes to see you. You and I will meet again soon. I am too old to play golf any more. My swing was proving ineffective. But I have taken up croquet instead. You must join me one day. I understand that all English gentlemen play croquet." I did not demur. "Such a delightful game, Mr Bellingham. Especially when your opponent is poised to push his ball through a hoop and you hit him away to the furthest corner of the field. A great test of character. I had Tiberio almost in tears the other night."

The old wretch gave a playful grin. He had not really changed. Was Golosina running the show now, as Gerald thought? Or was that only a ploy by Raro to take the heat off himself? That seemed more likely.

"Say a few Hail Marys for me please, Mr Bulstrode. Every night when you kneel beside your bed. The Church is still firmly on my side, you know. We are all sinners."

You more than most, Mr President, I thought, as I withdrew backwards – quite a tricky operation.

**

Elviro Raro had aged a bit too but she still had her mass of bright yellow hair, though I suppose it could have been a wig. In a country like Concordia, where most of the population were of native Indian or African descent, fair hair and skin were greatly prized. The First Lady had capitalised on this and, in spite of the onset of middle age, had managed to retain the appearance of a blonde bombshell. Admittedly she now looked best from a distance – like Balliol College, Oxford – but she retained vestiges of the wild beauty that must have so attracted young Captain Raro all those years ago, when she was a star turn at the Felicidad Follies.

"I remember you well, Sir Bellingham," she said with gratifying enthusiasm, "and your charming wife too. How is she? Such an enthusiastic supporter of our botanical gardens. We do not see much of the present British Ambassador."

"You are very kind, First Lady," I replied. "My wife is well, and sends her good wishes. How is your little boy?"

"He is not so little now, I fear. We are so worried for him here because of the security situation. These terrible terrorists have threatened his life. That is why we are keen to send him to your lovely peaceful country. I was indeed grateful for the suggestion you made through our ambassador in London."

"I hope that was helpful, dear lady. Father Manfred is an old friend of mine. He has helped to make my own son what he is today."

"I understand that you are also a valued ally of our ambassador. Hector Garcia is, I think, a fine representative of our new Concordia. Of course he is from the old upper class. What we call the oligarchs. Not my background at all, as everyone knows. Thank God we have at last eliminated all class differences here, I am happy to say."

She gave a smile of ineffable satisfaction. Rather rich, I thought, since this spoiled woman was living in the lap of luxury, financed by the spoils of the national treasury. But, with my customary aplomb, I continued to display a bland exterior.

"Hector has been in touch with your Father Manfred," she contin-ued. "We have decided to entrust him to the Disrobed Benedictines.

He will be leaving here almost at once. I want you to see him today to encourage him. The dear boy is so fond of his daddy and mummy that we fear he will be homesick."

"My wife and I will be happy to visit him at Calderbeck. We could take him out for a nice cream tea."

"That will be very kind of you. He will have two of our best security men with him. They will be living under deep cover. I do hope it will be all right."

"Trust the British, dear First Lady."

"And Almighty God, too, Sir Bellingham. Never forget Him, as they taught me in the Convent of the Little Sisters of the Poor, where I was once employed to wash the dishes. The Church in Concordia has been a great support to my dear husband. I have, however, had to warn the Archbishop that some of his younger clergy have been preaching subversive sermons under the influence of godless Marxism. I will not stand for that, you know." She stamped her tiny, elegantly shod foot.

"Your Disrobed Benedictines are not like that, I hope," she continued anxiously. "It is essential that my darling Dominic's faith should not be disturbed by Protestant heresies or even the current subversive tendencies within the true Church. My husband and I are traditional believers. We have a horror of such absurdities as women priests."

"You will not find any woman priests at Calderbeck," I assured her. "Women are employed there only to serve the meals and teach the viola. And, by the way, the brethren are known as Discalced."

"Between ourselves," added the First Lady, lowering her voice to a conspiratorial whisper, "it will do Dominic good to go away to a boarding school. Here he gets his own way all the time, because people respect his father and they seem to love me. That is not right for a growing boy. It could have a bad effect on his character. Only last week he ordered a couple of Danes to be shot because he did not like the way they were staring at him."

"Danish tourists?" I asked, appalled. "What was the reaction from Copenhagen?"

"Enormous dogs. But even so! The boy, sweet though he is, does need a firm hand. Please inform Father Manfred to that effect. What a good thing you came."

"I expect you know why, First Lady."

"Yes, I have heard about your project. As you know, there is certain … competition. But I am hoping we shall buy from Britain. I am a great admirer of your beautiful Harrods."

"If you could see your way to … using your influence."

"That slightly depends, Sir Bellingham. I have long lost interest in the things of this material world. My eyes are fixed on the prospect of joining the saints and the archangels around the throne of God. But others around here have different priorities. The French Ambassador, the Marquis de Marigny-Marmande, keeps dangling the carrots he will give us if we buy their equipment. I find that very shocking."

"Yes, indeed, dear lady. But we have to live in this real world of sinners. I think the British manufacturers too could be induced to offer … shall we say … an interesting consideration. Terms, of course, to be negotiated."

"We will talk of this again," said the First Lady decisively. "I might be persuaded to accept a donation for the Elviro Raro Foundation for the Ungifted. Cheques to be made out to E. Raro. The people are so pathetically grateful for one's feeble efforts."

"I know how they love you, dear lady."

"They feel I have a tender heart," said the First Lady complacently. "Even though I am now old and ugly."

"Nonsense, *señora*. You are extremely beautiful. You have the skin of a young girl. And your smile is bewitching." I remembered Disraeli's advice that flattery should be laid on with a trowel. On this occasion, it seemed to work.

"You are a dear man," she said, placing a hand gently on my arm. "My secret, I think, is quite simply, just give out love, as you stand by the bed of the invalid and the cot of the newborn." With the television cameras behind you, I thought cynically. "I do want you to enjoy your stay. I shall introduce you to my friend Casilda.

She has not been here long and is, she says, the widow of a Spanish nobleman."

I suspected a ploy but bent my head gracefully. "I must not take up more of your valuable time," I murmured.

"Would you like to come with me now to visit a leper colony?"

"No, thank you," I answered hastily. "I have another engagement."

"Leprosy is contagious, you know, but not infectious. You probably cannot catch it on just one visit. However, I will not press you, dear Sir Bellingham."

At this point the door was flung open and an uncouth juvenile sprinted into the room. I realised that this must be Dominic. He had certainly developed in the last three years. Tall, wide and muscular, he seemed unusually mature for a child of his age, with an incipient moustache and even the beginning of a straggly beard. I guessed that he must be bulging with testosterone and unhampered by moral scruples. The kitchen maids at Calderbeck, and perhaps the smaller boys too, had better look out. I did not envy Father Manfred his task in trying to restrain this natural phenomenon. Even his mother had heard about the Great Danes. What else had he slaughtered for pleasure? We were reintroduced and he took my hand in a crushing grip, grinning as the tears of pain came into my eyes.

"Here is my little darling," explained the First Lady, rather unnecessarily. "Dominic dear, this is kind Sir Bellingham, who will be another father to you when you are in England. He and his dear wife will welcome you to their beautiful estate."

I shuddered. How would this fearsome young brute go down in Little Bigney?

***

It all began peacefully enough, two days later. I had submitted a request to the Foreign Ministry for an interview with General Golosina, who would be the key figure in deciding on the new defence contract. No reply had yet been received, and Gerald had discouraged me by saying that probably none ever would. "Golosina is terrified of assassination," he explained. "Hardly surprising, considering all the widows and orphans he has created in this city alone. The Nevera leadership have sworn to get him. His bodyguards are twitchy as hell. They say he never sleeps two nights in the same bed. He won't receive foreign visitors, except from the American Mafia."

It was a discouraging prospect but I could not believe that the General would have forgotten me, especially as the First Lady had so graciously implied that she might be able to put in a good word for us. I decided to employ my free time with a visit one morning to the botanical gardens, which my dear Susan had so much enjoyed. It was delicious day before the heat became intense. I felt happily relaxed as I strolled beneath the deep purple of the bougainvillaea and the dark red of the luxuriant jacquaranda. The great royal palms waved above me and, in the near distance, a fountain splashed. I might have been back in some exquisite garden of the old world, in Granada or Marrakesh.

Suddenly I felt my arms seized from behind and some ominously sharp object being forcibly pressed into the small of my back.

"Don't resist," hissed a guttural voice into my ear, in Concordian Spanish, "or you're a dead man." I had no intention of resisting. Heroics are not in my style at all. They bundled me into a van without windows, and I was driven off at breakneck speed. The men wore masks, and appeared to be robustly constructed. I remembered reading somewhere that it was essential to establish some rapport with one's captors. Had not Pattie Hearst become quite a friend of her kidnappers? One is trained in the British Foreign Service to maintain one's sangfroid in all circumstances. At least outwardly. Inwardly I was quaking like the proverbial jelly.

"I was just admiring your beautiful botanical garden," I remarked casually. "Surely one of the jewels of Felicidad. And what a lovely morning."

"Belt up, swine," suggested the same harsh voice. "Or you'll get a kick in the kisser." I fell sagely silent. But they were taking no chances. I was instantly blindfolded and tightly gagged – a most uncomfortable combination.

After a short but ghastly ride, I felt the vehicle screeching to a halt. Rough hands were ejecting me from it and dragging me into a building. I was pulled down a steep flight of stairs into what was presumably a deep cellar, and pushed into a hard chair. There was an ominous pause. I sensed that the brutes were still there, pointing their guns at me, and that it would be disastrous to try to make a move. Then I heard a door opening, and realised that someone else had entered.

The gag was snatched from my mouth and the blindfold was removed. I found myself gazing into an only too familiar face. It was Silvester Marsala. I gave a gasp of horror. He responded with a wolfish grin. "I remember you," he said nastily.

"And I remember you," I retorted, mustering my natural dignity.

"My men didn't like what you were doing in the gardens," he explained. "Gazing around in a most suspicious way."

"I was enjoying the natural beauty," I explained.

"A likely tale! You stared at me in the plane too. As if you were trying to memorise my face. What's your name, Mister?"

"I am His Excellency Mr Ambrose Bellingham," I said, in my most magisterial manner, "formerly Her Britannic Majesty's Ambassador to the State of Concordia."

"You're a spy, aren't you? It's written all over you. From the British Secret Service."

"Nonsense," I protested. "The Secret Service is quite distinct from the Diplomatic Service. Our spies are people who haven't got the brains to become diplomats. Just as your State of Department are the ones who couldn't get into the CIA."

"We'll see about that, Mr Bellingham. Take him away to the Persuasion Parlour, Bruno. Give him a spell on the stretching table. That will make him sing."

The rough arms seized me again. I was about to be dragged away to the torture chamber in some remote corner of this sinister underground complex. I felt myself gibbering with terror. Then inspiration struck. Taking a deep breath, I gave out a piercing scream; not a half-hearted squeak but the sort of deep-throated bellow you would emit if you were strapped across a railway line and trying to stop an approaching express train.

"What's all this fucking noise?" enquired another voice, in heavily accented Concordian English.

"Nothing to worry about, General," said the unspeakable Marsala. "We're just going to warm up a suspect."

"I told you I want peace and quiet down here," protested the other voice. "This is my bunker, where I listen to music. Not the place for your little hobbies."

"We're not doing this for fun," protested Marsala. "The man is a spy, threatening your personal security. Aren't I meant to protect you?"

I peered into the semi-darkness of the horrible cellar. There was no mistaking it. That huge jowl, those flapping ears, that lumbering figure – it all belonged to none other than General Golosina. Since I had last seen him, he had grown flabby and looked out of condition.

"Tiberio!" I shrieked. The General looked at me in astonishment. "Ambrose Bellingham!" he yelled in reciprocity. "I heard you were in town and I was planning to receive you. But there was no need to go to such extremes in order to get into the Bunker."

"He was sniffing the flowers," explained Sylvester Marsala, "and gazing up at the sky. That's not regular for a man. We thought he must be a spy."

"The English are like that," said Golosina. "They love nature."

"I told you quite distinctly," I said, beginning to recover my cool, "that I have diplomatic status."

"You didn't look like a diplomat," protested Marsala. "Not when my team brought you in, whining and whingeing."

"You must forgive Sylvester," said Golosina, in the gently cooing voice he could assume when he felt like it. "He is doing a fine job for Concordia." I thought of the drug running. They were all in it together.

"Come with me, my dear Ambrose," continued Tiberio. "We

will try to make it up to you."

I followed him into another part of the cellar, enclosed behind a steel door. This proved to be a veritable Aladdin's cave, with velvet hangings, comfortable chairs and soft lights. And surely that gruesomely sadistic picture hanging on the wall was none other than *The Flaying of Marsyas* by Caravaggio, the only Old Master picture belonging to the National Gallery of Concordia?

"Removed temporarily for cleaning," explained the General, with a hoarse laugh. "What can I offer you?" He indicated a well-stocked drinks tray.

"A stiff whisky please," I gasped. "You might as well know I intend to bring a legal action against Marsala."

"That would be … inadvisable," commented Golosina smoothly. "We'e got the Supreme Court sewn up. At least we got to meet. I'm not all that accessible these days."

"So I heard."

"They know the Raros wouldn't last an hour without me. So the opposition are out to get me. I spend a lot of time down here in the Bunker. Planning my anti-terrorist swoops. Pleasuring my women. And listening to my Gesualdo tapes. At least I'm still alive so far."

"You haven't thought of quitting?"

"Sure, I have. But there's nowhere to quit to. People out there are trying to put me on trial as an enemy of the human race. Just because I try to hold this damned country together. It's all got worse since your time, Ambrose. We've had those fucking Tozudos for years. They have de facto control of the interior. I don't care about that. The area is only a swamp, and crawling with crocodiles. Then we have the Nevera rebels. I can cope with them too. Most of the coast is malaria-infested, and the Nevera seem to thrive on that. But Victor Fernandez is the last straw. He's an educated man, you know, with a Tozudo mother and a Nevera grandfather, or so he claims. He's getting the Tozudos and the Nevera to co-operate, and that's bloody dangerous for the Government. We're desperate for arms – you know that."

"You have our offer."

"And the American offer. And the French. We'll go for the best one."

"What exactly does that mean?"

"We should have to take account of … fringe benefits," said the General, with a wicked grin. "I am particularly interested in Our Lady's Refuge for Military Orphans. Poor little dears. I do Father Christmas for them every year, in a lovely red cloak. Excellent cover. A donation would be much appreciated, amount to be discussed. Cheque to be made out to T. Golosina."

"I take your point, Tiberio."

"I guessed you would. You were always good at understanding our little ways here. I remember how you used to let me win at golf. That meant the drinks were always on you at the clubhouse."

"It was a pleasure," I murmured.

"I don't get out on the golf course any more. Too risky. Just the occasional game of croquet with the President in his sunken garden. And I don't have much contact with your present ambassador. But I get nice letters from your boss Ludovic Molnar. He shares my taste for Early Music."

Both supreme crooks, I thought. But the decencies must be preserved.

"The President and the First Lady seem to have taken refuge in their Catholic faith," I remarked blandly.

"They've never been the same since they got that illuminated scroll from the Pope. I myself pin my hopes on … another power."

"Really?"

"I may tell you some day. We'll keep in touch, Ambrose. It's a pity you didn't get to see my computerised persuasion facility. Sylvester just loves tinkering with the controls, seeing how far he can go. Don't look so scared, old man. I got to you just in time, didn't I? They were about to strap you down. A bit of a joke that, you must admit."

I made a ghastly attempt to smile.

"That's what I like about you, Ambrose. Your British sense of humour."

Marsala and his brutes were waiting outside to lead me up to the world outside. No doubt steps would be taken to make sure that I could not identify the route again. He gave me a faintly apologetic grin, to which I responded with a glance of magisterial contempt. He would not dare to tangle with me again. Or so I thought.

***

"I am in need of peace and calm, Harry," I said. "That is why I decided to call on you."

"I am very glad you did, Ambassador," replied my host, Archdeacon Harry Wilderness of the Anglican Church of Saint Mary Magdalene. He had arrived in Felicidad long before my time, and we had become quite good friends when I was there *en poste*. I liked the respectful way in which he addressed me, even now that I was a Person of No Importance. He was a gentle-looking man, with the face of a slightly bewildered cherubim. The existence of an Anglican Church in Felicidad had always struck me as bizarre. After all, it was Spanish papist territory. But apparently, in the early twentieth century, Concordia had enjoyed a brief period of stability when it seemed a suitable headquarter for an English archdeacon, who had to minister to miscellaneous parishioners washed up from the British Caribbean territories plus those venturous British and American episcopalians who settled in Central America in search of money and sun. There had been a small, slightly seedy colony round the emerald mines until they were nationalised.

"May I offer you a dry sherry?" asked Archdeacon Wilderness. I accepted with alacrity, and we sat comfortably on his modest terrace. I felt soothed by the company of this mild and kindly person – qualities I had not been recently encountering.

"So you're still here, Harry," I said, "after all these years. Aren't you sick of Concordia by now?"

"I applied to become Bishop of Bath and Wells," he admitted. "I liked the idea of feeding the swans in the palace moat. But they only offered Bishop of Basutoland. I thought I might as well stay on in Felicidad. I didn't fancy the prospect of retiring to Saffron Walden with my invalid sister."

"Things seem pretty tense around here. Aren't you in danger?"

"Human life was intended to be dangerous, I think. We are all in the hands of God."

"There are some awful brutes in Felicidad," I said. "I have met some of them quite recently."

"There is good in everyone, I think. Deep down, but worth digging to get it out."

"You are an idealist, my dear archdeacon."

"Well, why not? People *can* live happily together. William Penn showed that when he was so decent to the Indians. And the Jesuits had a fine record in Paraguay. I long for the day prophesied by Isaiah. How does he put it? The lion and the sheep shall abide together, and the weaned child shall thrust his hand into the den of the basilisk."

"I don't think that point has yet been reached in Concordia," I said with a touch of cynicism. "What, by the way, is a basilisk?"

"A fabulous reptile, I believe. A basilisk glance means a touch of the evil eye."

"Sounds rather nasty," I said. "I hope they are at least decent to you here. Does your church get molested?"

"The Raros are very keen Roman Catholics, as you know. But I have had no trouble. So far."

"You should be very cautious, Harry."

"I agree, Your Excellency. Up to a point. But one has certain responsibilities. I cannot honourably be silent when I ought to speak out. I have prayed publicly for a restoration of public order."

"No harm in that. It will be taken to mean that you want the rebels defeated."

"I have also denounced the drugs traffic from my pulpit."

"That is thinner ice," I pointed out. "You must know that some high-level interests in this country are very much involved in the narcotics business."

"I can't help that," said the Archdeacon, with the sudden

obstinacy of a mild, but righteous, man. "Soon I shall have a chance to raise the whole issue in a wider form. The Archbishop of Canterbury, no less, will be visiting Miami, in the course of a tour of episcopal churches in the States. He has summoned me to meet him there. I hope to persuade him to point the finger at those responsible, with full geographical details."

"They won't like that here."

"Then they'll have to lump it," replied Wilderness with a gentle smile. Such, I thought, was the stuff of the martyrs.

"While you are here, Ambassador," he continued, "I hope you can attend the Talent Night Supper I am arranging to raise funds for our Organ Restoration Fund. It will be the greatest fun. Everyone has to do something to add to the entertainment. I shall be singing selections from Gilbert and Sullivan. And Mr Haverstock-Jones has promised to read from Kipling."

"My talents are of a different order," I murmured cautiously. Fortunately we were interrupted at that moment by the arrival of another visitor – a youngish man with huge spectacles and the enthusiastic appearance of an overgrown schoolboy.

"Allow me, Ambassador," said Harry, "to introduce Adrian Carr-Baxendale – one of our local residents. He arrived shortly after you left."

"What is your line?" I asked.

"I'm an ethnographer, researching the pre-Mayan inhabitants of the Nevera peninsula."

"The Nevera peninsula! Do you actually go down there?"

"From time to time. I've got a dig going on there."

"But is that safe?" I asked. "I thought the area was in the hands of the rebels."

"Not all of it. And the rebels don't do me any harm."

"But what about the Government in Felicidad?"

"They aren't interested. They know I'm only an innocuous scholar on sabbatical leave from the University of Hartlepool. Terribly interesting, the Stone Age Neveras, you know. Quite artistic in a sinister way."

"Sinister?"

"Noted for their gruesome human sacrifices. We have found their altars. And the implements."

"I seem to remember," I said, "that in the Mexico of the Aztecs, some of the victims were actually volunteers."

"If you'd ever witnessed a Nevera sacrifice," said Carr-Baxendale grimly, "I don't think you would volunteer."

"What a ghastly field of study," I said.

"It has its satisfaction. Partly as a way of understanding modern life in Concordia. It helps to explain the endemic brutality. You see, the old ways have never really died here. They have only been partially obscured by the efforts of the Catholic Church. It's all been transformed into voodoo. That's the real religion here. Whatever they may pretend to you, President Raro and his lovely consort are deeply under the influence of voodoo priests. Golosina even more."

It sounded perfectly possible. I remembered that Golosina had admitted to pinning his hopes on some mysterious power.

"What really scares the voodoo believers is when they see figures resembling undertakers' men in black frock-coats and top hats."

"Who are they?" I asked.

"The death spirits. Come to fetch their victim."

"I should like to know more about the current practice of voodoo," I said.

"I don't advise that," intervened the Archdeacon. "It could be dangerous."

"For my physical safety?"

"For the salvation of your soul, my dear Ambassador. Will you have another small glass of sherry?"

***

"Susan! Is that you?"

"Ambrose!"

"You sound grumpy."

"I'm not grumpy. Just sleepy. It's the middle of the night here in Little Bigney."

"Sorry! I forgot that."

"I got to sleep late. It was a mistake, having coffee and a pork pie. And the O'Callaghans are back. They've got some new flamenco CDs, which have to be played very loud with a lot of stamping."

"I'll ring off then."

"No, don't do that, Darling. Are you all right?"

"More or less. What about you, Susan?"

"Sharon is in the neighbourhood."

"What exactly does that mean?"

"She's installed up a tree, protesting against the Swaffham bypass. But she keeps sending her socks and undies down for me to wash."

"And Neville?"

"He's disappeared. On some secret mission abroad of great importance."

"Good."

"It's not good at all, Ambrose. I don't know where he is."

"That doesn't matter, Dear. Our son is a big boy now."

***

I felt slightly peeved by Susan's reaction. I had expected her to be overjoyed to hear my voice, not to fuss about the lateness of the hour. I was also put out by the fairly obvious desire of Gerald and Monica Haverstock-Jones that I should not be present for every meal at the Embassy. Each morning Monica would quiz me pointedly about my plans for the day, expressing the hope that I would enjoy the company of old acquaintances. These two negative factors may have influenced me into taking a somewhat unfortunate decision. My judgement is usually pretty sound but we are all human and liable to error, as I used to point out to my old chiefs.

It all started when I received a charming note on expensive scented paper from a lady styling herself Casilda, Condesa de las Rosas. She had heard about me, she said, from the First Lady, and would like to offer me hospitality. Would I care to attend a little informal dinner she was offering the following evening? She gave an address in Los Pinos, the most elegant residential suburb in Felicidad. It sounded respectable enough and I hastened to accept. With the Ambassador's agreement, the ubiquitous Potiphar agreed to drive me there on the night.

"You know the *condesa*, Potiphar?" I asked, as we swept up the drive of a palatial villa.

"Oh yes, Sir," replied Potiphar darkly. "Everyone knows the *condesa*."

I wanted to ask him what he meant by that but we had arrived at the front portico. The door of the car was flung open by a smartly dressed flunkey. I felt myself being urged up steps into a highly decorated entrance hall. In Concordia the rich are very rich, just as the poor are very poor. The *condesa* came forward to meet me. She was beautifully dressed, not exactly in the first flush of youth but with an eager, sympathetic expression in her dark eyes which I found instantly attractive. To my surprise, she led me upstairs to a small boudoir painted mainly in pink, like one of the more louche backgrounds of Boucher or Watteau.

"I know what you're thinking, my dear Ambassador," she said in English, in a rather deep, sexy voice. "Where are the other guests?"

"The thought did cross my mind, Condesa."

"I must be frank with you, Mr Bellingham. There are no other guests."

"Oh."

"Naughty of me, wasn't it? But I was afraid you would not come if I said it was only the two of us. The truth is that the First Lady spoke so warmly about you. She said you were a fascinating man, and I can see she was right. I wanted to enjoy you all by myself and get to know you properly. One can never do that at big dinner parties, can one? Will you have one of my special cocktails? A great favourite with my former husband. We call it a stingaroo."

The drink had a slightly bitter taste but was undoubtedly palatable. I could not help being flattered by the *condesa*'s explanation of her outrageous behaviour. At my age one can do with all the encouragement available. It was pleasant to receive confirmation that I had not entirely lost my virile charisma, developed in those distant London days when I had been a 'debutantes' delight'. We chatted agreeably enough and I found myself downing two more of the delicious stingaroos by the time that dinner was served. I felt slightly shaky as we tottered into a sumptuous dining room.

The meal was excellent, washed down by a copious supply of imported French wines of rare quality. I felt myself warming towards the *condesa*, who was proving to be an excellent hostess. It was a welcome change from the homely fare provided by Gerald and his parsimonious spouse at the British Embassy. When we retired to the little boudoir and I had followed the superb wine with a magnificent old brandy, I felt as if I were floating on a cloud, totally divorced from all earthly cares. By now I was calling her Casilda, and she was addressing me as Ambrose in her honeyed tones. I felt we were kindred spirits and this was an enchanting evening one would not lightly forget.

"I am very fond of the British," cooed Casilda. "I am a Catholic, of course, but sometimes I attend Evensong in your lovely Anglican church. Dear Mr Wilderness – what a delightful man." I was surprised to hear this, thinking they would not have much in common. Casilda was so obviously a worldly sophisticate. But life is full of surprises, as I have often warned Neville.

"We have an interesting British group about to descend upon us," she continued. "They are highly cultured people sponsored by Connoisseur Travel. Their leader is Lord Cumberland. I expect you have heard of him." I had. He was a high-profile aesthete-cum-aristocrat, who sometimes appeared on television at home at late hours, after the workers had presumably retired to bed. "They are doing a tour of stately homes, under my direction. I shall be offering them some of my stingaroo cocktails." No doubt they would return to Britain singing the praises of the delightful old-world atmosphere in the baroque mansions of Felicidad.

From that moment onwards, I did not feel equal to intelligent conversation. Swirling thoughts seemed to be raging round my addled brain and I was conscious only of the curvaceous charms of my lively hostess. By now we both seemed to have mislaid a certain amount of clothing, and I felt myself being pleasantly wafted upstairs towards a huge bed.

"You're beautiful, Casilda," I croaked.

"You're so handsome, so strong," she riposted. I knew what I wanted to do. It was only a question of making the effort. At that point I must have passed out.

When I awoke, it was broad daylight. I felt perfectly terrible, with an appalling headache and a ghastly singing in my ears. Had my stingaroos been drugged? And why did I have no clothes on? There was no sign of Casilda, but a supercilious attendant appeared with my garments freshly pressed and indicated where I could take a shower. He also brought coffee and croissants.

As I crept down the stairs, like some wounded woodland creature, Casilda tapped me softly on the shoulder. She looked as fresh as a daisy.

"Thank you, Darling," she whispered. "You were wonderful. I never knew that an Englishman could love like a jungle beast." It was a flattering suggestion and I only wished that I could remember something about the encounter.

Potiphar appeared miraculously at the portico. He did not seem in the least surprised at my precarious condition.

"Ambassador have lovely time?" he asked suggestively, as we sped through the traffic of mid-morning Felicidad.

"I expect so," I replied rather curtly. The man was obviously an experienced pander.

"Ah, there you are!" said Monica drily, meeting us in the entrance of the embassy residence. "Will you be wanting lunch?"

"No, thank you." I would never eat lunch again. She gave me a rather odd look. I began to feel doubts. My caper had not been entirely fair to poor, loyal Susan, stuck at home in Little Bigney. Well, nobody would know. Or so I thought at the time.

***

"We are inviting you to meet the minister, Ambrose," said Gerald Haverstock-Jones, with a marked lack of enthusiasm. "After all, you are our house guest. And you can be relied upon to supply a quantity of amusing badinage and airy persiflage. But remember please that you are no longer Her Majesty's Ambassador. Do not try to influence Dame Rosy in favour of your hare-brained commercial projects."

"You know me, Gerald. I can be silent as the grave."

"I do know you, Ambrose. That is why I felt it necessary to be so explicit."

The embassy residence was in uproar. Monica had raided the native market, accompanied by Potiphar and the doddery Felipe, and had returned with baskets full of cut-price fish and tired-looking mangos in preparation for an unaccustomed spurt of economical entertaining. Dame Rosy had arrived for her proconsular visit, accompanied by Trevor Pilkington QC and Selby Tritton MP. They were already wilting in the tropical heat, in spite of their attempts to dress for the ghastly climate. Dame Rosy had stepped off the plane in a flowery pattern geared to Henley; while Selby sported a natty dark blue summer suit and Trevor, being on holiday, had opted for long Bermuda shorts, revealing a pair of knobbly knees. I chortled inwardly at this manifestation of the English abroad. We English tend to find other nations funny. Perhaps we never look in the mirror.

Advance telegrams from the Foreign Office had stated that the Minister of State intended to avoid all personal contact with the Raro regime. Instead, she would wish to tour prisons, mental hospitals and other places where Raro victims might be found decaying or recuperating. Gerald, to his credit, had fought this absurd instruction, pointing out that Britain enjoyed diplomatic relations with Concordia and therefore a British minister could hardly visit Felicidad without paying a formal call on the head of state. Nor was it likely that she could gain access to prisons and other corrective establishments. He had deftly implied that we were not, in fact, running the place and never had, beneficial though that would have been for all concerned. Dame Rosy had reluctantly been forced to agree. Now, in the late afternoon, she returned to the residence after her brief visit to President Raro and his sprightly consort.

The minister was not in one of her sweetest moods. Gerald and Monica unwisely suggested that she should take a refreshing bath. After some minutes, a muffled scream was heard from the guest bedroom and a hand, fringed with imperious fingers, emerged round the door, while a commanding mezzo shouted for Trevor. The reason was obvious. The insane Teresita had struck again. This problem resolved, we adjourned to the Ambassador's study.

"My gorge absolutely rose, Trevor," proclaimed Dame Rosy, "at having to shake hands with that bloodstained tyrant. He had the TV cameras trained on us too. I hope the pictures will not be shown at home. Thank God I opted, in the end, not to bring out a television crew myself, though *Panorama* were awfully keen."

"You missed a trick, Darling," said the QC. "I had wrapped my hand in a handkerchief and told the head of protocol that I had sprained it while gardening in Hampstead."

"But you never garden in Hampstead, Darling. We have a man to do that."

"He was not to know."

"Surely you have to admit, Minister," said Gerald in his smooth, confident voice, "that poor old Raro looks quite harmless, when you actually meet him."

"Not at all," snapped Dame Rosy decisively. "I could see a definite aura of profound evil around his wicked little head."

"I thought he was rather polite," interjected Selby, braving her temporary wrath. He knew he was a bit of a favourite with the minister.

"You're the sort of man, Selby, who insists on seeing redeeming features in the most horrible tyrants. Hitler was a non-smoker. You shouldn't be deluded by the superficial. Of course they tried to butter us up. The President attempted to persuade me to join him in a game of croquet but I wasn't having that."

"His wife invited me to visit a leper colony with her," said

Trevor. "Hardly my idea of a holiday diversion."

"We must get rid of the whole pack of them as soon as possible," announced the minister in her stentorian tones. "My visit has already convinced me of that. It's simply a question of how. I'm inclined to favour a high-level bombing campaign, followed by an invasion by UN troops."

"I don't think this is the place to talk about that, Minister," said the Ambassador nervously. "We may well be under ... electronic surveillance."

"Bugging, you mean? The Office did warn me about that. They said the whole city is riddled with spies."

"Keep your big mouth shut then, Rosy," suggested Trevor.

"All right, but I shall certainly revert to the matter when I am back on home ground."

"My advice, Minister, for what it is worth, is to let sleeping dogs lie. The Raros have been in power for a long time. Nothing ever lasts. They will be out some day." Gerald gave a calming smile.

"You mean we should just stand idly by?" snorted the embattled minister.

"Ought you not to accept the President's invitation to see some of the achievements of his regime?" suggested Selby emolliently. "Such as the work of the Elvira Raro Fund for the Ungifted. And Our Lady's Home for Military Orphans."

"Certainly not. I never like to blur the clarity of my vision. One thing is certain, gentlemen. The regime is quite obviously repressive. You have only to drive through the streets to see the miserable condition of the people. I'm not at all inclined to agree to that arms deal proposed by Wedmore and Bassenthwaite."

"It's a great pity that you have not been able to meet General Golosina, the Internal Security Director," I pointed out, "owing to his absence in the interior. A gentle giant of a man, anxious to obtain humane control equipment so as to maintain public order with the very minimum of force."

Trevor Pilkington gave a disbelieving guffaw. "A bit fishy, that," he said. "We all know that Golosina is known as The Gorilla.

Amnesty have a huge file on him. And what's he doing in the interior? I thought that had been taken over by the Tozudo freedom fighters."

"I should have liked to meet some human rights activists," said Dame Rosy wistfully.

"You can't," pointed out the Ambassador. "They're not around."

"I would have been willing to take some cases to the International Court of Human Rights," said Trevor. "But I can't, if there are not complaints." And no fat legal fees either, I thought.

"Who *are* we meeting now?" asked Dame Rosy. "Not silly socialites, I hope. I do detest idle talk."

"The American and French ambassadors are coming in for a drink," said Gerald. "I thought you might like to compare notes. The Diplomatic Corps here is decidedly mixed. Most of the colleagues have been sent to Felicidad as a punishment for making some ghastly mistake elsewhere. But Homer Fairchild, the American, is a world authority on butterflies. The Frenchman, Jacques Marigny-Marmande, writes amusing satirical novels which have done him no good at all with the Quai."

"Did I hear you mention drink?" enquired Trevor Pilkington. "I should so love a whisky. A single malt if possible. I am rather partial to Glenmorangie. I suppose it's all on the poor old British taxpayer." I did not blame Monica for darting him a withering look as she bustled off to give instructions to Felipe. This was the type of freeloading official visitor I had most detested during my own career.

"Selby and I will take a turn in the garden," announced Dame Rosy, "now that it's the cool of the evening? Wasn't that when God walked in the Garden of Eden?"

"Be careful of snakes then," suggested her husband nastily. I am perceptive about these things and had already spotted that while the Clumber woman rather cared for Selby, effete though he might be, the Clumber man did not like him at all.

The meeting with the other ambassadors, which I was not invited to attend, could hardly be described as a success from my standpoint. Gerald told me afterwards that Homer Fairchild had made a deep impression on Dame Rosy by informing her of Washington's conviction that the Raro regime was at the centre of the drugs trade for the whole area. The Americans, he said, might well withdraw their support. The Marquis de Marigny-Marmande had also claimed, with a sophisticated giggle, that Paris, while taking their own decision entirely independently of the Anglo-Saxons, were unlikely to back the Raros any longer in their long drawn-out battle against the Tozudo minority and the Nevera rebels. Both ambassadors had assured Dame Rosy that neither of their governments were in the least disposed to sell arms to the wretched Raros. They had also strongly advised the British not to do so either.

"This ludicrous arms deal is clearly a non-starter," Dame Rosy had told Gerald later. "I can't think why I bothered to come here at all. You should have given me clearer guidance in advance. That's what we pay you diplomats for, isn't it? Not to go to cocktail parties." There had been a threatening tone in her voice. "You told me that if we didn't sell the wretched stuff, then the Americans or the beastly French would do so. Now I see that it's not true."

"But it is true," I complained to Gerald when we were alone. "Your diplomatic colleagues have fooled Dame Rosy completely. Of course they will sell arms if we don't. The silly woman has believed their lies."

"I expected her to do so," commented Gerald quietly.

"Then why on earth did you invite them round?" I asked.

"I had my reasons."

"I think I know why," I exclaimed in sudden fury. "You wished to scupper the defence equipment sale."

"I wanted some precision in British policy."

"You mean ... you didn't care for a lot of extra work."

"I am not accountable to you, Ambrose. Please remember, I am not on the payroll of Ludovic Molnar. Besides, the Raros are really not very nice."

"What about the unemployment situation in Greyburn? Doesn't that mean anything to you?"

"Not a lot," he said with a smirk. I could have socked him on the jaw, but instead contented myself with a look of ineffable disdain.

"I've got a bone to pick with you, Mr Bellingham," intoned Dame Rosy as we reassembled before dinner. "You shouldn't have encouraged me to come here. It's been a waste of time. I think I'll go straight home. I could make a surprise appearance at the Hospital Ball in my constituency on Saturday. It would give immense pleasure."

"Certainly not," said Trevor. "Now I'm here, I want to see some-thing of the country. Whom are we meeting at dinner?"

"Archdeacon Wilderness," put in Monica brightly. "He's absolutely sweet. And then there's Mr Carr-Baxendale, our local ethnographer – a great authority on ancient Nevera society."

"There's also Lord Cumberland," interjected Gerald hopefully. "He's just arrived with a group from Connoisseur Travel." He spoke with the enthusiastic air of an estate agent showing off a desirable property.

"I have encountered Lord Cumberland before," said Dame Rosy sourly. "He is a birdbrained aesthete with no political sense at all. Didn't he take his Connoisseur clients to visit Angkor Wat when the Pol Pot were in charge? These people are no use to me, Ambassador. I wished to meet Concordian opinion formers, the political elite."

"We had to do the best we could," riposted Gerald with admirable sangfroid. "You didn't want a social meeting with Raro supporters. And the opposition are dead or in prison or hiding in the jungle."

At the last moment, he had at least the sense to open fresh supplies of a rather ordinary wine. Lord Cumberland turned out to be an amiable peer, with whom I had an interesting conversation on Italian art of the quattrocento. The talk and the drink started to flow. Trevor was clearly out to enjoy himself at government expense and, after a time, even Dame Rosy Clumber began to relax her stern demeanour.

"I hear you have met my friend the Condesa de las Rosas," the Archdeacon told me.

"Yes," I replied cautiously.

"She has spoken most warmly about you. Between ourselves, she has just given me a most generous donation for our church's Organ Restoration Fund."

"I wonder what her motive could be."

"Disinterested generosity, I suppose," he replied in a tone of gentle reproof. "I must try to buy a little present for that dear lady when I go to Miami next week to see the Archbishop. I invited him to come here, you know, but he said he would rather not."

"There must be something to see," I heard Trevor Pilkington say to Adrian Carr-Baxendale. "Surely I haven't travelled all this way for nothing?"

"The country is brimming with interest," replied Carr Baxendale, "if you have a sense of the past. There's my own Nevera dig, where we have set up a small human sacrifice museum."

"We have that in England too," interjected Dame Rosy. "We call it Prime Minister's Question Time."

I looked at her in astonishment until I realised that she had actually made a joke. It was like hearing the cat speak.

"I shouldn't advise you to go there," said Gerald. "That coastal zone is rebel territory. You would be in danger of kidnap, Mr Pilkington."

"He could go halfway," pointed out Carr-Baxendale. "As far as the Sacred Grove. That's a very fascinating spot too. Classic voodoo country. The grove itself is surrounded by a river infested with crocodiles."

"I shouldn't fancy that," said the QC.

"It's not dangerous. You cross in a little boat."

"Even so," said Gerald, "it would be safer to go there as a group. Some Swedish ladies got lost in the area last year, and after that they were never quite the same."

"It so happens," said Lord Cumberland with a benevolent smile, "that our Connoisseur group is due to visit the Sacred Grove tomorrow. We shall have a good local guide, of course. The trip will start with a brief tour of Felicidad colonial homes, and then our air-conditioned bus will proceed along the coast road, with a shrimp lunch en route at the Golden Sands Hotel. It should be a delightful day. We should be charmed if you would join us as my guest, Mr Pilkington. You too, Mr Bellingham."

"Oh, do go, Trevor," said Dame Rosy. "You deserve a break from me. Selby and I will spend the time writing up my report."

Trevor frowned. "Poor Selby," he said with mock sympathy. "Doesn't he qualify for a day off in the country too?"

"There would be room for you as well," said Lord Cumberland amiably. "Two of our guest lecturers have collapsed with some local bug and will be unable to travel tomorrow."

Later, Trevor Pilkington said to his hostess, "If I may ask, where on earth do you get hold of this wine?"

"We buy it in bulk from a store in Trinidad. My husband saw it advertised in a mail-order catalogue."

"Jolly rotten embassy this," hissed Pilkington to me in a loud, carrying voice. "Better in your day, I expect. Not a drop of single malt in the whole establishment. Time to come to bed now, Rosy." The great lady got up with some difficulty. "If we stay any longer," he announced expansively to the company, "she is liable to start singing. And I join in."

***

"This is one of the most beautiful of our baroque colonial homes," proclaimed Casilda to the well-scrubbed group from Connoisseur Travel. "Once it belonged to the Spanish Governor but, after independence, it was taken over as the residence of our first president, the Liberator of Concordia, General Enrique Trabazon. He was born in Seville in Spain, and came here as a lieutenant in the Spanish army. But he became a convert to the noble cause of Concordian independence. He it was who defenestrated the Colonial Governor from the balcony of the town hall, shipping his mistresses back to Spain in a small boat which unfortunately sank in the mouth of the harbour. So he is our General Washington, and this is his Mount

Vernon. Note the beautifully decorated fireplaces, though in fact we never light fires in this benign climate."

Looking round at our select group, the Condesa de la Rosas, as she claimed to be, favoured me with a specially beaming smile. I had not intended to see her again and had forgotten that she was to entertain the Connoisseur group when I agreed to join them. Trevor Pilkington and Selby Tritton had also shown up in response to Lord Cumberland's gracious invitation. We were not travelling in the luxury bus, since the Ambassador had placed Potiphar and the official car at our disposal.

"What was the policy of General Trabazon towards the native Indian people?" asked Trevor Pilkington loudly and rather pointedly.

"He employed some of them as domestics," replied Casilda, unabashed. "Others were shipped off into the interior. He feared that they might suffer from exposure to European culture."

"Could that be one of the reasons for the Tozudo liberation movement in central Concordia today?" pursued Trevor.

"You may not know, Mr Pilkington," intervened Lord Cumberland in his usual bland tones, "that it is the policy of Connoisseur Travel not to involve our patrons in current political controversy."

"We shall now proceed to the Liberator's bedroom," said Casilda hastily, "and admire the lovely view over the gardens of the Bishop's palace."

As we trailed round the large mansions, the artful Casilda managed to get me alone in the small nursery on the top floor, once occupied by the Liberator's many children.

"I was expecting you to telephone," she whispered reproachfully.

"I've been rather busy."

"But you've not forgotten me, Ambrose?"

"How could I, Casilda?"

"I did so enjoy our evening together. You have such a lot of … er … stamina, for a man of your age. Let's meet again soon."

"Delighted, I'm sure," I murmured untruthfully. I owed it to poor Susan to keep this mature siren at bay.

I was rescued by the appearance of Selby Tritton, inspiring the *condesa* to recollect that she had to rejoin the rest of our group.

"This is all a waste of time," grumbled Selby to me. "We are doing nothing useful to promote the project in the way we agreed with Ludovic Molnar." No doubt he was frightened of losing his retainer. "Courage, Selby," I said cheerfully. "This is a land of the unexpected."

There seemed to be an over-superfluity of gracious colonial homes, shown in exhausting detail by the enthusiastic *condesa*. I could not help admiring the courage and vitality of the elderly patrons of Connoisseur Travel, who skipped along on their Zimmer frames, anxious to miss nothing on what might well be their last earthly journey. At last they boarded their bus, and we climbed into Potiphar's Jaguar, making our way along the coast towards the Golden Sands Motel. There we enjoyed a tasty seafood lunch, somewhat superior to the fare offered by Gerald and Monica.

"Is the wine on the house?" I heard Trevor asking with unblushing audacity.

After lunch, we took the road again towards the deep forest surrounding the Sacred Grove.

"We are now moving towards Nevera tribal territory," announced Casilda. "As you know, there are certain ... political problems in the area. So it is important that we should all keep together and that none should stray from the group."

"Are we in danger?" asked a beautifully dressed elderly lady who, much to my surprise at first, spoke English with a curious cockney accent. "We seem to be surrounded now with savage-looking men wielding guns."

"Those are our guards, Duchess," replied Casilda, "supplied by the authorities to make sure that no harm comes to us."

It transpired that the Duchess was of French aristocratic blood and had been taught English in Provence in infancy by her so-called governess, who was actually a nursery maid from Hackney.

Casilda's announcement had filled the high-born party with a certain frisson, the remote prospect of danger acting as a stimulant.

They boarded the bus with the vivacity of schoolchildren out for a treat, determined to look for crocodiles while crossing the river. Lord Cumberland had discovered a winning formula.

I thought the Sacred Grove was a bit of a disappointment, looking like a perfectly ordinary bit of dense forest. But Casilda, now attired in fetching green jungle boots, did her heroic best to keep up the interest.

"The Sacred Grove is a historic place in our culture," she intoned. "It has long been known as the resort of voodoo priests and prophets, practising a system of magical cults much older than the Christianity brought by the Spaniards."

"I don't see any priests," commented the Duchess.

"They reside deep in the forest," explained Casilda, "and only emerge at midnight to receive their devotees. Nobody else is allowed to know their identity."

"And the worshippers?" asked Trevor. "Who are they? The underprivileged native majority, I suppose?"

"That is a difficult question to answer," replied Casilda cautiously. "But voodoo is believed to exert a considerable influence in my country, even today." I recalled what Adrian Carr-Baxendale had told me about the ruling triumvirate being strongly under voodoo influence. Would it be worth returning at midnight to the Sacred Grove?

I mentioned this idea to Selby, who expressed a fear that we might tread on snakes in the dark. Potiphar must have heard us because he came up and volunteered to drive us back there that evening, armed with two powerful electric torches.

"Are you sure we shall be all right?" I asked him.

"You will be safe with Potiphar," the man replied with a knowing wink.

And so it happened that Selby and I, accompanied by the irrepressible Potiphar, stood that night in darkness in the Sacred Grove. We could detect shadowy shapes moving stealthily through the forest. Could they be the dreaded undertaker's men? It was an eerie experience, which I was now beginning to regret. Was poor Selby trembling with the unusual chill or with plain fear?

"Keep closely with me," said Potiphar. "I lead you into the forest to meet the voodoo high priest."

"I blame you for this, Ambrose," hissed Selby. "It's a damned risky escapade."

"We should have brought a black dog and a white cock to slaughter," whispered Potiphar. "But the priest may be willing to sell you some animals. Be careful to catch the blood in the pot he will give you."

I did not care for the sound of this at all. As we advanced further into the wood, an owl hooted and dark clouds covered the moon. All around, sinister rustling and tiny screams indicated that little creatures were dying. Nature, I knew, was red in tooth and claw. How I envied Trevor, who had declined to accompany us and was now presumably tucked up in bed with the cosily comfortable torso of Dame Rosy Clumber.

At last we reached a rude hut in the middle of the forest. Potiphar motioned to us to enter. I thought it ominous that he himself resolutely refused to do so. Had we been led into a trap? In such an emergency, I suspected that Selby would be of little use, his audacity being reserved for the floor of the House of Commons. The place where we now found ourselves was very poorly lit by the light of a small candle, but I felt it would be sacrilege to snap on one of our electric torches, which Potiphar had made us put out. Dimly I saw that the floor contained a quantity of unattractive fetish material such as bloodstained feathers, palm oil, and mysterious images.

A short squat figure muffled in heavy robes came forward to meet us and extended a hand in greeting. A white man's hand. I was pretty sure now that we were victims of an elaborate deception. Was this really the voodoo high priest? Could we dash through the forest and reach the river on the other side? The crocodiles would, with any luck, concentrate on Selby Tritton, who was wearing a pungent aftershave. I was about to propose an immediate escape to him, when the hooded figure spoke again.

"Good evening, Ambrose," said the voice. "And you too, my dear Selby." The mystery man threw back his hood and raised his candle so that we might see his face. We both gasped. It was Ludovic Molnar.

"I hope I didn't frighten you," he said courteously, "but this little deception is really quite necessary. I'd love to offer you a stiff drink but it wouldn't be quite in character. Don't look so nervous, Selby. I'm not actually proposing to slaughter a sacrificial animal. And the snakes are stupefied."

"You owe us an explanation," I said.

"It's quite simple," said Ludovic Molnar, with one of his familiar deep laughs. "This backward country is ruled by fear as well as greed. It's not enough to offer money to the ruling clique. You also have to scare them. I've got them all eating out of my hand now by using voodoo. This enabled me to persuade the President and his lovely wife, and Golosina too, that they have to buy arms from Britain and not from other countries. Of course I dress up, so that they don't recognise me."

"What about the French and the Americans?" asked Selby. "Do they have voodoo priests too?"

"Certainly not," crowed Ludovic. "They haven't cottoned on to this idea. Their mistake, I suppose, in failing to employ a Hungarian. All the poor French could think of was to send out a scratch troupe from the Comédie Française to perform boring old *Racine*. And the Americans caused a lot of offence by bringing a goodwill party of marines who got horribly drunk in the cathedral. With any luck, I think we are near success."

"Don't be too sure," I warned him, adding an account of the negative result of Dame Rosy's visit.

"You haven't seen the end yet," said Ludovic confidently. "Watch this space for new developments. I will give you both one piece of advice. Remember that the situation here is extremely fluid. We have to be prepared for … sudden changes. You would understand that if you had been raised in Budapest."

"You still haven't told us how you managed all this," pointed out Selby. "Even in Concordia, you can't just set up your stall in the middle of a forest and summon the head of state."

"That's my secret, Selby. Shall we just say that … I had my helpers. It's best for you not to know too much, in case you are ever kidnapped by the opposition and submitted to torture."

In that event, I could not help thinking, I should be glad to have as much information as possible, with which to propitiate my tormentors. But I decided not to deploy this argument for fear of looking feeble.

"It's been delightful to see you both," said Ludovic dismissively, as if he was saying goodbye in a London restaurant. "I wanted you to know that I am here, close behind you, and always on the job. Wedmore and Bassenthwaite should be proud of us all. Now Potiphar will take you back to the car. And I shall fade away into the forest."

"What part does Potiphar play in all this?" I asked.

"I didn't hear that," answered Molnar with a grin, suddenly blowing out his little candle and so disappearing completely. We stumbled back to the resourceful Potiphar, who put on the torches and led us back through the forest. Even with their light, it was hard to see our way, and we stumbled more than once with exhaustion until at last we saw the outlines of the official car. The whole dramatic episode had been nerve-racking in the extreme, and I was longing for my bed in the residence.

To our surprise and consternation, two shadowy figures were standing beside our vehicle. The taller of the two stepped forward into the light.

"Put out your torches," he commanded in American English. "We can see well enough by the rays of the moon." Potiphar immediately obeyed. I had the uneasy feeling that we were being manipulated in some way I did not wholly understand.

"I wanted to meet you," said the Dark Stranger, "to see what you look like. You are Mr Bellingham, I assume. And you must be Mr Tritton."

"You are right," I said, "but how do you know? And who are you?"

"All I need to tell you now," replied the Dark Stranger, "is that you will meet me again." This sounded rather sinister.

"I should warn you," I said firmly, "we are armed, and Selby here is a crack shot. He won the Queen's trophy in the army shooting contest at Bisley." I had no reason to believe this to be true, but in diplomacy there is occasionally much to be said for a resounding lie.

"I intend you no harm," said the Dark Stranger. "In fact, I wish you both well." He raised one hand in a kind of benediction. The two men moved backwards, disappearing into the forest. Potiphar motioned us to get into the car.

"What an extraordinary evening," I remarked. "Say nothing to the others, of course."

"I am not a complete fool," snapped the Member of Parliament. "Did you spot who that other man was?" he added.

"No."

"I'm almost sure it was that archaeologist fellow, Adrian Carr-Baxendale."

***

"Thank heavens the bloody woman has gone at last," said Gerald, referring irreverently to Her Britannic Majesty's Minister of State for Foreign and Commonwealth Affairs. "Taking her freeloading husband with her, not to mention the tame MP."

"They ate us out of house and home," wailed Monica. "Live-in guests requiring all meals do not come cheap."

Gerald darted me a quick glance. "She blamed you, Ambrose, for encouraging her to come," he said maliciously. "But of course that was only a smokescreen. The visit achieved exactly what she wanted."

"I can't think what that might be."

"My dear Ambrose, you are so delightfully naive. No wonder you never got further than Felicidad. Dame Rosy Clumber can now tell the House of Commons that in rejecting the proposal to sell arms to President Raro, she knows, for once, what she is doing.

Hasn't she visited the damned country, meeting its government and a wide spectrum of influential opinions?"

"But she hasn't," I pointed out.

"She has toured the prisons, encountering the unhappy victims of the current tyranny."

"She didn't."

"That isn't likely to stop her, Ambrose. The woman is a British politician, economical with the truth."

"They brought an awful lot of washing with them," complained Monica. "Poor Teresita has been absolutely overwhelmed."

"There has been bad news about poor old Harry Wilderness," continued the Ambassador, with a slight trace of satisfaction.

"Injured?" asked Monica.

"No. Found out." I wondered what on earth he could mean. Teenage girls? Little boys? Goats? The Archdeacon had always seemed so sweetly innocent. But everyone, like the moon, had a dark side.

"You'll remember," continued Gerald, "that Harry was due to fly to Miami to meet the Archbishop of Canterbury. Perhaps unwisely, he had gone around telling everyone here that he would advise the Archbishop to make a rousing denunciation of the drugs traffic, naming the countries involved, headed by Concordia. Well, there has been a sensation. Apparently his luggage was opened at the airport here and was found to contain a large packet of cocaine. He was arrested, and will appear before a magistrate in Felicidad next week. Concordian justice is remarkably rapid, you know. He could be facing a long prison sentence."

"But that is ridiculous," I cried. "Wilderness is surely the least likely man to be carrying drugs."

"Of course. He has obviously been framed by the drugs cartel in league with the Government. The perfect way to shut his mouth."

"So he's in prison now," said Monica. "How ghastly. I could send Teresita to him with some clean underclothes. She has quite a store, bequeathed by previous house guests who had to leave without them."

"I'm hoping to get him out on bail today," said Gerald. "He qualifies as a Distressed British Subject."

"You should be able to obtain some explanation from him," I pointed out. "It must be some simple misunderstanding. How, for example, did that packet ever get to be in his suitcase?"

"He refuses to say. It's all rather mysterious."

Two days later, I called on a chastened Archdeacon, now temporarily released through the good offices of the Ambassador. He looked rather the worse for wear.

"How very kind of you to come," he said sweetly. "It wasn't very nice in prison; I didn't have my pyjamas and there were dreadful screams all around me. People were doing things to each other. I'm afraid I've been an awful nuisance. The Archbishop can't understand it at all, apparently. He doesn't like wasting time. They had to take him to Disneyland instead."

"You are obviously innocent."

"Under the Concordian legal system, everyone is guilty of everything until proven innocent. And I can't possibly explain how the horrid thing got into my luggage."

"But you know?"

"Oh yes, I know."

"You can tell me, Harry. It will do you good to confide in an old friend."

"That is true. Perhaps I will. But you must promise me not to reveal this to the present ambassador. I do not want it to be used in my official defence."

"Why not?" Really the man was exceedingly obstinate. But then one knows the definition of martyrs: people who have to cope with saints.

"I do not wish to compromise the person who gave me that packet to carry to Miami. I foolishly agreed to do so as a personal favour, thinking it contained snapshots of a much-loved aunt."

"That individual must be rather a skunk to involve you in such a risk."

"All the same, I cannot damage the reputation of a lady."

"A lady?"

"You know her. It is our mutual friend, the Condesa de las Rosas. She pleaded so plaintively and she has been so generous to the church. I did not have the heart to resist."

It was as plain as a pikestaff. The duplicitous Casilda must have been working with Golosina and his cronies to neutralise the saintly Archdeacon, with his innocent trust in human nature. I did not like that idea at all. Did it not have implications for me too? I was of course an experienced man of the world and a much tougher target than the unworldly Archdeacon. But Casilda's behaviour towards me had been decidedly suspicious. Had she deliberately spiked my drink on that fateful evening? If so, that would explain the sensational way in which I had passed out. What on earth had happened when I was unconscious? Had I been photographed with Casilda in a state of undress? If the wretched woman was really working with Golosina, she could have passed any such embarrassing evidence to him. I imagined the unpleasantly flabby Chief of Police chortling over it with the unspeakable Sylvester Marsala, he of the rippling muscles.

We were sitting again on the residence terrace the following week. "Any news of the poor Archdeacon?" I asked Gerald.

"We have had to compromise," he replied. "Golosina has agreed not to press the charge in exchange for Harry making a large donation to the police orphanage."

"But the unfortunate man hasn't got a cent. You'll be paying the money for him, I suppose."

"Certainly not," snapped Gerald. "It will have to come out of the Organ Restoration Fund. That will clean it out completely. And Harry is finished here, of course. Even the Church of England has to draw the line somewhere."

I thought of the good, trusting Archdeacon, who had believed so strongly in human goodness. Did he still do so, I wondered, or was he bewailing the wickedness of the actual world?

"By the way, Ambrose," said Gerald blandly, "can we help you with your return air reservations?" I took this as a delicate hint, especially as I had noticed him and his wife exchanging significant glances in advance of this sally. You do not easily fool an old ambassador. Susan and I had cultivated a number of social ploys during our own embassy days, one of the most effective being the conducted tour of the residence, culminating in the front door.

"I shall be leaving quite soon," I replied, with my customary sangfroid. "But I hope you will kindly allow me to stay over the Concordian National Day and accompanying celebrations. I understand that these will include a new gala production of *Aida* by the State Opera, with real camels and specially imported elephants."

"If you want to," snapped Gerald ungraciously, "though I should have thought you would have had your fill by now of such ghastly functions."

"We were rather thinking of your dear Susan," chimed in Monica in her dulcet tones. "She must be missing you."

That made me feel a bit of a cad. How I bewailed the day when I had met the ineffable Casilda.

***

We were seated in the Diplomatic Tribunal in the choir of the Cathedral of the Divine Compassion in Felicidad, an historic building originally constructed by the Spanish conquistadors as part of their civilising mission in the Americas. The high altar had been especially dedicated to Our Lady of Victories, in gratitude for the successful outcome of the Battle of the Mangrove Swamps, more recently known in progressive circles as the Corpus Christi Day Massacre. It was the annual High Mass, celebrated on the occasion of the National Day – the high point in the local ecclesiastical calendar. All Felicidad was there, or at least that section of it not languishing in General Golosina's prisons.

Gerald, as reigning British Ambassador, was seated in the front row, accompanied by his peevish consort and wearing his full diplomatic regalia complete with sword. I had sported the same in my own day, but my outfit was now reposing in my wardrobe back home in Little Bigney, having been rejected by the local Oxfam shop as unlikely to suit their customers. I now planned to offer it to the amateur dramatic society for their production of *HMS Pinafore*, the next attraction after *Aladdin*. How are the mighty fallen!

In the same row I detected the stout frame of Homer Fairchild and the slimmer torso of Jacques Marigny-Marmande. I myself had been relegated to the back row with a Second Secretary from the Dominican Republic and a huge woman from Haiti, somewhat to my chagrin. I am far from stuffy or *protocolaire*, but humility does have its limits.

Opposite us sat the serried ranks of local high society. I had scanned them in vain for a sight of Casilda as we arrived. Surely she would not have willingly missed such an important occasion.

"I do not see the Condesa de la Rosas," I had remarked to Gerald with studied casualness before we took our seats.

"You are not likely too, Ambrose. I understand that she fled the country this morning. It transpires that she is no more a Spanish *condesa* than I am."

"Then what is she?" I asked, with a feeling of dread.

"A go-go dancer from Buenos Aires."

"What is a go-go dancer?" asked Monica. "I have always wondered."

"I don't really know myself," replied Gerald hastily. "The sort of woman, I suppose, whom one would not introduce to one's mother."

I boiled inwardly. To think that I had wasted my attentions on a low-born slut from the Boca. If one is going to fornicate, one should at least do so upwardly.

Now the action was starting. The great organ wheezed into life. Trumpeters pealed out of the west door. The massed bands of the Concordian Grenadiers broke into a rousing march by Sousa. Regimental banners were paraded up the nave. Then came the small figure of President Raro, accompanied by the more opulent frame of his spirited consort. Ignacio looked rather quiet and withdrawn, but this was more than made up for by the antics of the First Lady, who waved to the other worshippers in her usual film star manner, bowing to right and left in queenly style. The Cardinal Archbishop came forward to greet them and usher them to their special thrones placed in front of the high altar. It was, I have to admit, an occasion of some magnificence.

The mass proceeded without incident. The Archbishop's sermon was noteworthy for its laudatory references to President Raro and his benevolent government. He even included a special message from the Holy Father thanking the President for his recent decision to accord to Our Lady the Mother of God the honorary rank of major-general in the Concordian army. This was hardly the kind of low-decibel Catholicism practised by Father Manfred and the rugger-playing Benedictines of Calderbeck Abbey.

"It will take us ages to escape from all this scrum," pointed out Monica, as the presidential entourage disappeared down the nave after the concluding benediction.

"At least we can rely on the faithful Potiphar," said Gerald. "He'll be stationed bang in front of the west door. If we could only get there."

The organ was now pealing out something rather showy by some French Romantic composer, with lots of difficult pedal work. The diplomatic corps – hardly the flower of their profession and now avid for drinks before lunch – were spilling out into the choir, almost pushing each other but not quite. I clung tightly behind Gerald and Monica, in spite of reproachful glances from the stout lady from Haiti, whom I had unfortunately kicked in the confusion.

Suddenly, outside the west door where the presidential party had disappeared, we heard a terrible noise. Clearly there had been a huge explosion of some kind.

We all threw ourselves to the floor. It was no time for heroics. A general massacre was to be anticipated. I resourcefully took the opportunity to cover myself with the curvaceous torsos of the British Ambassadress and the lady from Haiti. One should never discount the value of a well-fed woman.

"Move over, Ambrose," shouted Gerald. "There is room for me too under Monica."

We lay cowering in silence for some ghastly minutes. I thought of my impending and violent death. Gerald's obituary would be in *The Times*. Would there be room for mine too? Would Lady Moggeridge and the Harrison Bedfords attend my memorial service in Little Bigney? Perhaps I should have repented my sins and prepared for eternity. But my mind does not work quite like that.

Suddenly a loud voice came through a portable speaking trumpet. I recognised the gravelly tones of General Golosina. He announced that a bomb had been detonated outside the cathedral in a cowardly attempt to assassinate our much-loved President and his lady. By the grace of God, they were totally unhurt and had now left for the presidential palace. Two dastardly criminals had been arrested, and would be treated appropriately. The military were in complete control and there was no more danger. The congregation should disperse at once. For security reasons, the presidential reception in the town hall had been temporarily postponed. Long live our beloved Concordia! Long live President Raro!

Tired and frightened, we began the search for Potiphar. Monica gave me a sharp look and I wondered if she had resented being treated as a human sandbag. At least I would be leaving the country soon and need never see the Haverstock-Joneses again.

***

It was the day before my planned departure. Gerald and Monica had gone to some lengths to ensure that this should not be delayed. They had spoken pointedly of how they would soon get their residence straight after all the interruptions. Gerald had loudly ordered Potiphar to take me to the airport, while Monica had instructed Teresita to make sure to have all my laundry ready in time. They seemed only too anxious to get rid of me. I could not think why. I had done my best to provide amusement and had, so far as I knew, only one social fault: a propensity to hold forth vivaciously during breakfast.

An eerie calm prevailed over the city of Felicidad. There had been no more bombs. The suspected terrorists had disappeared, not surprisingly, inside General Golosina's penal empire. Soldiers were much in evidence throughout the town. Gerald thought they had been brought in, to cow the population, from their barracks in the suburbs. It was rumoured that some foreign agitators had recently arrived but these too had abruptly vanished. For the time being at least, the Raro regime had won a reprieve.

I decided to have a nice walk along the seafront. It had a certain faded charm, with its green bandstand and decorated iron seats like some Edwardian spa. I mused over my mission. It could hardly be considered a success. We had done nothing to tame the savage heart of Dame Rosy Clumber. Ludovic's euphoria in the Sacred Grove was hard to understand. But at least I was going home. I thought of the tasty doughnuts that Susan made for tea. Suddenly, as I turned the corner, wrapped in thought, I ran straight into a most unwelcome figure. It was the American Mafioso Sylvester Marsala, accompanied by two of his gruesome thugs.

"We've been looking for you, Mr Bellingham," he snapped. "General Golosina wants to see you urgently."

"Then I will come voluntarily," I said with dignity. "There will be no need this time for your blindfolds, gags or other stage properties."

The man looked at me sourly. They had a car waiting at the end of the promenade, and we were driven off at breakneck speed, narrowly missing a couple of presumably expendable old ladies. Marsala did not frighten me so much now, because I sensed that Tiberio Golosina wanted me alive and in one piece.

"I suppose you were involved in that miserable business with our unfortunate Archdeacon," I remarked by way of conversation.

"The guy was very foolish," snarled Marsala, "trying to damage a vital commercial interest. He was lucky not to get any bones broken."

"Well, he's out of your clutches now. As I too shall be soon."

"I wouldn't bank on that, Bellingham. My principals back home never lose interest in a marked man. You'll be on our database."

I shuddered and then broke out into a cold sweat. It was almost a relief to find myself once again in General Golosina's well-equipped underground bunker, gazing at the only too familiar and well-lived-in face of the Chief of Police.

"Welcome back to the command centre, Ambrose," he said courteously, motioning me to take a seat. "How kind of you to drop in. Just let me turn off the Monteverdi. Were you enjoying the blooms in the esplanade gardens? The red hot pokers are at their best."

Was this a sinister reference to the awful way in which King Edward the Second of England had met his untimely death? My nerves were in tatters.

"I understand you will be leaving us soon," he continued. "Just in time, perhaps."

"What exactly does that mean, Tiberio?"

"There's a big job for you to do at home. As you may have noticed, we had a little contretemps here recently. But the powers that rule our lives have mercifully preserved our president and his first lady. And they are here to stay, mark my words. Indeed, their regime is now stronger than ever. The assassination attempt has reminded our people of the threat of anarchy and chaos. They are now more likely to support the existing authorities. Tell that to your government, please."

"I'll do my best. But I am only a poor, broken-down senior citizen with absolutely no influence."

"Nonsense, Ambrose. Our ambassador in London reports that you are received in the highest ruling circles. This is your great opportunity. To combat the terrorist threat, we are now in need of a very quick and large consignment of control equipment. Your charming colleagues in Wedmore and Bassenthwaite know very well what we require. I have spoken to the President and the First Lady, and I am authorised to tell you this. We have definitely decided to accept the British offer."

"You are turning down the French and the Americans?"

"Yes. It will be a pleasure. I long to see the face of that oily French Ambassador, the Marquis de Marigny-Marmande, contorted with Gallic chagrin. And Mr Fairchild can go back to his butterflies. Are you not pleased?"

"Indeed, Tiberio. But there remains one little local difficulty. To obtain the permission of the British Government."

"That is up to you, Ambrose. I know you will succeed."

"Why?"

"We have received guidance to this effect from … certain mystic Powers resident in this city, on which we place total reliance. They were very insistent that we should buy from your great country. This is, of course, dependent on the fruition of a private financial arrangement which I have already mentioned to you in the strictest confidence."

"Yes, indeed," I agreed enthusiastically, lost in admiration of Ludovic Molnar, that clever old Hungarian crook.

"I hope we can rely on you, Ambrose, to push these arrangements through in a manner beneficial to all parties."

"You certainly can."

"I am glad to hear that. It will help me to defend your interests here."

"My interests! What do you mean?" I asked.

"A slightly tiresome situation has arisen. An over-zealous official in the Bureau of State Security has got hold of some silly photographs in which you play a starring role. Until I told them to hold their hand, my stupid subordinates were planning to use them in a way which you could have found … unnecessary."

He handed me a large brown envelope. The pictures inside were all of me and the *condesa*, in a state of undress, performing sexual contortions of almost acrobatic complexity.

"Amusing, eh?" chortled Golosina. "I didn't know you were still up to that."

"Not amusing at all," I retorted frostily, "but we are doing nothing illegal."

"That is hardly the point, my dear Ambrose. My foolish colleagues thought it would be fun to ask our embassy in London to send copies of these works of art to your dear wife in her country seat."

The thought filled me with horror. I imagined poor, loyal Susan innocently opening these foul pictures. How on earth would I explain them? I have survived a number of awkward situations in my time but this one might well defy even my talent for self-disculpation. It was only too clear. This ghastly man had me at his mercy, and we both knew it.

"I feel sure you can restrain your subordinates," I croaked.

"Perhaps. Provided that certain conditions are fulfilled."

"What are those?" I asked nervously.

"First, the arms deal must go through quickly, on the terms agreed. I do not wish to fail my admirable charity already mentioned to you. It is greatly in need of fresh resources."

"I will do my best, I promise."

"I do not doubt that. There is a second condition. You know my colleague Sylvester Marsala, and no doubt have already guessed about his valuable weekly transport link with Miami. We are also seeking to include your own beautiful country in these arrangements."

"I'm not taking any of your packets." Strip-searched at Heathrow! That would be the final step in my downward mobility.

"We do not ask you to. But there is a problem. Your customs authorities have conceived the bizarre notion that narcotics are being transmitted to London from Felicidad in the diplomatic bag sent to our embassy."

"That would be an abuse of ambassadorial privilege," I commented sharply.

"Indeed it would. And our ambassador, Mr Hector Garcia, a gentlemen of ancient family, would certainly not connive at any such nefarious arrangement. But your people take a low, cynical view and we suspect that they have found some way to examine our diplomatic bag while not appearing to do so. This must be stopped at once."

"Who is to do that?"

"You, Ambrose."

"I have told you, I have no influence."

"Then you must acquire some. Straight away. It is the only way I can control my headstrong young officials acting, as they conceive it, in our national interest. Concordia is a poor country and we need … all the resources we can get."

"This is disgraceful blackmail."

"I don't care for words like that, Ambrose. Surely we can discuss the problem quietly between gentlemen? Assure me at least that you will do your best. That will buy us a little time."

"All right, I'll do what I can over that matter too," I said bleakly, inwardly fuming at the duplicitous Chief of Police, the false *condesa*, the revolting Raros and the whole pack of them. At all costs, I must protect Susan. I saw now that my marriage to that delicate creature was what really mattered in my life. In old age, I would need her badly to bring me meals in bed, fend off creditors and summon doctors to treat my expected cornucopia of geriatric ailments.

Suddenly we heard a scream directly below us. I stared at Golosina in horror.

"What on earth is that?"

"Don't worry, my dear sir. The holding cells are down there. They are probably only disciplining some refractory prisoner."

"Like the men arrested for trying to blow up the President?"

"They are not actually … with us any more," he replied smoothly.

"Who were they?"

"That is a matter of state security. But I can tell you that the villains were very helpful in volunteering information. Before they … er … left us. We have proof now that the attack was masterminded by the war criminal Victor Fernandez. Just wait till we catch him! But the people in the cells now are some foolish young foreigners who came especially to our country in order to cause trouble."

"What will you do to them?"

"Probably we shall simply expel them, after a short but intensive course of political re-education." He gave a sinister laugh. "By the way, one of them happens to be English. I think he would like to meet you."

I had better things to do than involve myself in petty consular problems associated with some juvenile ne'er-do-well backpacking round the globe. That was all the fault of his slack, spineless parents. But I could only agree. One does not wish to appear heartless.

"I fear that our facilities are not of the most modern," said Golosina. "But we are asking our Americans friends for aid, so that we can construct a state-of-the-art penitentiary of which the nation can be proud."

With this preparation, he led me down to some appalling cells, which appeared to be well below the waterline. A gaoler flung open the door of one of them. In the dim light of a small window, high up on the wall, I could just make out a solitary prisoner wearing heavy chains. The man shambled towards me. I gave a shriek when I saw his face.

It was Neville!

"Hello, Dad," he said casually. "I was expecting you earlier."

"Neville! What on earth are you doing here?"

"I came here on a human rights action programme. To get rid of the tyrant."

"Hush, Neville," I suggested hastily. "The Chief of Police here doesn't want any of that talk."

"It's awful here, Dad. Worse than school. The food is terrible and there are rats. You've got to get me out." How like today's younger generation, I thought: despising their father's position in society but keen enough to avail themselves of it when in trouble. I felt tempted to say this, but decided it was not the right time. Poor Neville did look rather dreadful with his long greasy hair and scarred fingers.

"I think my son would like to leave," I explained to Tiberio, who was looking at us sardonically.

"They all want to go. I can't think why, when we have such a hospitable hotel here."

"Come on, Tiberio. You know we've got a bargain, you and I. I'll take him with me and see he keeps out of trouble." The fellow was a great, harmless booby of thirty-six and I tried to imply that.

"Very well," announced the Chief of Police. "He can depart with you. Straight away."

"I must have my personal stereo back," said Neville, without a trace of gratitude. "The gooks took it away when they gave me a delousing shower."

"Nonsense, Neville. No time for that. Let's get out at once." The capricious Golosina might change his mind at any moment. "I'll take you back to the residence, and you can have a nice hot bath."

"That will not be possible," said Golosina firmly. "We're escorting you both directly to the airport." Had he known all along that Neville was my son?

"I must have my luggage," I said. "Two valuable cases in the best pigskin. I left them at the residence."

"They will be given to you at the airport," said Golosina. "With your air tickets. No time to lose. I might start to regret my clemency."

There was no help for it. We stumbled up into the open air and Marsala pushed us into a car. To my astonishment, the driver was none other than Potiphar.

"What on earth are you doing here?" I asked.

"Do not worry, Sir. Everything is under control. Your luggage is in the boot. And your tickets are here." Potiphar's calm efficiency was certainly suspicious. For whom was he working? I did not really mind leaving at once, though it would prevent me from saying goodbye to Gerald and Monica. It was a loss I could well bear, though I did not care for the thought that I was being, in effect, deported. I should not be able to leave farewell tips at the residence for old Felipe and the mad ablutionist Teresita. But at least that would be an economy, and I should not be coming back.

I glanced at the tickets and noted with relief that, while I should of course be travelling Jacquaranda class to Miami and first class to London, Neville had been booked in the tourist pen on both flights. That was just as well. A decidedly pungent aroma emanated from his person, and I did not wish to sit next to that. At the airport we were placed in the VIP lounge and closely guarded by the same large men with machine guns.

"No need to tell Mum about the state of the cells, Dad," said Neville, as I unenthusiastically lent him one of my best silk handkerchiefs to wipe his nose. "You know how she worries. And how she feels about rats."

"I agree," I replied blandly. "There are lots of things we don't have to bother your dear mother about."

3

"I'm not going to nag you, Neville."

"Thank you, Dad." He looked unconvinced.

We were sitting in the train to King's Lynn. I had suggested to my promising son that he might care to return directly to his squat in North London, but he opted to come with me to Little Bigney in order to see his mother and hopefully receive news from her about the whereabouts of the unspeakable Sharon. At least he had cleaned himself up in the Gents at Kings Cross, and now looked slightly less like an inmate of General Golosina's grim penitentiary. I had bought us both first-class tickets, which I intended to charge to my expense account with Molnar Enterprises.

"There is just one thing, Neville."

"I thought there might be, Dad."

"Why did you burn your passport? But for my timely intervention at London Airport this morning, you might have been refused admission to the United Kingdom. No other country would have taken you then. You would have had to circulate round the airways of the world for the rest of your life, like that unfortunate Flying Dutchman. Did you not consider that?"

"I wanted to make a protest, Dad. I was disgusted with the way the British Government are sucking up to those bloodstained tyrants in Concordia. That made me ashamed of being British."

"There is no question of sucking up," I retorted with dignity. "Just normal diplomatic relations. I suppose you went there on purpose to wreck my deal."

"I'm not malicious, Dad. You don't understand us: Sharon and me. When we see on the telly about injustice abroad, that makes our blood boil. We have to do something about it."

"You must have a low boiling point."

"It's your own fault, Dad, sending me to the Benedictines. They made us think of everything in ethical terms."

"You can't blame it all on Father Manfred," I said. "Some of your school-friends have turned into quite solid citizens. I met one at the Voyagers the other day: Jaime Damiel, a charming young man from a distinguished Spanish family, I believe. He remembered you well."

"He was rather wet but he had a pretty cousin called Isabella, who came to visit once. She went down like a bomb with us sex-starved schoolboys."

"Well, you aren't a schoolboy any longer, Neville. I hope you are giving some serious thought to your future. Your dear mother won't be there for ever to do your laundry. By now your partner is sure to be pretty notorious in our locality. A number of my friends are rather in favour of the Swaffham bypass, and feelings will be running high. May I suggest that you collect her and take her away."

"I'll have to ask Sharon, Dad."

"Don't let that girl ruin your life, Neville. Why don't you strike out on your own? You seem to enjoy foreign travel. A number of reputable organisations run schemes to recruit late entrants. You could, for example, join the British Secret Service. They take candidates whose intellect is not up to the rigorous standards of the Diplomatic Service. The main requirement is a talent for fiction."

"Thank you, Dad."

"Or you could apply to become a representative of the British Council."

"Don't you have to be cultured for that?"

"Not any more. Nowadays they concentrate on balancing their budgets. If all else fails, you might try the BBC. They are scraping the bottom of the barrel these days."

"Don't worry about me, Dad. I'm a bit short of cash at the moment. Lost my personal stereo in that dungeon from which you so kindly rescued me. But I've got an idea for making a killing."

"What exactly might that be?"

"You'll find out. All in good time."

"Well, please keep away from my field of activity in future. The world should be big enough for both of us."

"I just need a spot of help to enable Sharon and me to get back into our squat."

"More money, you mean?"

"That's about the size of it."

"I'm not giving you another penny, Neville."

"Don't be like that, Dad. After all, we have to work together. To protect Mum."

"I don't know what you mean."

"I heard Golosina talking. About some woman you had in Felicidad. Wasn't she called Casilda?"

"Absolute nonsense," I blustered. The boy gave me a steely look.

"Another five hundred would do it," he said calmly. I looked with horror at the young viper we had spawned. Then I slowly nodded in dignified acquiescence. The great thing in diplomacy is to know when you are beaten.

***

"It's lovely having you home, Darling," said Susan. I was sitting in a deckchair on the lawn, while my beloved wife bent over a flowerbed she was weeding with her usual diligence. It is always a pleasure to see a woman work.

"I suppose you missed not having a man around the house."

"It was not so much that," she replied, straightening up with some relief. "But when you're away, I always worry about you. You're so absolutely hopeless on your own."

I responded with one of my Delphic smiles. The idea that I am not fit to cope by myself has been central to my wife's thinking throughout our marriage. I have done nothing to discourage this illusion. Long experience has taught me that the more feckless you appear to be, the more you get done for you.

"This time though," she conceded, "you seem to have excelled yourself."

"What exactly do you mean, Dear?"

"I suspected that you had some dark secret, Ambrose. Why else would you have gone back to that horrible place? And now it's all become clear."

Dark secret! The blow almost made me fall off my chair. So she knew about Casilda! Who could have told her? The duplicitous Neville, I supposed. Unless Golosina had carried out his threat to forward those photographs. I felt myself growing hot and cold at the same time – an unusual sensation which I do not recommend.

"What has become clear, Susan?" I asked nervously, inwardly ravaged by the gnawing of a guilty conscience.

"Why you went back to Felicidad, of course. Somehow you had discovered that poor Neville would be going there to make trouble. So you flew there yourself in order to rescue him. That was magnificent, Darling. I didn't think you had it in you."

Deeply relieved, I gave one of my diplomatic all-purpose smiles. If Susan cared to believe that, it was all right by me. Women like to imagine that they are married to a hero – a satisfaction notably missing up till now in Susan's life. She would carry my fame all round the upper social circles in Little Bigney.

"Sharon said you would be no use to Neville when we heard you were both in Concordia. She was sure you would collapse under the threat of violence. Now she can see for herself how badly she underrated you."

"I am used to being underrated," I commented with dignity. "Have you been seeing much of Sharon?"

"Only when she brings her bloomers down for washing in the middle of the night. She's still up a tree, you know, though I hear they are sending a detachment of Grenadier Guards down next week to flush her out. She had been more than a match for those unfortunate local policemen. Trevor Pilkington, no less, has sent a message of encouragement. He arranged for a team of photographers to provide evidence of harassment for the European Court of Human Rights."

"Neville has promised to take her away, as soon as he can get her down."

"I shan't be sorry," admitted Susan. "Even though she is our boy's other half, I find Sharon awfully unsettling. She's so worried about the future of the world. I haven't got time for all that, now that we're so busy in the garden with the preparations for the new greenhouse."

"Greenhouse?" I asked nervously.

"Yes, Dear. You did say we could have one, now that you're getting all that money from Mr Molnar. There's a lot of work to be done, levelling the earth and digging the drains."

"How much are you spending?"

"Not a penny so far. I've only signed the contract, in our joint names. Just a few thousands. It will be chickenfeed, now that we are so rich."

"We are not rich, Susan," I explained patiently, seeing here a fruitful opportunity for the most dreadful misunderstanding. "We are only getting a one-off payment for my services to Mr Molnar. In fact, we haven't had anything yet, except expenses."

"Don't worry, Darling. Rowley was awfully pleased to hear that you are in the arms trade. He says there's a lot of money in that."

"Rowley? Who the devil's he?"

"Admiral Harrison Bedford, of course. He and Griselda have been so kind since you went away. In fact, I've seen quite a lot of them."

"I wish to have nothing to do with that precious couple."

"You're cross about the amateur dramatic society, I know. Rowley feels bad about that too. He thinks now they may have acted in too much of a hurry. They want to read your plays again, if you would be willing to give them another chance."

That was Susan's doing, I knew. It would explain why she had bothered to chum up to the stuffy old sea dog and his withered spouse. My darling wife had sacrificed herself for me. How fortunate I was to have such a helper in the long pilgrimage of human existence.

Suddenly Neville appeared on the terrace.

"Come and watch the telly," he shouted. "Great stuff! There's a riot in Whitehall."

It looked more like a pitched battle to me. Two gangs of thugs were slugging it out under the Cenotaph, to the palpable distress of a handful of police, mostly young female postgraduates, inadequately protected with riot shields.

"Is this something new since I left?" I asked.

"They're fighting over the Ziggurat," explained Susan. "We get it most nights. They still can't agree about the figure to be put on the top. It's Tony Blair now against Margaret Thatcher."

"The battles of the past," I said sadly.

"No, Dad, the battles of the future. The very fabric of society is collapsing." There was a manic glint in the boy's eye. How on earth could Susan and I have produced such a nutter, when we ourselves were polished and urbane?

***

"Have some more smoked salmon," suggested Ludovic Molnar as we picnicked on the terrace during the long interval. He had generously invited me to join his party at an exclusive performance in the newest country opera house, nestling below the Mendips. I was glad of the food and, even more, the freely flowing champagne. The offering that night was a rarely performed gem of the Venetian baroque, rendered on period instruments. In my experience, works that are rarely performed are so neglected for some jolly good reason. *The Triumph of Chastity* by Salvator Cacciatore was no exception. Nor had I taken kindly to the period instruments, which involved the irritating rattling of the theorbo and the painful growling of the violone. Molnar had been warmly welcomed by our landed host. I suspected that the cultured, but wily, Hungarian had been a generous benefactor to the enterprise. He was clearly adept at mingling business with pleasure.

"How are you enjoying the opera, Ambrose?" he asked.

"It is … interesting," I replied cautiously. "A change from the usual repertoire."

"Cacciatore has been undervalued, I think," said Ludovic. "He was a protégé, you know, of Cardinal Ettore Campo, from whom the modern word 'camp' is derived. A very unusual prince of the Church, even for the early seventeenth century. He used to make progresses around the Veneto in his scarlet litter, looking for artistic talent to foster. The young Cacciatore was discovered on his father's farm beside the Brenta, playing to the cows, on a home-made chitarrone, a rude passacaglia of his own composition. Added to this, he was extremely beautiful, with strikingly long eyelashes. The Cardinal took to him at once and brought him back to Venice to join his household. There the young genius composed several operas and sacred works before unfortunately being drowned during a storm on the lagoon. *The Triumph of Chastity* is his best piece, though difficult to perform since it calls for five virtuoso castrati. Or nowadays, counter-tenors, I fear. Some believe that the story and title was intended as a slight hint to the Cardinal, some of whose diversions were of a fleshly nature."

This was a new side to my employer: dedicated patron of culture as well as ruthless dealer in weapons of destruction. I had been charmed by Ilona, his hostess for the evening, clearly one of his discreet stable of well-bred mistresses. They had also invited Susan but she had insisted on remaining at Little Bigney. Neville and Sharon had left the locality, and no longer needed constant vigilance. But Lady Moggeridge required support for the village flower show, where Susan had high hopes for her treasured blue-moon roses. Our party was completed by Selby Tritton and his young wife Lucretia, an extremely silly woman with a marked tendency to giggle inanely. Hector Garcia and his wife were also present, but with a Latin American diplomatic party. They would be joining us for a nightcap after the show. I was looking forward to that. The end of the show, I mean.

"Nora Vallombrosa is excelling herself tonight," continued our host. "Though one has to admit that her figure is somewhat luxuriant for the largely undraped role of Venus. Nor does the music lie quite naturally within her tessitura."

"Her tessy what?" asked Lucretia Tritton. Selby looked uncomfortable, and Ludovic pretended not to have heard.

"So good of you to invite us, Ludo," said Selby in his usual sycophantic manner. "Lucretia is mad on early music, aren't you, Dear?"

"I played the recorder at school," contributed Lucretia. "They asked me to give up the violin."

"I owe you gentlemen an apology," grinned Ludo. "I'm afraid I gave you both a bit of a scare when we last met in Felicidad. What did you think of my little *coup de theatre*?"

"A master stroke," I said warmly. "It certainly seems to have done the trick. When I left Concordia ..."

"In rather a hurry, I believe," interjected Ludovic snidely.

"I had completed my mission," I added with dignity. "Our contract was in the bag. The Government of Concordia had decided to award to Wedmore and Bassenthwaite a massive order for defence equipment. What more could I have done?"

"That's all very well, Ambrose," snapped Ludo, "but nothing has happened since. We're all been back here for some time but the bloody contract is completely stalled. We want action."

"Wedmore and Bassenthwaite did their stuff all right," bleated Selby. "They put in the usual application for an export licence and export credit guarantee. I know it was favourably received by the Department of Trade and Industry. But, once again, it seems to have been held up in the wretched Foreign Office."

"Those diplomats should be shot as traitors," opined Ludo. "Look, girls, you talk among yourselves. Frocks or hats or something. We men need a word."

Ilona meekly engaged Lucretia in amiable chatter, apparently unfazed by Ludo's old-fashioned male chauvinism. I wondered whether she would take her revenge some day. One could imagine the tyrannical tycoon being lifted from a nice hot bath, like Marat, with a bleeding dagger through his chest.

"It's perfectly simple," continued Molnar. "Selby and Ambrose, you must together seek a confrontation with that bitch Dame Rosy Clumber. She can hardly refuse to see you. We know for sure that she's the one holding the project up. In fact, I gather that since her trip to Felicidad she's keener than ever to get rid of the Raros. Counterproductive, that visit. If we're not careful, we shall all lose a great deal of money. I'm not paying anybody anything if I don't get anything in."

It was brutally clear. I was in danger of losing my fat bonus, part of which Susan had so unwisely dedicated to the purchase of that massive greenhouse, where she planned to cultivate the finest orchids north of Madeira.

"It's not just the money," wailed Selby. "One's heart bleeds for Wedmore and Bassenthwaite and all those excellent folk in Greyburn. I suppose their best hope now is to concentrate on riot control equipment for police forces coping with the Ziggurat protesters."

"They will also have to develop the sado-masochistic side of their business," said Ludovic. "It's been a profitable sideline for some years. You'd be surprised how many old gentlemen write asking for handcuffs. They have built up quite a mailing list, with some distinguished names. We might be able to sell it to the tabloids some day."

"It might be best for Ambrose to beard Dame Rosy alone," said the spineless Selby. "He's the expert on Concordia and I'm rather busy now drumming up enthusiasm for the parliamentary delegation to Felicidad. That tiresome Nancy Greengrass has pulled out. She got a more tempting offer to visit crèche facilities in Saint Petersburg with an evening at the Kirov."

"Nonsense, Selby," snapped our paymaster. "This is no moment to give way to abject fear. We know you're terrified of Rosy Clumber. But she won't eat you. In fact, she's got a weakness for you. You send her into hot flushes." The unfortunate Member of Parliament darted a nervous glance in the direction of his vivacious wife, now squealing with inane laughter. "We've got to move quickly," continued Ludo. "Too much time has been lost already. We have to keep the Raros and the Golosinas in play. Otherwise they'll turn to the horrible Americans or the duplicitous French. I'm relying on their ambassador here to fight our corner in his own country."

"What about another dose of voodoo?" I suggested. "That was wonderfully successful last time."

"I'm getting too old for amateur theatricals," snapped Ludovic rather sourly. "We'd better go back in. I hear them tuning up the arch-lutes. Don't want to miss the beginning of the second act. A delicious dialogue between the gods and goddesses about the value of chastity. With viola pomposa obbligato."

The rarely performed work droned on. At least, at the end, the promised champagne appeared. Ludovic was not the type to econo-mise with one of the cheaper brands. The Concordian Ambassador, dapper as ever with a crimson bow tie and cummerbund, came over to reintroduce his wife – a high-born Catalan lady who reputedly had never visited Concordia. He came straight to the point.

"What news from the Foreign Office about our defence order?" he enquired of Ludovic.

"It won't be long now," replied Molnar smoothly. "We are in close touch with Rosy Clumber. I had hoped that she and Trevor Pilkington would have been here tonight among my guests. But they have been obliged to attend a rally in Walthamstow. It's a protest in support of revolting pygmies in Brazil. Ambrose and Selby have an appointment to see her very shortly." Ludovic had a wonderful way of massaging the truth.

"You'd better hurry," advised the Ambassador. "I understand from Felicidad that your American competitors have now enlisted the active help of Sylvester Marsala. And you know how close he is to Tiberio Golosina. Sylvester's activities have … shall we say … world-wide ramifications."

I had a momentary vision of a Mafia hit squad descending upon Little Bigney. But that was too absurd.

"Point noted, Ambassador," said Ludovic brusquely, with a meaningful glance towards Selby and myself. He turned with ineffable charm to chat up the Ambassador's lady – a tight-lipped female who looked as if *The Triumph of Chastity* were right up her street. Selby and his wife, meanwhile, were coping with the blooming Ilona, who did not appear as if chastity was a speciality with her at all. I was left with Hector Garcia, who deftly drew me to one side.

"I have a message for you, Ambrose," he said, "from our mutual friend General Golosina. He wonders whether you have been able to do anything yet about my diplomatic bags."

The question took me unawares. I found myself stammering – a rare situation for me. Long practice has rendered me abnormally articulate, like most trained diplomats.

"You must surely remember," continued the Ambassador implacably, "that you very kindly volunteered to General Golosina that you would be willing to assist us in this way. All we seek is the normal immunity granted to diplomatic missions."

"I would love to help," I said cautiously, "but I am only an old retired official. I count for nothing in Whitehall today."

"Nonsense, Ambrose. Your modesty is perfectly charming. I have always admired your lovely English understatement. Such a contrast to those brash Americans. But you do not fool me. I know that you still have *enchufes*, as we say in Spanish, into the very heart of the British Establishment." *Enchufe* is an all-purpose word, literally meaning an electrical plug and denoting a direct connection with the target area. Felicidad is a great place for *enchufes*. I gave a wintry smile.

"I haven't forgotten, Hector," I said. "I'll do my best."

"That would be wise," he countered smoothly. "We are not disposed to drop the matter. If you are to see Dame Rosy Clumber shortly, why not take the problem up with her?"

It was not an inviting prospect. Dame Rosy would want to know why I was interfering in the delicate matter of covert intelligence. But I could see no alternative, and accordingly gave Hector a slight nod of acquiescence. What else could I do when faced with such brutal blackmail? The only other way to neutralise the threat would have been to come clean with my own darling Susan, presenting my brief romp with Casilda as a momentary aberration brought on by loneliness and alcohol. But that would have been unspeakably painful for us both. How could I bring myself to shatter my dear wife's innocent trust when she had occupied herself in my absence by cultivating the awful Harrison Bedfords for my sake. I was prepared to sink low, but not as low as that.

"How did you enjoy the opera this evening, Hector?" I asked, neatly changing the subject with my customary aplomb.

"Ghastly," replied the Ambassador. "Perfectly ghastly! The things one does for one's country."

At that moment I was relieved to see the aristocratic Lord Cumberland approaching with an ancient lady who had once been a high-profile ambassadress in Paris. I had pleasant memories of the affable proprietor of Connoisseur Travel.

"How nice to see you again, Mr Bellingham," he said politely. "I would rather like to pick your brains about Concordia. We thought of organising another visit there. But it is too late in the evening now. Would you care to lunch with me one day?"

"That would be delightful," I said. "Whenever you like." I was in residence at the Voyagers, and welcomed changes of fare.

"Come to the Sheridan next Thursday, if you're free. We could meet in the bar about twelve thirty."

I accepted with alacrity. Any appearance at the Sheridan might help to get my name at last before the Candidates Committee. It would do me no harm at all to be seen there in the company of Lord Cumberland, a prestigious peer descended from a serving wench in Long Acre and one of the more louche of our Hanoverian monarchs.

***

The Sheridan is not a particularly grand club. It is not a place where you meet dukes, but it is well known because its members keep it that way. They are mostly successful actors, media moguls, television pundits and denizens of the upper reaches of the law – show business being the underlying theme. I felt thoroughly at home there as I stood supporting the bar with Lord Cumberland. Unlike the Voyagers, the Sheridan is not strong on retired diplomats and spies, and I liked that. My former colleagues, well aware that my career climaxed in Felicidad, tended to eye me with amused indifference. As Lord Cumberland plied me with a huge gin and tonic, I took the opportunity to inform him that my name had been down in the candidates book at the Sheridan for many years and I could now do with some support. One had heard horror stories of candidates whose election had been approved only after their demise. I did not want that to happen to me.

"Of course, my dear fellow," said the proprietor of Connoisseur Travel. "I shall be delighted to sign your page. You will remember Adrian Carr-Baxendale, whom we all met in Felicidad." To my surprise, I found the distinguished Nevera scholar standing at my shoulder, dressed in a sober London suit with respectable tie.

"I'm here to give a series of lectures at the University of Hartlepool," he explained. "Can't afford to lose touch with the academic world."

"What aspect of ancient Nevera society will you be dealing with?" I asked politely.

"Death," he replied promptly. "The Neveras were strong on different forms of death. You could say it was their speciality. Ritual sacrifice, capital punishment, death by torture, assisted suicide, culling of unwanted children. It's a fascinating area," he added ghoulishly.

"I thought Mr Carr-Baxendale might well be able to help us in future enterprises," explained Lord Cumberland. "Connoisseur Travel specialises in the scholarly approach. Our patrons are not just out to enjoy themselves. We aim to stretch their intellectual boundaries. Some even say that they need an ordinary holiday to recover after returning from one of our mentally arduous tours."

"There are some wonderful things to see in the Nevera lowlands," said Carr-Baxendale invitingly. "Sacrificial altars, burial mounds, decorated tombs."

"All rather grim," I pointed out.

"The Neveras were like that. They had a strong sense of the danger of being alive. They were afraid that one day the sun would fail to rise unless the gods were propitiated by a regular diet of succulent youths and comely maidens."

"As you will remember, we were advised not to go as far as Nevera tribal territory on our last visit," said Lord Cumberland. "It was considered too dangerous. So we had to content ourselves with the Sacred Grove."

"That was the Embassy's doing," said Carr-Baxendale with a wry smile. "Gerald Haverstock-Jones isn't exactly the sort of ambassador who encourages people to take chances."

"If you take chances," I said, "you don't get to become an ambassador."

"Shall we go down and eat?" suggested our host with his customary urbanity.

The three of us sat at one of the small tables lining the large dining room. Members of the club were guzzling at the long centre table. Sir Emrys Merioneth, a great old ham from the past, was noisily consuming a bowl of soup. That would be something to tell Susan. And there was Trevor Pilkington QC in the middle of a group of eminent lawyers which included the Lord Chancellor, no less.

"What will you have?" asked Lord Cumberland hospitably. "The potted shrimps are quite good here. And so is the lamb. I can recommend the club claret. I chose it myself." He ordered a satisfactorily large meal and we sat back to enjoy ourselves, doing our best to shut out the braying laughter emanating from a media team at the next table. The Sheridan is nothing if not social.

"And now to work," said Lord Cumberland. "One is not allowed to talk business in the club but I suppose it's all right to pick your brains, Ambrose." Flattered, I indicated that these were available for that very purpose.

"What I need to know is this. I'm very tempted to include Concordia again in our programme for Connoisseur Travel next year. The country has a certain novelty value with a dramatic, if somewhat bloodstained history ..."

"And an original artistic tradition," added Carr-Baxendale.

"As you say. Just the thing to appeal to our cultivated patrons. Remember, these are the sort of people who were taken to Venice and Florence in their cradles, who celebrated their twenty-first birthday on the Great Wall of China, and selected Borobudur for their honeymoon. They've seen it all, done it all. So they are easily bored. We in Connoisseur Travel have to keep dreaming up new projects. I am getting tired of Antarctica. That's why I was so delighted to discover Concordia. It's not exactly on the beaten track."

"You could say that," I agreed drily. "People don't even go to the emerald mines now that they've been nationalised."

"As you know," said Carr-Baxendale, "there's a wealth of interest in the Nevera lowlands. And marvellous Bronze Age temples if you could only get into the interior of the Tozudo heartlands. I went there once but was put off by the headshrinkers and the killer bees."

"Security does seem to be the overriding problem in Concordia," agreed Lord Cumberland. "One would have to choose our routes very carefully, as we did this year. But there is one overriding question, and that's where I need your help, Mr Bellingham. Leaving aside little local difficulties like the headshrinkers, is the country generally safe for tourists?"

"That all depends," I countered sagely, "on the stability of the regime. Without it, there would be a complete breakdown of law and order. And facilities too. Even hotels like the Waving Palms could find their water cut off, their sewage uncollected."

"Exactly," agreed our host. "So I must have the answer to one key question. Are the Raros likely to stay in power? What is your considered view about that?"

"I will give you an answer, to the best of my ability," I replied, flattered at being appealed to as a pundit. "The Raros are not popular. But they are ruthless, especially their henchman General Golosina. They have totally destroyed the opposition, whose leader is broken and reduced to hiding in the bush. So the Raros will last, at least for some time. As I have told the Foreign Office, they may not be very nice but they are the best Concordian government we've got."

"Thank you, Mr Bellingham," said our host. "It is most helpful to get such a clear and unequivocal view. Do you agree, Mr Carr-Baxendale?"

"I don't disagree. I'm an anthropologist, you know, not a diplomat or a politician. I tend to stop at five hundred BC."

"Well, that's splendid and I am most grateful to you both," said Lord Cumberland. "We shall definitely go ahead with another visit in the near future. We can schedule these things quite quickly." He beamed with pleasure.

"If you ever need a guest lecturer ..." I suggested.

"I shall certainly bear you in mind, Mr Bellingham. Most of our lecturers are eminent scholars but we do include the odd diplomat." It seemed an unfortunate turn of phrase.

Suddenly a figure loomed over us. It was Trevor Pilkington QC, whose legal group had clearly broken up.

"Is this a reunion of the Felicidad mafia?" he asked jovially. "Do you mind if I join you for coffee? The Lord Chancellor has had to go and sit on the woolsack."

"Do sit down," said Lord Cumberland. "Perhaps you would like a glass of brandy? You will remember Mr Bellingham and Mr Carr-Baxendale." Pilkington nodded affably.

"I am expecting to pay a call on your wife very soon," I said by way of conversation.

"Don't let her bully you then," replied the great human rights defender cordially. "She's become very bossy since she went to the Foreign Office. The trouble is: I'm seldom there to keep her in order. We are both extremely busy, and only meet for our Sunday afternoon walk to the Vale of Health."

"You must be involved in some fascinating cases," said Lord Cumberland.

"They never stop," replied Trevor Pilkington cheerfully. "One can only do one's little best to alleviate the inhumanity of man to man. Or, very often, to woman, or in-between. At the moment I am representing an unfortunate gay couple who were denied a church blessing on their relationship. The vicar refused simply because the client wanted to dress in white as a bride. The wretched cleric objected because my client happens to have a luxuriant beard and a bushy moustache. He feared that this would expose the Church to ridicule."

"You will obtain exemplary damages for the bearded bride?" I asked.

"That is certainly my intention. But victimisation does not stop there. Half my cases derive from a failure to accept different patterns of culture in our multiracial society. Only recently I represented an Indian family who were denied their right to expose their son's widow to the age-old practice of suttee or widow-burning on a funeral pyre. They were planning to hire the Alexandra Palace and give her a tremendous send-off."

"What view did the widow herself take?" asked Lord Cumberland drily.

"She was against it. Perhaps that is why the High Court found for the opposition. Too many of the judges are white and public school, you know. They argued that if we allowed suttee, we would also have to permit thuggee: the equally venerable local practice of disposing of opponents by garrotting them unexpectedly with a silken cord around the throat. A *reductio ad absurdum*, I protested. Some of the Bench are quite hopeless. They have even refused to allow a Chinese father to bind his small daughter's feet in the traditional Chinese way. I argued in vain that this was an inalienable human right dating back to the Ming dynasty. It's an uphill struggle, but one never gives up the fight." He accepted a second glass of brandy and gave us a brave smile.

***

Selby Tritton and I had arrived a little too early for our appointment with Dame Rosy Clumber at the Foreign Office. It was a fine day and we stood placidly on the pavement in Whitehall. In my youth one could have walked up Downing Street to enter the Foreign Office, but now the Prime Minister was barricaded away from the humble public. Perhaps that was one of the reasons, I thought, why our leaders invariably became so badly out of touch with the very people who had elected them. You now had to approach the Office through King Charles Street, and we stood on that corner.

Suddenly I saw a vendor selling copies of the evening paper. I was mesmerised by the contents of the poster. It said in bold type 'Envoy's Son Reveals Details of Torture Gaol'. Hastily buying a copy, I read the contents with increasing horror and bewilderment. The paper was serialising a forthcoming book which would describe the appalling experiences in Concordia of a blameless youth called Neville Bellingham. This was the first of several planned instalments. Neville had described in graphic detail the odious repression practised by the Raro regime, and the hideous cruelties inflicted in their subterranean prisons. Neville himself was depicted as a courageous and even heroic fighter for human rights. There was a large picture of him, beard and all, and it was made only too clear that he was the son of a former British ambassador to Concordia.

"I hated the way that Dad and Mum had to suck up to that odious regime," he was reported as graciously remarking, "and I resolved that I at least would stand up for the poor and the oppressed. That was what got me into trouble."

I seethed inwardly. Here was this wretched boy again, scuppering my best-laid plans and probably condemning me, his unfortunate old father, to return to my old life of rustic penury. It was all so typical of Neville. There has been something wrong with the lad from the start, when he had taken to bringing wounded badgers into the kitchen and giving away my loose change to evil-smelling tramps, like Saint Francis of Assissi. How he got like that it was hard to say. My own people have always been robustly normal. As I have often remarked to Susan, there must be a rogue gene on her side of the family.

I had encouraged Selby to read the piece over my shoulder. "We could have done without this," I said with outward calm.

"Very damaging," he agreed. I did not point out the obvious conclusion that now Ludovic Molnar would blame me. People who think that others should have brought up their children better have not had the experience of coping with a confirmed rebel like Neville with the brain of a pea and the obstinacy of a mule. Ludovic might well penalise me in revenge by refusing to pay my promised bonus. He could even cut off my expenses, and then I would be obliged to slink back to Little Bigney, spending the rest of my miserable life within earshot of the hateful O'Callaghans. And how would we cope with the expenses already incurred by Susan over that wretched greenhouse?

As we turned away from Whitehall, I noticed an elderly man carrying a sandwich board which proclaimed boldy, 'End scandal of drug regimes in Central America'. The fellow's face looked familiar, and then I saw that it was none other than our former Archdeacon, Harry Wilderness.

"Harry!"

"Mr Bellingham!" he countered courteously. Selby too had of course met him in Concordia.

"What a coincidence," I said.

"I don't always believe in coincidence," replied Harry. "These things can be planned by a higher power. You know they sent me home. I couldn't get anything else. The Archbishop thinks I am an unguided missile. I had to go to Saffron Walden to live with my sister."

"I hope you're happy there," I said.

"It's rather quiet. My poor sister is extremely deaf, so we can't talk a lot. I am fairly busy with rehearsals for *Iolanthe*. But I come to town whenever I receive a call. Like today."

"You've seen my son's piece in the evening paper?"

"Indeed. An excellent contribution."

"Perhaps you'll go back to Felicidad some time."

"I should love that. But it won't be possible so long as the present regime are in power. Things will change though. Mark my words. And now you must excuse me, gentlemen. I've done my stint for the day and am off to the Athenaeum for tea and hot buttered crumpets with the Archbishop's chaplain. I want to tell him what I would have said, if I had ever managed to meet the Archbishop himself in Miami."

I found the meeting disconcerting, following so hard on the revelation of Neville's disloyalty. And now we had to face Dame Rosy, a woman of supremely confident ignorance. I entered the archway of the Foreign Office with some trepidation. The lights were on already throughout the fine Palladian building. Lord Palmerston had been wise to substitute it for the original Gothic design, subsequently utilised for the construction of Saint Pancras Station. Come to think of it, there was one essential factor in common between the two organisations. You had to stay on the rails.

***

Dame Rosy Clumber had a large, expressive face, not always on asset in politics where, as in poker, you have so much to conceal. Her demeanour was far from welcoming as I entered her impressive office. But she softened perceptibly on registering that I was accompanied by Selby Tritton.

"Do come and sit beside me, Selby," she purred. "And you, Mr Bellingham, please take a seat too. I know exactly what you're going to say to me. You've come here to lobby me on behalf of Wedmore and Bassenthwaite for their wretched arms contract for Concordia. I don't know why you bother. I've heard all your arguments already."

"It has become urgent, Dame Rosy," I said. "As you know, the Government of Concordia have now put in a firm order. But if it cannot be fulfilled promptly, our competitors will rear their ugly heads again."

"The Americans," added Selby, "and the perfidious French."

"I don't go along with these xenophobic sentiments," said Dame Rosy. "Foreigners can hardly be blamed for not being British. Trevor buys his shoes in Florence, and we are both devoted to French cooking."

"The fact remains," I pointed out, "that we have an obligation to support British industry."

"That point is not lost on me, Mr Bellingham. I hear a lot about it from the Chief Whip and the Member for Greyburn. It happens to be a marginal constituency. I know all about the problems encountered by Wedmore and Bassenthwaite. Their Mr Atkinson is seldom off the line to my private secretary. But I have to look at the broader picture. And that is Britain's place in the world. As my husband reminds me, it is essential that we should be seen to be on the side of the angels. What really matters is our support for human rights."

"I am all for human rights, Minister," I said. Selby was cowering beside Dame Rosy on the sofa, and I could see that I should have to do most of the talking. "And I admit that the regime in Concordia does leave something to be desired in that respect. But they are coping with huge internal difficulties, and I think they deserve our support."

"You have said all that to me before, Mr Bellingham. But on that earlier occasion you had the advantage over me. I had not then been to Concordia to see the situation for myself. But now I have, as you well know. It was not an enjoyable visit."

"The Raros would have done a lot more for you, Minister, if you had been willing to accept their hospitality. The First Lady was all agog to welcome you at her Home for Wayward Females. I am told that they dance a sprightly cancan."

"I saw quite enough," snapped the Minister. "It was perfectly plain to me that the unfortunate people are groaning under a most tyrannical regime. They have been herded into prisons, concentration camps and fake psychiatric clinics. Trevor and I saw it all with our own eyes."

"But you didn't, Rosy," protested Selby, with a rare flash of spirit provoked by her outrageous lie. "You never entered a single one of those establishments. I was there too, don't forget."

"I was all set to visit them. In fact, I demanded to do so. But the British Ambassador failed to include those items in my programme. To be honest, I was not impressed by Mr Haverstock-Jones. He seemed just the kind of diplomat who gives the Foreign Office a bad name: far too eager to please his host government, and quite lacking in fighting spirit."

"He has long experience in the Middle East," I pointed out. "They rather drained his fighting spirit there."

"So they tell me. I have made enquiries of the Personnel Department since my return. I understand that he failed badly in Damascus, and was sent to Felicidad as a punishment. Apparently we retain the embassy there as a place to park out elderly duds who have to be hidden away until we can get rid of them."

This was really too much. I gave Dame Rosy one of my steely glares. Selby cleared his throat in gentlemanly embarrassment.

"At least my visit has had one good result," continued the harridan. "It has helped me to make up my own mind. It is now absolutely clear to me that the Raro regime must be removed. It is only a question of how this is to be done. The best plan, I still think, will be to bomb them from a high altitude. Then our brave boys won't be at risk. We shall have to carry the Americans with us, of course. The Royal Air Force will need to fly out of their airfields."

"Have you discussed this with the Ministry of Defence?" asked Selby pointedly.

"Indeed I have. I am afraid they were inclined to shilly-shally. They invited me to clear the project with the Foreign Secretary first. Apparently you are not allowed to embark on hostilities below cabinet level. Unfortunately I have not so far been able to engage the Foreign Secretary's full attention. He is dreadfully occupied with resisting the machinations of our European partners. And the Prime Minister is completely tied up with the Ziggurat. He's terrified that it's going to go on the same way as that damned Dome."

"You mean, the bitter argument over the figure on the top?"

"Not only that, my dear Selby. The financing is now in grave doubt. We have been obliged to rule out contributions from the tobacco companies. And from a rather dubious Danish conglomerate who run massage parlours."

"I feel sure," said Selby cautiously, "that the Raro Charitable Foundation would be happy to make a generous donation towards the cost of the Ziggurat."

"An excellent idea," I agreed. "The Raro family are great lovers of Britain, and the Ziggurat would be just their thing. As you may know, their only son is now a pupil with the Discalced Benedictines at Calderbeck."

"I am aware of that," snapped the Minister. "We were consulted by the Home Office about the need for the child's bodyguard to carry automatic weapons. I am sorry we had to get involved."

"I'll sound out the Ambassador then about a donation," said Selby hopefully.

"Indeed you will not. To accept their money would be politically very damaging. It would wreck my career. Besides," she added with less vigour, "it would be morally wrong. You ask your own son, Mr Bellingham. I see he has just written an excellent piece about his experiences in the Concordian penal system."

"I think you should consider carefully the repercussions of your bombing project, Dame Rosy," I ventured. "Wouldn't you kill a lot of innocent civilians?"

"You can't make an omelette without breaking eggs, Mr Bellingham. At least they would be dying in a noble cause. I am prepared to make that sacrifice on their behalf. What is your suggested alternative? We cannot just stand idly by."

"So it is your intention now to announce that the export of defence equipment for Concordia will not be permitted?" At least that would put Wedmore and Bassenthwaite out of their misery, I thought, and allow them to concentrate on alternative lines of production.

"That would certainly be my intention," said Dame Rosy. "One does not send arms to a country one is intending to bomb, though I believe we did in Iraq. But, as I have told you, I cannot get the Prime Minister and the Foreign Secretary to concentrate on these issues at this moment. There are counter-pressures from small-minded people who put employment and prosperity in our own country above moral considerations. The outcome is yet to be seen. But at least you know where you stand with me. We look forward to seeing you and Lucretia next week, Selby. So kind of you to invite us to your niece's christening. Goodbye, Mr Bellingham. If we don't meet again, I wish you a happy retirement." It was an obvious way of signing off. She got up rather ostentatiously and rang for her private secretary to show us out.

"There is just one more small point, Minister," I said.

"Yes, Mr Bellingham," she snapped with ill-concealed impatience.

"The Concordian Embassy here are somewhat disturbed," I said with rather less than my usual aplomb. "They fear that somebody at the airport is tampering with their diplomatic bags before they can get hold of them. That, of course, would be a breach of diplomatic privilege."

"I know nothing about that, Mr Bellingham. You must address your enquiries to some other quarter."

"I mention the matter for the sake of my successor in Felicidad. If this goes on, the Concordians might well take reprisals by opening our own diplomatic bag."

"I view that threat with equanimity," opined the Minister. "Their bag contains large quantities of heroin. Ours will no doubt be full of baked beans and copies of Hansard. And now, you really must excuse me, gentlemen. I have to work on my speech to the League of Young Female Achievers. They are collecting money to commission a figure to be erected in front of Somerville College, Oxford. You may know that in Constanta, Romania, there is a Roman statue entitled *The Thinker and His Wife*. Ours is to be called *The Thinker and Her Husband*."

"What a character!" I said to Selby as we stood outside in Whitehall once again.

"Political life was so much gentler before we had female liberation," he ruminated. "Women in public office today all have one thing in common. They are so awfully manly."

***

"I'm so glad you've come, Ambrose," said Father Manfred, lighting his pipe. "Can I press you to a single malt?"

"You may indeed." I always enjoyed the hospitality of the

Discalced Benedictines. Outside the darkening window, with curtains undrawn, the broad waters of the river Calderbeck flowed peacefully towards the Irish Sea. On the other side of the estuary rose the dark shape of Great Combe.

"We are in rather desperate straits," continued the monastic headmaster. "That's why I rang you and begged you to come. After all, it was you who landed us with the problem."

"I gather that young Master Dominic Raro has not fitted in very well here."

"That's an understatement, my dear Ambrose, a considerable understatement. God knows, we have had some difficult boys here in my time. One thinks of the young Earl of Kendal, who went beagling by moonlight. Or Luke Chatterton, now lead singer for a pop group called, aptly enough, the Screaming Queers. I have had a great deal of experience in quelling youthful high spirits and even outright disobedience. I had been warned in advance that the Raro lad would not be easy to manage. But nothing had prepared me for the hideous reality. The boy is nothing short of a monster."

"I thought you took the view that all human beings are children of God."

"That may be true in theory. But, if Almighty God created young Dominic, it must have been on an off-day."

"What exactly is wrong with him?"

"Oh come, Ambrose, you've met him yourself. He's supposed to be a child but you've only got to look at him to scent danger. He's precociously well developed, as you know. He has a very definite moustache and the beginnings of a flourishing beard. I invited him to shave but he pointed out that he's still in the junior form. He's already in the throes of adolescence, consumed, it would seem, by an overpowering sexual urge. We are simply not used to that sort of problem in children of thirteen."

"You must be understanding, Father. They grow up earlier in these warmer climates. Juliet was only fourteen."

"Maybe. And look what happened to her. I'm terrified that something will go dreadfully wrong."

"Please be more specific."

"The boy has a very small brain and his English is limited. That makes him an appalling nuisance in the classroom. He lolls at the back, making faces to amuse the other boys. And he simply refuses to accept orders. Poor Father Clement, his mathematics teacher, was recently discovered in tears. It's so bad for the discipline of the whole school."

"You must be firm, Father Manfred."

"Firm?!" almost shrieked the headmaster. "You haven't heard the worst yet. Dominic has formed a small group of cronies among the larger boys, and he uses them to terrorise the smaller ones. Not for nothing is he known in the school as the Wolf Man."

"Surely we have to see these things in proportion. According to Neville, there was always bullying at Calderbeck. I believe it happens at all public schools. It used to accustom boys to the subsequent rigours of the Brigade of Guards and the Stock Exchange."

"I am not speaking of mere bullying. A few of the smaller boys have been withdrawn from the school already, some of them rather the worse for wear. Mrs Hibbert-Smith is threatening an action against the Community, though our doctor has assured her that her precious Julian's injuries are more dramatic than life threatening. If we lose more pupils, that could have awful effects on our cashflow."

"It is quite simple, Father. You must punish him."

"Punish him?! Don't imagine I haven't tried. But we have no real sanctions left in this degenerate age. I gave him five hundred lines to write out, but he produced some extremely rude words, some of which were quite new to me. In fact I had to have them explained by Mr Snowshill, our games master, who used to be in the Navy. How I long to give him six of the best, as we did in the good old days. Now let me tell you about his sex life."

"Sex life?! I thought children were sent here to protect them from worldly temptation."

"You must be pulling my leg, Ambrose. Dominic is a heaving mountain of testosterone. We have had several painful incidents. Miss Manners, who teaches the oboe, and is highly strung at the best of times, was ambushed by him one night behind the music rooms, after a performance of the Verdi *Requiem*. He drew a knife and insisted that she display her somewhat exiguous breasts. Worse would have happened if Mr Snowshill had not passed by at that moment. Miss Manners has not been the same since. It has even affected her embouchure. Then there was a rather ghastly episode with one of the more forward local girls who work in the kitchens. She is spectacularly pregnant, though fortunately she cannot quite remember who the father might be. There are apparently a wealth of candidates."

"At least the boy seems robustly normal."

"I have my doubts, even about that. I have had to remove him from a dormitory, where he was opening up a variety of fresh experiences to the younger boys. Now he sleeps in the isolation wing. I just pray that we don't have another epidemic of scarlet fever. They say he also takes an unhealthy interest in the farm animals. Where will it all end, I wonder? There is no provision for this kind of thing in the Rule of Saint Benedict."

"Surely the bodyguards can help?"

"Have you seen them? They are Neanderthal brutes, speaking not one word of English and posing, most unconvincingly, as the boy's uncles. He orders them around as if he were a dictator himself. The trouble, you see, is that he has always had his own way. People have been afraid of him because of who his father is. So he is completely unused to discipline. There is even talk of his practising voodoo at midnight in the chemistry labs. Just think of the possibilities, Ambrose. We may be facing massive public humiliation, ruinous court cases, a stinging rebuke from the Holy Father himself. Kindly advise me what to do."

"I think you should keep calm, Father Manfred. The Benedictine Order has had to cope with a number of problems over the centuries. The Huns, the Mongols, Vatican Two. View this matter against the long perspective of human history."

"That is what Father Abbot advises." Abbot Juniper, rather than the headmaster, was the head of the whole Community. "But even he is shaken. In fact he has slipped off for a retreat at a convent of reclusive nuns on an island in the Hebrides without a telephone. I need some positive suggestion very badly."

"I'll tell you what," I said brightly. "Tell the boy there is a security alert. The opposition are coming to murder him. Send him off to your centrally heated hermitage in the hills with his minders and a nice basket of goodies. Meanwhile, I will contact urgently my friend the Ambassador of Concordia and ask him to implore the boy's parents to transfer him urgently to some more permissive school where his little ways will fit better into the liberated ethos."

"It might just work. But I suspect that the boy's mother will insist on his staying here. She was so keen on his being brought up in a traditional Catholic atmosphere."

"Then you must tell her that you will only take the boy back on one condition. It is that the Raro Foundation endows that new computer centre you have been wanting for so long."

"But that would be blackmail, Ambrose."

"That's not a word I care to use, Manfred. But you must admit, we have there the genesis of a solution. Take the long view. The business school will be the making of Calderbeck for future years. That's all young people want to know about these days. And young Dominic won't last for ever. I should guess that he's pretty accident prone."

"I could never connive at injury to the boy."

"Of course not. But you never know. Sometimes providence does step in. I don't see that child ever making the sixth form."

"If he does," said Father Manfred, "I shall be a shattered husk by that time. I sometimes regret, you know, that I didn't enter one of those nice quiet Trappist monasteries where they keep bees and don't allow any talking."

***

"At the request of the First Lady," said little Hector Garcia, "I have consulted urgently the eminent educational advisers Blackfoot and Pride. They have put forward a number of alternative suggestions for a school to which young Dominic might be transferred with the minimum of fuss. But none of them seems at all satisfactory. Just look at these. An academy in deepest Dorset run on progressive lines. The boys and girls are encouraged to develop their personality. Condoms are freely available, and creative sexual expression is a key element in the curriculum."

"It would be like letting a drunkard loose in a brewery," I said.

"Then there's a rationalist establishment in Aberdeenshire where the children are trained to liberate themselves from the intellectual shackles of organised religion. Think of the effect on the First Lady, with her intense devotion to Saint Térèse of Lisieux, generally known as the Little Flower. And her special medal for outstanding services to the Holy See. They have even broadened their search to include other countries, but without success. There's a military school in North Carolina where they specialise in boys who need to have military virtues instilled as a matter of urgency. Reveille is at five o'clock, followed by an hour's run in the pinewoods, and then a compulsory cold shower."

"I can't imagine Dominic lasting there."

"From Australia we hear of a pioneer school in northern Queensland where the boys spend their spare time clearing bush land of immense zoological interest. It contains eight separate varieties of poisonous snake."

"If they send Dominic there," I commented, "I should be sorry for those snakes."

"It is all so very worrying," said the unfortunate Ambassador, glancing out of the window of his huge embassy residence in Belgrave Square, so grotesquely out of proportion with the actual resources of penurious Concordia. "The First Lady is almost out of her mind with anxiety. You know how she adores Dominic. She simply cannot understand why they are being so nasty to him at Calderbeck. The Raros had hoped that the saintly monks would make allowances for the exuberance of youth."

"Exuberance?!" I echoed grimly. "It is getting worse every day. Mrs Hibbert-Smith has sold her story to the *Daily Mail*. And there has been an unexplained combustion at the hermitage. They have had to move the lad with his bodyguards down to the toolshed behind the monks' burial ground. Father Manfred telephones every day. He has even found a way to send me E-mails at the Voyagers."

"I am at my wit's end," wailed the Ambassador. "It seems impossible to find an alternative school which would take Dominic and which he would agree to go to. Is he to return home? That would be a terrible blow for his unfortunate parents. We wondered, my dear Ambrose, whether you and your wife would care to invite the child to stay at your country mansion for a time. His bodyguards would come to look after his material needs, and we could engage a robust tutor to develop his mind. I know of a Jesuit theologian who used to be a major in the Commandos."

"That would be delightful," I countered promptly, "but unfortunately it would not be possible."

"Why not, Ambrose? You did assure the First Lady, I understand, that you would take an avuncular interest in the boy while he was over here in your country. She was relying on your help in the hour of need."

"It is all most unfortunate. My poor wife is suffering badly," I said hastily, "from acute attacks of lumbago. Our elderly butler has just retired, and we are busy building a gazebo at the end of the west wing. The place is in uproar."

"A pity," said Hector smoothly. "One would not wish the Generalissimo and the First Lady to lose interest in your beautiful country. As you know, your French and American rivals are always on the watch for opportunities. I understand that the French run a military *lycée* on a small island off Tahiti. It has no airstrip, and the boat calls there only once a month."

The threat was palpable. Find a solution, or lose the arms contract for good.

"You should consider the other alternative I mentioned to you, my dear Hector. Offer the Discalced Benedictines a huge bribe to keep Dominic at their school."

"A huge bribe? Surely that would not be very British."

"You wouldn't call it that, of course. So many of these things are a matter of semantics. I happen to know that the school are desperately in need of a new computer centre. They would certainly accept a generous gift for the Raro School for Business Studies, to be constructed between the Abbey church and the swimming bath. They have all the plans drawn up. Unfortunately the donor originally planned, a Croatian business tycoon of immense piety, is now serving a lengthy sentence for misappropriation of official funds."

"How much would that cost?" asked the Ambassador cautiously.

"A mere four millions," I said lightly. "Pounds."

"Four million? That is a lot of money. Perhaps they could offer something less ambitious. A new grand piano, perhaps, for the assembly hall."

"You won't get away with a Bechstein."

"A scholarship then for a pupil unusually gifted in athletics or the martial arts?"

"They will take nothing less than a computer centre. The school has got to modernise, you see. The parents are insistent these days that their children should be equipped to earn a living in the global marketplace. They have had enough of Latin and literature."

"Four million pounds!"

"It has all been costed," I said firmly.

"I suppose I shall have to put that to the First Lady, though she will not be pleased. Sylvester Marsala and his associates might be able to raise some funds. Perhaps we could auction off some of the First Lady's shoes. But what makes you think that this enormous donation would enable Father Manfred to keep Dominic, if he is so intolerable?"

"Nobody is intolerable," I retorted, "if you just grit your teeth. The gift would liberate other resources, which could be helpful. A house could be rented for young Dominic in the village, and he could live there with his minders, attending the school as a day-boy. The great thing is to keep him away at night from the boys' dormitories and the quarters of the female domestic staff."

"You'll ask Father Manfred to agree to that?"

"I'll do my best."

"I sincerely hope so, Ambrose. After all, you and I are professional diplomats of long standing. Between the two of us, we ought to be able to sort out any problems posed by a child of thirteen."

"This is no ordinary child, Hector."

"I am sure I can rely on your full co-operation," concluded the Ambassador urbanely. "And I do hope there will be no more trouble with my diplomatic bags. If so, that could have some relevance for your four million." I took his point. I was to connive at their smuggling. Then, for good measure, he got in another blow.

"Do you ever hear these days," he asked with deadly gentleness, "from our mutual friend, the Condesa de la Rosas?"

***

"Sharon is sick with worry," said Susan when I went back to Little Bigney for the weekend, as the Voyagers virtually closed down. "She keeps ringing hysterically from Stoke Newington. Neville has disappeared again."

"No doubt he has departed on some new foreign adventure," I commented cynically. "Try the heart of darkness."

"He went off without a word, leaving the poor girl with nothing to live on. They've spent all that money he got from the newspaper. She has already had to pawn those silver candlesticks we gave them for Christmas. And the heartless householder is trying to charge them rent at last. If this goes on long, she may have to take a paid job."

"My heart bleeds for her."

"It's terribly distressing. If Sharon was obliged to go back to office routine, she might have to reduce her work for the planet. Her campaign for the badgers. Even her voluntary activities to stop influenza in mice. You know how tremendously she cares."

"Sharon is quite mad."

"Don't be harsh, Darling. It doesn't suit you. When is our money coming through from Mr Molnar?"

"Quite possibly, never."

"Oh dear! Rowley Harrison Bedford says you should never trust a Hungarian. He once commanded a patrol boat on the Danube."

"That man is a fascist bigot. I'm surprised you bother with either of them."

"I'm only doing it to help you, Darling. You know how influential they are in the village. We had a nice day trip to Norwich while you were away. Griselda did a lot of brass rubbing in the church. She's got a thing about crusader knights."

"Griselda is a silly little mouse. A woman ought to stand up for herself against a brute of a husband."

"You've never encouraged me to do that, Dear."

"I don't need to," I said with an affectionate smile. "You're not married to a brute, are you?"

***

"It is agreed," said Father Manfred when I visited him again. "I have managed to communicate at last with Abbot Juniper on the Isle of Mingulay. He has sanctioned the compromise plan. We accept the generous donation for the Raro Business Centre. And Dominic is to remain here, but as a day-boy. That was rather a clever idea of yours, Ambrose. The day-boy wheeze, I mean. I have told him that he is excused afternoon games, which he never much enjoyed. He goes home each day at three thirty, and we breathe again. Until the next morning."

"And what news from the village?"

"I try not to think about it. At least we have reduced his activities on school premises."

We both heaved a sigh of relief.

"Well done, Ambrose. The Community is grateful. You have proved yourself to be most resourceful in the emergency. I am surprised you did not go further in the Diplomatic Service."

"So am I."

"We should like to show our appreciation in some tangible way. As you know, we possess no great stock of this world's goods. But there is something we have decided to do for you."

What could he mean? A case of champagne? Or a box of the best cigars?

"Father Abbot met a charming, but distressed, youngish man on his island in the Hebrides," continued Father Manfred. "An old boy of the school, in fact, with a somewhat chequered past which I remember only too well. The man, under the persuasive influence of Father Abbot, has surprisingly decided that he would like to enter the novitiate here, in order to train to become a Benedictine monk. I was rather against it myself since I was far from convinced that this particular postulant would be quite suitable. But Abbot Juniper's word is law at Calderbeck, and the young man has just joined the Community as a novice."

A dreadful suspicion darted across my mind. No! That would really be the last straw.

"He is here now, Ambrose, and would like to see you. May I introduce our new Brother Cyprian?"

A young clean-shaven novice entered. It was Neville! "Hello, Dad," said Brother Cyprian.

"This is an awful shock, Neville. Are you sure you are doing the right thing? You're not just trying to gather material for another of your contributions to the tabloid press?"

"Of course not, Dad. It's great here. No money worries, regular meals, early bed. And a sort of inner glow of spirituality, a glorious feeling of sanctity."

"That won't last," said Father Manfred with a grin.

"The meals, you mean?" asked Neville.

"No, the feeling of sanctity."

"What about Sharon?" I asked pointedly.

"I've renounced her," replied Neville smugly. "I've taken up celibacy. It's a lovely new feeling. You should try it some time, Dad."

***

"I'm desperate for a stiff drink," wailed Lucretia Tritton. "I didn't want to come this evening but Selby insisted. Isn't it fearsome?"

I had to agree that the Concordia State Folklore Troupe were an acquired taste. We were attending the first night of their season at Sadlers Wells. With his usual ingenuity, Ludovic Molnar had managed at last to obtain sponsorship from Pontifex and Cuthbert, who imported Concordian bananas, and the company had been accommodated at a cut-price hotel on the wrong side of Euston. The house had been liberally papered, as the phrase goes, by giving away seats to friends of the management, but even so the enthusiasm of the audience had been muted. The folkloric performers were only too generous with their services. We had just survived the first half, lasting for two hours. Now, after the interval, we were promised another hour and a half. I felt quite stunned by the drumming, the harping and the conch-blowing, the conch being a monotonous instrument not unlike the didgeridoo beloved of the Australian aborigines. The dancing also presented a problem, the vigorous peasant boleros of the Nevera coast being incompatible with the graceful tarantellas from the Tozudo interior. Indeed, the two main tribal groups within the company were palpably at odds with each other, scowling malevolently from opposite sides of the stage. There were rumours of knife fights in the chorus gentlemen's dressing room.

"These folklore dos are all the same," I said to Lucretia. "They lose all their fun when presented so clinically in a London theatre. We should be sitting in some tropical glade in the hills of Felicidad, watching the rising of the moon, sniffing the hibiscus, listening to the humming of the crickets and the cry of the jackal, and sipping some delicious sherbert with a strong alcoholic content. Then I could bear a few hours of that conch-blowing."

"You sound quite poetical, Ambrose. Selby never talks like that." She gave me a provocative glance but I am too old a hand to fall for feminine wiles, the episode with that wretched Casilda having taught me a lesson.

"The second half should be even livelier," said Ludovic Molnar, bustling up to us with his usual enthusiasm. "We are promised a wrestling display by the all-girl team assembled by the First Lady, customarily known as the Amazon Warriors. They have been trained by the American marines. You will see some magnificently developed torsos." Lucretia privately made me an elegant gesture of disgust.

"It is a great pity," I said, "that the Generalissimo and the First Lady could not be here this evening."

"It is not for lack of trying, my dear Ambrose. We requested a visa for them from the Foreign Office. The Ambassador even went to beard Dame Rosy Clumber in person. But she refused in the most offensive terms. Then we tried to obtain entry for General Tiberio Golosina. After all, the Amazon Warriors are part of his defence forces, personally selected by him for the First Lady in a series of raids on … sorry, visits to … the tribal villages. But his application was rejected even more abruptly. Never mind: the Folklore Troupe are making a tremendous impact tonight on the English cognoscenti. That will help to turn British opinion in our favour. Don't you think so?"

"They are making a superhuman effort," I conceded. "I have seen nothing quite like it on the London stage."

"The great thing is to keep the impetus going," said Ludo. "At least Dame Rosy has never quite been allowed to turn down our application, and the Raros still want to buy from Britain. One does not easily concede defeat. I still have some interesting initiatives up my sleeve. And thanks to you, Ambrose, the Raros are more involved than ever now with the saintly monks of Calderbeck."

"Work will start shortly on the new Raro Business Centre," I said.

"You have done well, Ambrose. But I must admit I had thought of diminishing or even cancelling your expense account because of the apparent lack of progress in the defence equipment contract."

"That would be a definite blow, Ludo. I might be reduced to going home to Little Bigney."

"To your charming wife?"

"She is charming," I agreed, "but we get enough of each other at weekends. She finds my personality rather ... pungent for every day."

"Very well. Stay on at the Voyagers then, with my blessing. At least," he added with a sinister grin, "for the present." How well he combined the threatening with the urbane!

The Ambassador drew me aside. "Isn't this show appalling?" he hissed. "Simply a bunch of ignorant peasants with their brutish pastimes! I hate to think that you British will be judging my beloved country from their primitive caperings. Concordia is a highly civilised nation!" Little Hector Garcia groaned theatrically and gulped his champagne.

***

"Good evening, ladies and gentlemen," said Lord Cumberland. "It is indeed a pleasure to welcome you all here to our offices in Half Moon Street. We continue now with our series of lectures on little-known but fascinating countries to be visited by Connoisseur Travel during the next season. Last week we heard Archdeacon Grant-Edwards on the Orthodox churches of the Lake Baikal region of inner Siberia. Next week it will be Professor Luke Fosdyke on the buried cities of Bessarabia. Tonight, we have a great treat, as we dedicate the evening to the stimulating, though seldom visited, country of Concordia. The renowned scholar and archaeologist Adrian Carr-Baxendale will speak about the rich Nevera culture he is currently unearthing. Then, after a complimentary coffee break, with my favourite ginger biscuits, we shall hear from Mr Ambrose Bellingham, formerly Her Britannic Majesty's Ambassador in Felicidad, about the gracious houses built there in colonial times."

There was polite applause. I looked around me. They were elderly ladies and gentlemen of the old school, presumably eager to mop up their spare cash with expensive travelling so that it would not eventually fall into the clutches of their in-laws. There was an air of distinction about the gathering. I recognised the faded beauty of the Marchioness of Angmering, once a society charmer noted for *affaires* with heavyweight boxers. And surely that was old Lord Helvellyn, the former Home Secretary remembered for his involvement in the notorious miscarriage of justice known as the Horsham Nineteen. At least I should be among my own kind.

"The Nevera world was grim," began Carr-Baxendale with ghoulish enthusiasm. "Treason, backstabbing, human sacrifice."

"Not unlike British politics," commented Lord Helvellyn, in an audible aside which provoked a titter. This, I thought, would be a not uncritical audience. At least I had managed to negotiate a fee for my appearance.

"Felicidad is not of course one of the world's art centres," I began, when it came to my turn, "but it does contain some charming mansions. These are all tucked away in the elegant residential suburb of Los Pinos, developed in the last days of the colonial era and the earliest years of independent Concordia. The houses are all set in extensive grounds and contain spacious drawing rooms. The bedrooms are also of interest. Several of them include an unusual feature: an outside staircase leading down from their balconies to the lawn beneath. These are thought to have been built in order to provide an emergency escape route in the event of the unexpected return of an irate husband or father."

"We could have done with that at Cambridge," chortled Lord Helvellyn.

"May I ask a question?" asked the Marchioness of Angmering, delicately raising a beringed paw.

"Certainly," I agreed.

"I understand that the Condesa de la Rosas owns one of the most beautiful of these villas. I encountered her in Barbados and she seemed perfectly charming. Shall we have a chance of meeting her?"

Over my dead body, I thought, but did not say.

"Is Concordia perfectly safe for visitors?" enquired a thin lady with spectacles in the front row. "I heard they were killing each other."

"There is a system of guided democracy," I replied, "under a benevolent dictatorship. It was a system much admired by some of the most eminent Greek philosophers."

"It is part of the ethos of Connoisseur Travel," chipped in Lord Cumberland hastily, "not to become involved in politics."

***

"A very strange thing has happened," said the Ambassador of Concordia. "Your friend Father Manfred naturally invited President Raro and his lady to attend the ceremonies connected with the official start of work on the Raro Business Centre at Calderbeck. Somebody has to lay the first stone, and he thought this would be beautifully done by the First Lady."

"I encouraged him to do so," I said. "But it was only an act of courtesy. We knew perfectly well that they would never get a British visa."

"So I thought," agreed Hector Garcia. "In fact we had already received a notification of refusal. But then yesterday I was summoned to the Foreign Office. Dame Rosy did not seem quite her usual confident self. I could see that something unusual was happening. Then she blurted it out. The Raros are to be given a visa after all, for the express purpose of visiting the monastic school at Calderbeck."

"How extraordinary, Hector."

"It will be a private visit, of course. No question of staying with the Queen. But the Government will be obliged to take some notice of the party. After all, the President is head of a state with which you have diplomatic relations."

"Dame Rosy must have been furious. Presumably she had been overruled by the Foreign Secretary or even the Prime Minister. Perhaps the Pope has intervened."

"She certainly looked extremely flustered. Why has this happened, Ambrose? I thought I understood your system."

"There must be wheels within wheels," I agreed. "Maybe our brilliant friend Ludovic Molnar has produced another of his miracles. Could it have something to do with the emerald mines? Their shares went right down after nationalisation but they must still be theoretically held by somebody."

"I have tried in vain to find out about that," said the Ambassador. "The remaining British interest in the mines is held by a mysterious trust but their legal adviser is very coy about the real ownership. Anyhow, the great thing is that the Generalissimo and his lady will actually be here with us in Britain. I feel faint with joy."

"It's tremendous," I agreed. "The First Lady will carry all before her with her gracious charm. And what a coup for Father Manfred! Will General Golosina accompany them to conclude the arms agreement?"

"Not if I have my way. Tiberio will be needed at home. To keep the lid on the cauldron."

"The British Government can hardly refuse the defence deal now," I pointed out. "That would be illogical after accepting the Raro regime as a more or less respectable government. I long to witness Dame Rosy's chagrin." And I should be quite rich. It was a delightful thought.

***

"This matter has been mishandled," protested an elderly Tory member. "Here we are, going on a parliamentary delegation to Concordia just at the very time when the president of that nation is paying a visit to Britain. How do you explain that, Selby?"

I had been invited to join Selby, in his capacity as chairman of the Anglo-Concordian Parliamentary Group, for a meeting with the proposed delegation. They were in restive mood and Selby, no tower of strength at the best of times, seemed badly in need of support. Nor was the presence of Dame Rosy Clumber much of a help. As in her meeting with the Ambassador, she seemed to have lost much of her usual marmoreal composure. She was, moreover, strangely silent. As all the members were backbench MPs and peers of little importance, I found it impossible to recognise many of their faces.

"There is no problem," said Selby. "We have arranged that the delegation will be received by President and Mrs Raro on the very day of our arrival. The President will give us an account of the achievements of his regime, while the First Lady will show us a fascinating film about her charitable work. Then the Raros will leave later for London while we are on tour in the Nevera area. So you will not miss anything."

"I hope we shall see the concentration camps," said a tough-looking lady in black, who might have been Valery Ship-Godwin. "And the prisons where they torture people."

"I am sure we shall get a very interesting all-round view of current developments in Concordia," replied Selby evasively. "Perhaps Mr Bellingham can tell you more."

"I am so glad you are not confining your visit to Felicidad," I said hastily. "The countryside is spectacularly beautiful, with its wealth of semi-dormant volcanos and abundant natural fauna."

"Is it dangerous?" asked a nervous-looking man. "What about swimming?"

"You do have to be a little careful," I admitted. "Make enquiries about bathing in the sea. There could be sharks. And the rivers have large black leeches which cling to your flesh. The swimming pool at the Waving Palms Hotel should be safe, unless they have run out of chlorine."

"Can you confirm that all expenses will be paid?" asked a jolly-looking man who might have been the Earl of Templeton.

"I can," said Selby enthusiastically. "And we shall be travelling Jacquaranda class on the national airline from Miami. Their stewardesses are noted for their exquisite courtesy."

"But what about the real question?" chipped in a crisp voice from the back. "Perhaps Dame Rosy can answer. Why on earth, after all these years, are the villainous Raros being let into Britain?"

"We have decided that much good could flow from admitting the Raros, so that they can see for themselves the virtues of our democratic system, with our independent judiciary and a police force open to public scrutiny." Dame Rosy did not sound at all convincing. How could one explain this extraordinary volte-face?

***

It was a glittering occasion. Ludovic Molnar had hired an upmarket boat, and we were on our way down the river to Greenwich. A contingent from the London Symphony Orchestra were playing *Eine Kleine Nachtmusik*. Delicious food was being served, and the drink flowed copiously. Nothing but the best to welcome to London that eminent couple the President-Generalissimo of Concordia and his gracious lady. Everyone knew that Molnar had footed the bill but, for the look of the thing, the nominal host was the Ambassador of Concordia. The tiny man kept hopping around in an ecstasy of excitement. For him, it was a dream come true.

Gerald Haverstock-Jones was there too. "Hello, Ambrose," he said gloomily, "I thought you might be around. The measly old Foreign Office agreed to pay my fare to be on parade for the visit, but they refused to stump up for Monica, so she has had to stay behind in Felicidad. Our finances have been badly hit by an expensive party we had to give two days ago for that wretched parliamentary delegation. What a gang of freeloaders!"

"How is your dear Monica?" I asked, with my usual courtesy.

"Surprisingly chipper, thank you." What high jinks had that well-upholstered beldame been planning, in Gerald's absence, with the sprightly Potiphar? I thought.

"I called on the Personnel Department today," added Gerald. "Tunis is vacant, you know. A lovely residence given to HMG by the Bey. But they say I'm too old for a transfer. Just my luck!"

"I expect you know Mr Greg Atkinson of Wedmore and Bassenthwaite?"

"Indeed we do know each other," agreed Greg, with his usual bluff cordiality. "The Ambassador kindly entertained me to a nice cup of tea when I made my recce to Felicidad. And now it looks as if the deal will really go through at last. There is much rejoicing in our neck of the woods. You'll be seeing a lot more of me and my team, Mr Haverstock-Jones."

"That will be delightful," replied Gerald faintly.

"We hope to be busy once again," added Greg. "It's been tough, these lean years without a nice juicy war. Now we are tendering too for the restraining equipment needed for the Ziggurat. That's a grand project. What a pity it isn't on the river!"

"The Dome was on the river," I riposted, "and a fat lot of good it did them. Why on earth should the Ziggurat require your restraining equipment?"

"The authorities are determined that the queues should not get out of control, as they did at the Dome. They've called for tenders for all sorts of things that are just up our street: truncheons, handcuffs, hoses for spraying ice-cold water, even helicopters from which troublemakers will be lassoed." He spoke with loving enthusiasm. One could not help admiring the sheer professionalism of the man. "See you gentlemen soon at Greyburn." With a cheery wave, he was off towards the buffet. Gerald sloped towards the champagne bar.

I spotted Susan gazing over the side of the boat as we glided by the lighted towers of the City. I gently put my hand on her shoulder, and she reacted with a start.

"Oh," she said, "it's only you."

"I do hope you're enjoying yourself, Darling," I said in my usual solicitous way.

"It's all right." She had not wanted to come, but I had insisted. A thrusting tycoon, such as I had now become, need the support of a decorative and obliging consort.

"Rowley's birthday party was this very evening," she added mournfully. "He did so want me to be there."

"Look, Dear, I appreciate all those efforts you are making for my sake with those appalling Harrison Bedfords. But there's no need to overdo it. You can't bury yourself for ever in Little Bigney, now that we are going to be rich. Why don't you make yourself useful? Come with me and chat up the First Lady. You remember how much she always liked you."

We pushed through the throng to where Elvira Raro was holding court, with her vivacious laugh and quicksilver fingers.

"Dear Sir Bellingham," she cooed in her Concordian Spanish, "how delightful to see you again. And this is your beautiful Lady Bellingham, as lovely as ever. I do admire the way you English ladies retain your delicate complexions. Even into advanced old age. How wonderful it is to be here in your great city. I long to visit the principal cultural centres: your Harrods, of course, and your famous Bond Street."

"I expect you plan a little shopping, dear lady," I said.

"Just a little. The stores of Felicidad are so poor. But I do not know how I shall manage with my wretched English." I gave Susan a sharp dig in the ribs.

"I should be glad to accompany you, First Lady," she said at my prompting.

"That would be extremely kind of you. I enjoy bargaining and you can help me beat their prices down. The Embassy have hired a Rolls Royce for me, so we shall travel in comfort. You and I, Sir Bellingham, will meet again at the monastery of the Disrobed Benedictines. Hector has told me how ingenious you have been in calming Father Manfred. I have met many priests, and I know they are apt to become overexcited. It is their terrible burden of celibacy, you see. How I long to see my beloved child again. I had hoped that you might be able to welcome him to your mansion, but I understand that it has not so far been possible." There was a faint note of reproach in her well-modulated voice.

"We have been otherwise engaged," I said hastily. "But we long to receive Dominic for his next half-term holiday." Susan looked surprised but I dug her in the ribs again. She complains that there are better methods of covert communication but I have found none so effective. Leaving my dear, loyal wife to plan with the rapacious First Lady a mammoth raid on the most luxurious shops at the expense of the Concordian taxpayer, I edged my way forward in order to pay my respects to President Raro in person. It is one of the golden rules of diplomacy. If you have the luck to be invited to an occasion where important people are present, make sure that they know you are there.

I had spotted the gnarled old face of the President, looking more than ever like a saintly recluse, and sipping a small glass of orange juice. I had managed to dislodge a couple of stout women and was moving into the range of the head of state, when I found my way blocked by a large, unfriendly figure. It was none other than the unspeakable Sylvester Marsala.

"Security!" he boomed in his gravelly voice. "Oh, it's you, Bellingham. I remember you well."

"I remember you too," I riposted cautiously. There was no point in alienating this odious thug, who had clearly been brought over to protect the Raros. That was not surprising. There had been an ugly rumour about possible protests against them by the human rights industry. Marsala might well have denied me access to the great man, but happily, at that moment, the President happened to notice me. He beckoned me forward with a trembling hand, and his Mafia henchman was obliged to welcome me into the VIP circle. I was surprised to see that it contained Dame Rosy Clumber but I assumed that she was only carrying out her minimum official duties. She looked unusually ill at ease.

"Good evening, Sir Bellingham," said the aged statesman in Spanish. "I am so happy to be here in your splendid country."

"What on earth is he saying?" enquired Dame Rosy, whom I suspected of being resolutely monoglot.

"He is delighted to see me again," I said boldly. "He considers me to be one of the finest ambassadors ever sent to his country."

"It didn't sound like that," snapped the Minister of State.

"You might be able to help me," continued the Generalissimo in his squeaky voice so inappropriate in a mass murderer. "I should love to play croquet while I am here. Please could the British Government set up some facilities?"

"He wants to play croquet," I explained to Dame Rosy. At least that was better than some other outlandish potentates, who tended to demand girls, or even boys.

"Hell's bells," snorted Dame Rosy.

"Is your husband here?" I asked politely.

"Certainly not," she retorted. "I'm only here because I have to be. It's the bare minimum the Government can do." It was hard to think of her as a bare minimum.

"Nothing would induce Trevor," she continued, "to accept the hospitality of these dreadful people."

"What is the dear lady saying?" enquired the President, giving her a gentle smile.

"She is explaining," I said hastily, "how sorry her husband is to miss this truly delightful occasion."

"I remember," said the President, "his gardens in Hampstead. Perhaps they have a croquet lawn? What is that huge building?"

"It is the Tower of London. We are just passing the Traitors' Gate."

"We could use a facility like that in Felicidad," commented the President wryly.

I found myself being deftly led aside, and was soon staring into the eager face of Ludovic Molnar.

"It's going splendidly, isn't it?" he whispered. "The chief of the defence staff is here. And the director of the British Museum. But there are some inevitable absentees. Selby is in Concordia with his parliamentary delegation. And Lord Cumberland is also there with this Connoisseur group. I understand that he has taken Adrian Carr-Baxendale as a guest lecturer. Your Archdeacon Harry Wilderness has gone with them. He is to talk on primitive religious cults."

"I am glad to hear that," I said, slightly surprised that Molnar should be so well informed. "It will be a nice change for Harry from life with his deaf sister in Saffron Walden."

Suddenly the innocent delight of our evening cruise was shattered. A fast motorboat loomed up beside us, and we heard the noise of offensive chanting. The boat carried a huge banner, in Spanish and English, exhorting the bloodstained Raros to go home at once. The distinguished visitors and their diplomatic hosts looked appalled. The crew of the motorboat consisted of ill-dressed young people with unkempt hair, shrieking obscenities in tones of bitter malice. Prominent among them, and presumably their leader, was a scruffy-looking young woman yelling ruderies through a microphone. The sort of female who used to sit beneath the guillotine in revolutionary Paris, happily knitting as aristocratic heads rolled into a bloodstained basket.

Something about the girl seemed vaguely familiar.

"Is that someone we know?" I asked Susan.

"Yes," she replied crisply. "It is Sharon. Very nearly your daughter-in-law."

***

The First Lady had decided to skip the President's visit to Wedmore and Bassenthwaite, proceeding directly to Calderbeck College in order to have more time with her beloved Dominic. Dame Rosy Clumber had also retired to the more refined atmosphere of the Foreign Office, presumably with some relief. But the two ambassadors had arrived in Greyburn to accompany the aged President, together with the *eminences grises*, Ludovic Molnar and myself. We had received a splendid welcome. The town had declared a holiday, the workers and their families being out in force in their grimy streets to welcome the party from Concordia. Luridly coloured banners extolled the value of Anglo-Concordian friendship, in the expectation of the early signature of the lucrative arms deal. It would breathe new life into the whole region, as the Mayor emphasised in his address of welcome.

Greg Atkinson was in excellent form at the substantial lunch. It had been preceded by a lengthy grace from the Bishop of Dunnerdale, in which he tactfully invited Almighty God to bless the hoped-for co-operation in the cause of peaceful and stable government. The President, with his wafer-thin, parchment-like skin, looked like an exhausted Byzantine saint. But his lack of animal vivacity was amply compensated for by the enthusiasm of Sylvester Marsala, who quickly established a highly professional rapport with the senior management of the British firm.

"You've got some lovely stuff here," he said to Greg Atkinson. "It quite makes my mouth water. Look at the beautifully crafted handles of those bullwhips."

"We used to sell a lot to South Africa," said Greg nostalgically.

"But times change. One has to keep abreast of the market. Most of our discipline equipment now goes to ladies with addresses in Soho and Amsterdam. And to think that we started by making muskets for the Blues."

"My boss General Golosina will be delighted with these new toys," said Marsala with one of his ghastly smiles. His face could have made him a fortune in the horror movie industry. "He may well put in a repeat order. I love the water cannons and the electrified nightsticks. I shall recommend you, Mr Atkinson, to some of my American friends. They do big business."

The implication was obvious. Wedmore and Bassenthwaite could be in line to become a major arms supplier for the American Mafia. Greg gave his honest, northern grin. At some point they would have to discuss the amount of the bribe for Marsala.

"We are most grateful to you, Ambrose," whispered Greg to me after tea. "I wonder if you would consider becoming a non-executive director of our company."

"I should be delighted," I said with enthusiasm.

"It really does look as if our finances have taken a turn for the better," added Greg happily. "We're a strange business, you know. I was looking through the accounts the other day. The original families sold out some years ago. Then most of the shares were bought by a lady named Amanda Beachcroft, who lived in Cheltenham. But she died and I don't know who inherited her estate. The income is paid to a firm of solicitors on behalf of a trust."

"It might be worth following that up," said Molnar, never backward at putting his oar in. "Knowledge is power. You can examine any British will if you apply. They are all in the public domain. Just write in and send the fee."

"We must move the President on," said Hector Garcia, "or he will be late for compline at the Abbey."

***

"What a delightful place this is," said the First Lady as we stood on the terrace outside the great Abbey church at Calderbeck, looking across the green playing fields towards the estuary. "So full of the peace of God. I felt that strongly at High Mass this morning in the Abbey. Your dear Abbot Juniper looked like an archangel in his pretty robes."

Unfortunately, at that moment a group of junior boys ran by on their way from the rugger field, muddied, oaf-like and screaming with laughter. Father Manfred smiled.

"Peace is not the main quality you associate with an English public school," he said mildly, in passable Spanish.

"I feel sure you will turn the children into little saints," gushed the First Lady. "That has never been our objective," said Father Manfred drily. "I should not consider it a viable ambition."

"I was just telling the headmaster how beautiful this whole valley seems to me," explained Elvira Raro to her somnolent husband. "An ideal place for our dear Dominic to be brought up safely, and pumped full of Christian ideals under the patronage of Our Lady and Saint Jude."

"Beautiful grass," said the President. "Do you have a croquet lawn here?"

"The President is tired," said Sylvester Marsala. "I'll take him back to the abbot's guest room for a rest before the ceremony." He led the unprotesting statesman away. The formal dedication of the Business Centre would take place that evening, with prayers and speeches followed by a reception.

"How have you found Dominic?" asked Father Manfred.

"It has been wonderful to see the dear little fellow again," replied his besotted mother. "But I'm not sure he is very happy as a day-boy. He finds the company of his two security guards somewhat irksome. They are not intellectuals, you know. Dominic misses the innocent fun he used to have with the other children when he slept in a dormitory."

"Innocent fun?!" Father Manfred almost shrieked.

"I do understand the problem," continued the First Lady.

"Dominic was being bullied by the British boys because he is not English. But I think he has gained the courage to bear that. Perhaps he might now return to the school as a boarder, so as to enjoy the full range of the traditional activities?"

"Certainly not," snapped Father Manfred. "Have you forgotten our agreement? No power on earth could oblige me to take that youth back into the boys' dormitories. And we are accepting girls next term!"

"My dear Father Manfred," said Elvira, deploying the charms so well honed during a lifetime of deception, "you really are an old bear. I may appeal over your head to Father Abbot."

"I should not advise that, Madam. Father Abbot may look like a guileless innocent but he knows a lot about evil."

As a practised diplomat, I sensed that this would be a good moment to change the subject.

"You may be interested to know, dear lady," I said brightly, "that my only son is now a member of this Community."

"A member of the Community? I should not go as far as that," said the headmaster, still in a slightly grumpy mood. "The young man recently joined us as a novice. But he would have a long way to go, if he were to remain long enough to take his final vows."

"There is something discouraging about your use of the subjunctive, Father Manfred," I said. "Are you suggesting that my Neville might not make the grade?"

"As you know, Ambrose, I have always considered Brother Cyprian as slightly dubious monastic material. I am not the Master of the Novices myself but one hears reports. Our vows comprise poverty, chastity and obedience. He is quite strong on poverty. He might even manage chastity at a pinch. But obedience is not exactly his cup of tea. It was a mistake on his part to argue publicly with Father Abbot last week on the theological implications of Original Sin, just when the Cardinal happened to be visiting. Novices, you know, are the midshipmen of the monastery."

"What have you done with Brother Cyprian?" I asked. "I was hoping he could meet the First Lady."

"He has retired for a week to the hermitage," replied Father Manfred. "By mutual agreement. To take stock of his position."

"Poor boy!" said the First Lady sympathetically. "I suppose he is surviving on bread and water."

"Certainly not," said Father Manfred. "That is hardly the Benedictine way. He has taken a crate of beer, a supply of frozen pizza, and a stack of comedy videos."

"I hope the place is fortunately situated," said Elvira. "My husband and I attach great importance to that, you know. The Chinese call it feng shui. We have learned these lessons from a teacher in Concordia." Could this be another of Ludovic's ploys?

"I remember," said Father Manfred. "You sent someone to examine the site of the new business school before the work began."

"It is essential to choose a place where the evil spirits cannot reach."

Father Manfred and I exchanged glances. I knew what he was thinking. For all her protestations, this woman was, at heart, a pagan primitive.

"If my poor boy is obliged to continue living in the village," she went on, "I should like to have his house ritually blessed. Perhaps Father Abbot would oblige. And I'm going to do something about those bodyguards. We might leave Mr Marsala here to look after Dominic. He would be a fatherly influence, would he not?"

"An excellent plan," I said. The woman was no fool. The adult brute and the teenage thug would make a fine pair, richly deserving each other. Father Manfred's worn face relaxed into a sardonic smile.

***

I was having a delightful wallow. The water was decidedly hot but not quite scalding. Generous use of Susan's special bath salts had produced a delicately scented foam. We have a large bath in Little Bigney and I had been able to insinuate the whole of my substantial person under the soothing water except for the area from the chin upwards. There is something about a bathroom which inspires me to sing. I had embarked on a series of bass-baritone arias from the better-known operas, partly to annoy the O'Callaghans, who tended to bang rudely on our dividing wall, especially when I treated them to the Wagnerian items in my repertoire. I believe in loving one's neighbour, but I drew the line at the O'Callaghans.

There was good reason to sing. The Raro visit, though comparatively low key, had been a success. They had not lunched at the Palace or dined at the Mansion House. But they had done the essential things. Admittedly, my hope that the arms agreement could be signed during the visit had not been realised. Dame Rosy had continued to stall and Foreign Office approval had not yet been forthcoming. But I felt that this must be only a question of time, and I assumed that we could now count on success. Meanwhile, the Raros had returned to London for further shopping, and I had gone home to Susan for the weekend. It was delightful to think how many people would be infuriated when the arms deal went through: Dame Rosy Clumber, who had tried so hard to keep the Raros out; her sanctimonious husband, who made so lucrative a living out of human rights; and our hateful foreign rivals Jacques Marigny-Marmande and Homer Fairchild, who had attempted to scupper our bid in Felicidad. One could visualise their chagrin. Now Ludo would make me rich. Could one just afford a short lease on a little penthouse in Mayfair? Then Susan could stay mainly at Little Bigney and do her gardening, while I developed a new career as arms salesman, boulevardier and man-about-town. It was an enchanting prospect. I filled my lungs and burst into a Verdi fortissimo.

"Oh, do stop that awful noise," shouted Susan through the half-open door. "There's something very important on the television news."

I climbed out of the bath, snatched my robe and slippers, and sprinted into the bedroom.

"Arsenal beat Chelsea by two goals to nil," the announcer was intoning.

"What's so special about that?" I complained in pique.

"You've missed it, silly. There's been a revolution in Concordia. The army under General Golosina collapsed without a fight."

"Who's in charge?" I asked.

"Victor Fernandez, now styled the Liberator, after the original Liberator from Spanish rule. But it sounds pretty chaotic. The Raros have been declared enemies of the state. General Golosina has disappeared. People are worried about the British parliamentary delegation now visiting the country."

"Oh, Christ!" I groaned. "What about my bonus?"

"Really, Ambrose! There could be murder and rape. And all you can think about is your bonus."

"You underrate me, Susan," I retorted with dignity. "The trained mind is capable of thinking about two or three things at the same time."

"In that case, I'm glad I haven't a trained mind."

I gave Susan one of my withering glances. She always used to be so pleasantly docile in the old-fashioned, feminine way. It was one of her chief charms. Had some malevolent influence been encouraging her to take a more independent line during my absences?

"I must go at once to London," I said.

"What on earth for?"

"To offer my expertise to the Foreign Office."

"Come on, Ambrose, you're only an old retired diplomat. Rowley never gets summoned to the Ministry of Defence."

"I am not at all surprised," I riposted, with some asperity. "You seem to be forgetting that I am now a director of Wedmore and Bassenthwaite. The national interest is involved. What is to happen to our contract now?"

"You mean, we may not be rich, after all?"

"We may be as poor as church mice. With a large, unnecessary greenhouse to pay for. Not to mention that pearl necklace you seem to have ordered for yourself."

"If you're going back to London, I might pop up to Calderbeck and visit poor Neville. Rowley has offered to give me a lift as far as Kendal. He has to call on an aunt in the Trossachs."

"You can't bother Neville," I said. "He's still in the hermitage."

"How awful! Solitary confinement!"

"It was good enough for the desert fathers, my dear."

"Then why can't I be a desert mother?"

Susan could be tiresome. But then Socrates, asked why he had married a troublesome woman, explained that horse tamers needed to practise on the most spirited animals.

***

"Why are there no military men here?" wailed Dame Rosy Clumber. "I particularly wanted the chiefs of staff to be represented today, at major-general level at least. But I can't get them interested. They argue that it's nothing to do with them. So all I have are three ambassadors." She looked round with distaste.

"Two ambassadors actually," chipped in Gerald Haverstock-Jones. "Hector and I are representatives of the two governments involved. At least he was until yesterday. But Ambrose is my predecessor, now retired."

"I represent Wedmore and Bassenthwaite," I said, having agreed with Ludovic that he had better remain in the background, where he was so much at home.

"Merchants of death," snorted Dame Rosy. "At least that unspeakable arms contract will not go through now. I was so right to resist it from the start. Now let us pool our knowledge. What exactly is happening in Concordia? You ought to know, Mr Garcia."

"I have telephoned to Felicidad," said the little Ambassador, "but the line is very bad, continually interrupted by the sound of gunfire and awful screaming."

"Gunfire?" echoed Dame Rosy, in tones appropriate for Lady Bracknell when referring to a handbag. "I understood that the revolution was bloodless."

"So I believe," replied Hector nervously. I suspected that he was hedging his bets, not yet being sure of the eventual outcome. Like the Vicar of Bray, he would hope to remain Ambassador to Britain, even under the new dispensation.

"The Army did not fight," continued Hector, "so there was no war. But you know how it is after a revolution."

"No, we don't, Mr Ambassador," said the Minister of State. "We haven't had a revolution in this country for three hundred years."

"There will be old scores to pay off," explained Hector. "People roaming the streets with rifles and machetes looking for those who have seduced their wives or deflowered their daughters. We are an excessively manly race. And then there are the tribal hatreds which always come out on these occasions. You know how bitterly the Tozudo in the interior and the Nevera on the coast hate each other. There could be a lot of killing."

"I thought that the Liberator, as we should now call him, had managed to reconcile the Tozudo and the Nevera," said Gerald. "Isn't that why he succeeded in toppling the Raros?"

"He had perhaps done so at the leadership level," said Hector. "But there will still be great danger for unfortunate individuals caught by rival tribal gangs. I understand that the Liberator has not yet been able to restore order fully in Felicidad, much less in the rest of our country."

"It sounds a very tricky situation," said Gerald. "The Embassy must be evacuated at once. I am terribly worried about Monica. She is prone to nervous collapse."

"Nonsense, Ambassador," snapped the Minister. "The Embassy will certainly not be evacuated so long as protection is needed for British nationals. How on earth could I explain that to the House? You will fly back to the danger zone this very day. And I am sure that your wife will have a useful role. Producing soup or blankets or whatever diplomatic wives do on these occasions. I am very worried about the British parliamentary delegation, now in Concordia. They may be only unimportant backbenchers and elderly peers. But if they are massacred, I shall be strongly criticised in the Commons. That could be highly damaging. The Government will not want to have a whole bunch of by-elections at a moment when the Treasury have not had time to prepare the usual pre-election giveaways."

"We must hope for the best," I said with encouraging calm. "Their leader Selby Tritton is an experienced campaigner."

"I am not in the habit of hoping for the best, Mr Bellingham," boomed Dame Rosy. "In politics one always prepares for the worst. Poor dear Selby! I am very concerned about him. Remind me to telephone Lucretia."

"There is news at last of the parliamentary delegation," said the Ambassador of Concordia. "It is good. They have taken refuge in the cellars of the British Ambassador's residence."

"You call that good news?" Gerald almost shrieked. "Monica will be having to feed them. They will be demanding drink too. We have no allowances for that kind of emergency."

"My private secretary has just reminded me of another group you all seem to have forgotten," said Dame Rosy. "I refer to Lord Cumberland and his party from Connoisseur Travel. Aren't they in Concordia too at this very moment?"

"Indeed," I said. "As you know, they love to get off the beaten track, in order to see monuments of cultural importance. Mr Carr-Baxendale was taking them down to the Nevera lowlands in order to study prehistoric funerary monuments."

"I understand that they have vanished without trace," said Dame Rosy. "That should be your immediate task, Mr Haverstock-Jones. After making sure that the parliamentary delegation are perfectly comfortable and have all they need, you are to proceed directly into the Nevera tribal heartlands in order to rescue the Connoisseur party. Take that driver of yours, Potiphar. He would be a good man in a scrap."

"That would be extremely dangerous," pointed out Hector Garcia. "The Nevera are deeply inhospitable. They cut off heads. If you are lucky." Gerald darted him a look of anguish.

"I don't mind about the danger," said the Minister. "If we lose the Connoisseurs the Government will be highly criticised. Lord Cumberland is a distant relation of the Royal Family. He has been shooting at Balmoral, I think. And some of those tiresome society people have the kind of relations who keep firing off letters to the

Daily Telegraph. We must take any risk to get them back safely with all the limbs they started out with. I hope this will teach Lord Cumberland not to gallivant around foreign parts without taking any account of the local political situation."

"Are you quite sure," I asked Hector, "that Fernandez is going to last? Has there been any further news about General Golosina?"

"He fled into the interior," said Hector. "He had Tozudo family connections, you know, and reputedly a kind of baronial fief on the other side of the swamps. The problem would be to get across them without meeting the headshrinkers and the man-eating crocodiles."

"It looks, then, as if we shall have to deal with this Fernandez man, the so-called Liberator," said Dame Rosy. "Is he a good thing?"

There was a silence. Hector seemed reluctant to answer. "I believe he is an excellent dentist," I opined at last. "He trained in South Bend, Indiana."

"That is hardly the point, Mr Bellingham," snapped the Minister. "Has he the strength to beat down opposition, and the political skill to run the country?"

"We shall see," said Gerald. "Time will tell." Dame Rosy looked as if she did not consider this contribution very useful either.

"We must get to him quickly," she said. "That's another job for you, Mr Haverstock-Jones. I hope you are taking notes. Tell this Liberator from me that he must immediately arrange a democratic election and install a people's government, dismantling at once the whole apparatus of dictatorship. That is what Britain demands. We also insist that he returns our emerald mines."

"He will have a lot to do," muttered Gerald unhappily.

"If he needs an adviser, I could send out my husband, a noted defender of human rights. As a matter of fact, Trevor is involved already. He has filed an application to the High Court today to have General and Mrs Raro arrested as violators of international criminal law. I understand that they left Claridges this morning in rather a hurry, but we shall track them down. Do you know where they are, Ambassador?"

"Certainly not," replied Hector hastily. "The hotel have sent me a huge bill but fortunately the First Lady left behind her a very considerable quantity of expensive clothes and shoes, which can be sold."

"It is an awkward time to have a revolution," commented Dame Rosy. "A pity we had no warning. Then we should not have all these tiresome and influential British people in danger. But I must say, Trevor and I rejoice at the downfall of that ghastly dictator. It is a triumph for the human spirit. That's what I shall tell the House."

***

"Thank God it's only you, Ambrose," said Ludovic as I arrived at his exclusive residence.

"Who on earth did you think it might be?"

"One never knows. You look exhausted. Have a strong brandy. This is a terrible disaster, you know, just when we had the contract in the bag. To think of all the efforts we made to cultivate the Raro regime."

"Where are the Raros now?" I enquired.

"Don't ask me. Why should I know?" He seemed strangely defensive.

"And Marsala? What about him?"

"I talked to the headmaster this morning. Sylvester Marsala has disappeared, with his bodyguards. Taking the boy with him."

"Dominic? You mean he's been kidnapped?"

"It's not quite clear who kidnapped whom."

"How extremely worrying."

"I don't see why we need to worry. Marsala has plenty of influential friends. And Dominic was getting too big for Calderbeck."

"That's one way of putting it," I said.

"There must be money to be made from these retired tyrants," mused Ludo. "If one could only establish a comfortable place of refuge for them. Sorry, we can't waste time on fantasies. The great thing is to salvage the contract. You have to fly back to Felicidad, Ambrose. See the Liberator and encourage him to renew the deal.

Before the filthy French get to them. He will need defence equipment just as much as the other gang. Deploy all your charm."

"Can't you go, Ludovic?"

"I have … other problems to take care of there. I've got this airline ticket for you. You fly to Miami as usual."

"It's World Traveller class," I protested. "A euphemism for the horrid tourist pigsty."

"First and Business were fully booked. Never mind, Ambrose; you ooze dignity wherever you sit."

"How on earth am I to obtain access to the Liberator?" I asked. "I've never seen the man in my life."

"Are you quite sure of that?" riposted the wily Hungarian with one of his enigmatic smiles.

4

"So you are here again, Ambrose," remarked Monica Haverstock-Jones with a certain lack of enthusiasm.

"Yes, Monica, I am back in sunny Felicidad. It was kind of you to invite me to stay again."

"We had no alternative," said Monica ungraciously. "The Waving Palms Hotel was wrecked by looters during the revolution. As you will have heard, the whole city was in chaos."

"Monica had a ghastly time," commented Gerald.

"You refer to the danger?" I suggested.

"No," replied Monica. "The expense. Those awful British parliamentarians quartered themselves in our basement, as you know. We had to serve them three meals a day plus morning elevenses and afternoon teas. They have consumed all our tins of baked beans and our boxes of shredded wheat. And they didn't seem at all grateful, even when I opened the Concordian claret. They actually had the nerve to blame the Embassy for failing to warn them about the revolution in advance."

"Thank God they have gone home," said Gerald with relief. "Selby Tritton was no use at all in controlling them."

"There was a horrible Viscountess, who appointed herself as a sort of shop steward," said Monica.

"Was she the one who kept complaining about the service here?" asked Gerald. "When poor old Felipe was splitting his sides to satisfy their every whim. And Teresita was ironing all night. It was a happy moment when Potiphar took them away in the British Council's minibus."

"The Foreign Office must give us a special allowance," said

Monica. "To make up for all we had to spend."

"I've told them that already," said Gerald. "But you know how mean they are."

"We shall have a miserable retirement then," moaned Monica. "Reduced to travelling up from Bournemouth by long-distance bus for the occasional senior citizens' matinee at the National Theatre. Alexander is making much more than we do already. Sacheverell and Bulstrode gave him a magnificent Christmas bonus. And if Cressida wins the Booker prize, she won't exactly be poor either."

"Never mind, Dear," said Gerald, "we still have some more time to go here on full diplomatic allowances. Let's hope we don't have more house guests foisted on us." I thought this a bit pointed.

"I'm not having the Connoisseur Travel people here," said Monica shrilly. "Lord Cumberland can take them all straight home."

"They would have to get back to Felicidad first," said Gerald. "It's all very disturbing."

"Where are they now?" I asked.

"How the devil should I know?" retorted Gerald peevishly. "Somewhere in the Nevera lowlands, I suppose. That's where they went, to gawp at a lot of silly tombs. Now we hear they have been kidnapped by a splinter faction of the rebels who don't realise that the revolution is over."

"I thought that the Minister of State instructed you to proceed to the area in person, in order to rescue the group."

"I didn't fancy that," said Gerald calmly.

"Quite right," chipped in Monica. "The Foreign Office pay a miserable pension to widows. Lady Sampson has had to move out of Cheyne Walk."

"There was no need for me to stick my neck out," said Gerald complacently. "They've got two perfectly capable local guides with them. Adrian Carr-Baxendale and Harry Wilderness. Besides, anyone can see that Cumberland is one of nature's innocents, verging on the complete booby. He should be safe enough."

"I've never thought of innocence as a protection," I said. Gerald was really being rather slack.

"Don't fuss, Ambrose. Who is in charge here? As soon as Potiphar got rid of the parliamentarians at the airport, he was under instructions to take the minibus down the coast road to rescue the party from Connoisseur Travel. You can always reply on Potiphar. Why do you think we brought him from Egypt? He got Aunt Mabel out of a pyramid once when she was locked in after closing time."

We were sitting on the veranda before dinner. Soon the mosquitoes would start biting, and we would have to retreat inside. Until then we could enjoy the well-tended tropical garden with its wealth of purple bougainvillaea, red flame trees, hibiscus and white frangipani.

"There's no point in my sprinting all over the country," continued Gerald defensively. "This is where I am needed most. It is essential for British interests that I establish friendly relations as soon as possible with the new revolutionary government."

"And have you done that, Gerald?"

"Not exactly. Of course I have made it clear to the Foreign Ministry here that I should like to pay a call on the Liberator as soon as possible. He's appointed himself President, you know. Once he assures us that he intends to restore parliamentary democracy, we shall be able to recognise his regime. But the Ministry have not yet been able to give me an appointment. So far as I know, the other diplomatic colleagues haven't had any better success. But London won't understand that. You know how they always expect miracles."

"Why is the Liberator being so coy?"

"That's what puzzles me," said Gerald. "I should have thought it would only help him to get in touch with the representatives of potentially friendly countries. The Foreign Ministry have hinted that he's not too keen on me personally. Apparently I am seen as having been too close to the Raros and their discredited dictatorship."

"But that's monstrous," protested Monica. "We were only civil to those ghastly people because they were running the country. Ambrose, before our time, was far keener to suck up to the Raros. That's what everyone has told us."

"It's not the whole story, I agree," said Gerald. "My hunch is that Fernandez is uncertain which way to jump. It's not easy for him. The situation is very tense. Golosina is reputed to be still holding out in the interior. Remember the Liberator's background. He's a dentist, with no political experience. In opposition, he spent most of his time in hiding. He had a few things in his favour. His mixed Tozudo and Nevera blood. His hatred of the Raro regime. And, above all, his reputation for honesty – a rare asset in this part of the world. That's all. So I expect he feels very much at sea, uncertain where to turn next. I only hope he doesn't turn to Jacques Marigny-Marmande or Homer Fairchild. That could be the end of your bloody arms contract, Ambrose."

"Pascale Marigny-Marmande says that Jacques is unwell. A touch of that amoebic dysentery he first contracted in Cambodia," contributed Monica brightly.

"Oh, good," said Gerald with equal heartlessness. "We must hope for the best."

"We have given up dressing for dinner since the revolution," said Monica. "By the way, Ambrose, there is one small point I ought to mention. As you will remember, you left here in rather a hurry last time."

"I do remember," I countered drily.

"In your haste you must have forgotten to leave any tips for the staff. So Gerald and I had to give them something and pretend it was from you. Potiphar had driven you around so much, Felipe had served you all that drink, and Teresita had washed all those shirts and underclothes of yours. I've got a little note of it here."

"A sterling cheque would be quite acceptable," added Gerald.

"Thank you for reminding me," I replied with dignity. "I'll settle the matter at once."

I was longing to go into dinner. The mosquitoes were starting to nip my ankles, and Happy Hour with Gerald and Monica was not an occasion anyone would wish to prolong. Suddenly a very strange sight appeared. A large, ungainly vehicle entered the residence garden and drew up boldly outside the front door.

"What on earth is that?" Monica almost shrieked. "It should have gone round the back, to the service entrance."

"It is a dustcart," said Gerald, "of the type usually employed in Concordia for the collection of the more unsavoury varieties of rubbish."

"Then why is Potiphar driving it?" asked Monica, legitimately enough.

With a cheery wave in our direction, Potiphar got out of the filthy truck and went round to open its rear door. Slowly and painfully, a procession of ghostly figures emerged, looking not unlike those unfortunate prisoners in *Fidelio* who stumble out of their underground dungeon to the strains of uplifting music. They were all extremely dirty, and their collective stench was overpowering.

"How dare you, Potiphar?" shouted Gerald. "This is not a reception camp for refugees. Take them straight away to the delousing centre run by the Red Cross."

"Really, Ambassador," said one of the gruesome apparitions. "This is not quite the welcome we expected."

"Watch your step, Gerald," I whispered. "That is Lord Cumberland." This could be none other than the distinguished group of visitors from Connoisseur Travel. It was appalling to see them brought so low. Several, I recognised at once. That withered hag, straight out of the first scene in *Macbeth*, was surely a dowager duchess who had once been a Woman of the Bedchamber to the Queen Mother. That old fellow relieving himself on the front lawn looked awfully like our most senior living novelist, famous throughout the English-speaking world for his thirteen-novel series describing his action-filled schooldays at Harrow. And could that haggard figure in torn jeans really be the chairman of the board of the Royal Opera House? This was indeed a posse of petulant cognoscenti, elderly but still articulate, and with an enormous potential capacity for causing trouble.

"We have had the most ghastly time," croaked Lord Cumberland. "Could I have a very large gin and tonic, please?"

"Me too," said the Woman of the Bedchamber. "No need to

bother too much about the tonic."

"They might enjoy sitting in the garden," said Monica resource-fully. "Felipe could bring out drinks. We make delicious lemonade."

"I need a hot bath," snapped the novelist.

"You might have warned us, Gerald," said Lord Cumberland reproachfully, "that there was going to be a revolution. We always try to keep out of politics."

"I found it rather an interesting new experience," commented Archdeacon Wilderness cheerfully. "It helped me to understand how Saint Peter and Saint Paul must have felt in similar circumstances."

"At least we got to view the exquisite Nevera death cells, the decapitating altars and the torture garden," said Adrian Carr-Baxendale.

"Yes," agreed Lord Cumberland, sinking exhausted onto the front porch. "All went well at first and we saw some lovely things. But then these appalling brutes appeared. My Spanish was too pure for them, and Adrian had to interpret. We were held under conditions of extreme discomfort."

"The accommodation was disgusting," said the chairman of the board, more used to his box at Grand Tier level, "and the heat intense. Thank God we are all too unattractive to rape. We should be there still if this resourceful fellow had not arrived to liberate us."

"Well done, Potiphar," said Gerald. "But what has happened to the British Council minivan?"

"Bad men ask for van," explained Potiphar, with his usual knowing grin. "No van, no prisoners. We start walking home, and then I find this old truck."

"You should really have telegraphed for instructions," said Gerald. "You cannot dispose of government property without Treasury approval."

"That's so typical of your bureaucratic attitude, Ambassador," growled the Woman of the Bedchamber. "You only sent your chauffeur. Why didn't you come yourself?"

"I agree," said the novelist. "I shall be writing to *The Times* about the whole ghastly episode."

"I suppose that Connoisseur Travel will be making us a full refund for the whole of this dreadful tour," said a determined voice from the back of the group of filthy spectres.

"We shall look into that," said Lord Cumberland emolliently. "But remember we promised you unusual experiences off the beaten track. A good lawyer could argue that you have had exactly that."

"Let us hope that you will be able to leave for England," said Monica, "with all possible speed. Now, if you care to discard all your clothes, our excellent Teresita will subject them to intensive scrubbing."

"That's not possible," moaned Lord Cumberland. "We only have what we stand up in. All our baggage was lost."

"I should never have brought my mink coat," said the Woman of the Bedchamber. "But I was advised that it might be chilly at night."

"We are desperate for food," said Carr-Baxendale. "And drink." Gerald and Monica groaned as the unsavoury and rapacious group rushed like lemmings into the residence dining room, where a harassed Felipe was seen to be laying out an emergency supper.

"This is financial disaster," I heard Monica mutter.

"I'd like a long, cold beer pretty quickly," said a little man to me rather sharply.

"Would you indeed?" I retorted. "I don't think you realise who I am."

"Yes, I do. You're Bellingham. I've seen you hanging around the Sheridan. Your name should be coming up soon."

With horror, I noticed that the fellow was wearing a Sheridan club tie. What is more, I realised now that he was chairman of the selection committee for the election of new members.

Blackballed for the Sheridan! Could there be a worse disaster?

***

After the rather fraught atmosphere at the Embassy, even after the noisy departure of the disgruntled party from Connoisseur Travel, it was pleasant to sit with Harry Wilderness in his tiny garden, admiring the cavortings of the scarlet cardinal birds.

"This is such a peaceful place, Harry," I said gratefully.

"I don't think that peace is only to be found in places," said the Archdeacon. "It's more in people. You have to carry peace around inside you."

"Our poor ambassador is in a dreadful state today. He has just heard that both the American and French ambassadors have been granted interviews with the Liberator. But no word has come for him. That could be very serious."

"Perhaps I might be able to help," suggested Harry. "I was having supper with Victor Fernandez last night. He was charming, as usual. Quite giggly even. It's delightful the way he is still simple and unspoiled even though he is now so powerful."

"How do you know him, Harry?"

"I was a patient of his for years. He insisted on giving me check-ups twice a year, and then we used to have tea and chat about life. He's an excellent dentist, you know, trained in the States. His fillings were quite painless, and he was so clever with injections."

"He could be a great help to us."

"He has already been good to me. He has promised to reverse those unfair proceedings against me and return my donation to the police orphanage."

"He can't do that on his own authority," I pointed out.

"Oh yes, he can. It's a benevolent dictatorship now. That could be a rather nice system, as Aristotle pointed out. So I shall be able to compensate the organ fund. I only got back here, you know, thanks to Lord Cumberland, who kindly paid my fare as a guest lecturer. But now that I have been reinstated, the Archbishop of Canterbury has agreed that I should resume my duties here. Such a relief after Saffron Walden."

"I'm so glad, Harry."

"It's what I once told you, Ambrose. I may call you that now, may I not, since you are here in mufti, as it were? We may be approaching that happy day foreshadowed by the incomparable Isaiah. The calf and the lion and the sheep shall abide together. And a little child shall lead them."

"We shall see," I said cautiously. "I don't think the time is yet ripe here for the weaned child to thrust his hand into the den of the basilisk."

***

"It's too bad," wailed Monica. "Uprooted again. And we lose all our allowances."

"Bloody hell," added Gerald, for once moved to emotion.

"What on earth has happened?" I asked.

"I have been declared *persona non grata*," he shrieked. "The present bunch have said they won't do any business with me. We have to get out straight away."

"That's a shame, Gerald."

"I know who fixed it. Our fucking French allies. Jacques has given the Liberator the Grand Cross of the Légion d'Honneur or something. Now they'll collar the arms contract. And perhaps the emerald mines too."

"It's a disaster," I agreed. "Harry Wilderness knows the Liberator well, he tells me, and could have easily wangled an appointment for you. If you had just asked him."

"Thank you, Ambrose," retorted Gerald, with cold sarcasm. "That's a fine time to tell me. When it's too late."

"If you could only meet Victor Fernandez," I said, "and deploy your charm, you might persuade him to change his mind."

"I could come too," suggested Monica, "and weep. I am very effective when I weep."

"I keep telling you both," riposted Gerald petulantly, "it's too late. I have spoken to the Foreign Office on the phone. They consulted the ghastly Clumber female, and she has instructed me to return home at once."

"There could be a silver lining to that cloud, I suppose," ventured Monica. "Now the Office will have to post us somewhere else. I don't care where – even Lagos or Aden. Nothing could be worse than Felicidad."

"They have taken a decision about that already, Monica. We are not going anywhere else. I am to retire from the Service."

"Oh, how awful!" moaned Monica. "We shall be obliged to live off your miserable pension. And I shall have you around the flat all day, staring at the sea and looking at your watch."

"Don't be pessimistic, Monica," I said firmly. "Gerald is still young and sprightly. He might well obtain some non-executive directorships and develop a splendid career in the City, with a flat in the Barbican."

"Do you seriously mean that, Ambrose? Retiring from Felicidad, I shall not be considered much of a catch."

"Well, look at me," I said. "I am now a director of Wedmore and Bassenthwaite and have embarked on a potentially most lucrative future."

"I take your point, Ambrose. If anyone is willing to employ you of all people, then I should not lose hope. There may be something in that. You had better start packing, Monica."

"What is to happen here?" I asked. "Your first secretary, that silly girl with all that red hair, is hardly capable of running the Embassy at this tricky time."

"The Foreign Office have thought of that already," said Gerald grimly. "There is nothing like an emergency to concentrate their tiny minds. They have appointed someone to take over from me, on a strictly temporary basis."

"Really, Gerald? Who on earth is that?"

"You, Ambrose," he said with an unfriendly grin.

"Me! But I am retired."

"You have been brought back to active service with effect from today. That is, if you agree. You have to give them an answer at once."

"I didn't know that was possible. Isn't sixty the mandatory retiring age?"

"Apparently they are allowed to make an exception for officers of unusual value. In other words, when they are absolutely desperate and scraping the bottom of the barrel."

There was another, more serious, objection. Surely I could not be allowed to represent Her Majesty's Government when I also worked for Wedmore and Bassenthwaite? It was a pity that I had just reminded Gerald about my directorship. But apparently he had not yet focussed on that problem, and perhaps was now too self-absorbed to do so. I would play it long and lie low about my direct personal connection with the murky world of arms trading.

"You are welcome to this damned place," added Gerald. "Monica and I are getting out as soon as possible."

"We shall have to stay a night or two in London with Cressida," said Monica despondently. "I hope she isn't having one of her artistic parties. Do you remember that impertinent young man with the goatee beard who thought I was the charlady?"

"Oh, by the way, Ambrose," said Gerald with feigned insouciance, "I am to tell you. You will draw the full salary and allowances from today."

"*Our* salary!" moaned Monica. "*Our* allowances!" There were tears of rage in her eyes. Gerald too was staring at me with sullen fury. I felt tempted to retort with a malicious smirk, but was too much of a gentleman to do so.

"Of course there is one point the Foreign Office haven't thought of," said Gerald, more cheerfully. "If the present regime here don't accept me, Ambrose, perhaps they won't want you either. It's all a bit of a dog's breakfast, isn't it?"

It was perhaps at that moment that my dreadful toothache started. I remembered with horror that the only reputable dentist in the whole of Concordia was the head of state.

***

"Open your mouth wide, Mr Bellingham," said Victor Fernandez. "Oh dear, that's a nasty big cavity you've got. No wonder you were in some discomfort. I shall have to drill it and fill it straight away."

In his capacity of Liberator, he had not yet moved into the presidential palace but was living in his old small flat above the surgery, where we now were. I owed my emergency introduction to Harry Wilderness, who had sent him word that I was in pain. He had agreed to see me at once as an act of human solidarity. Potiphar had driven me to the surgery, though it meant that I had been obliged to send the somewhat disgruntled Haverstock-Joneses to the airport in one of the town's elderly taxis.

"We must keep in touch," I had said insincerely, as I gave Monica's leathery cheek a perfunctory peck.

"So glad to leave everything in your capable hands," said Gerald sarcastically.

The bodyguards knew I was expected, and I was ushered into the Liberator's modest quarters. A tall, somewhat saturnine man came forward and shook me by the hand. The shock was immense. It was none other than the Dark Stranger whom I had encountered so oddly at midnight in voodoo territory.

"I can see you are surprised, Mr Bellingham," he said in American English, with an unexpectedly light and gentle voice. "Yes, I am the man you met that evening in the Sacred Grove. It is a pleasure to see you again. How is your respected superior?"

"Dame Rosy Clumber is well enough, I believe."

"I don't mean her," said Fernandez. "I was referring to your real employer, Ludovic Molnar. As you will have realised, it was he that I was going to see that night. I had to be careful since there was a price on my head and the Raros were completely ruthless. I owe a lot to Ludovic, you know. He kept in touch with me all that time I was on the run, and helped me to set up … various secret arrangements." That old fox Molnar, I thought. It was starting to become clear that he had been hedging his bets and had never taken me fully into his confidence.

"The British community in Felicidad, though small, has been very helpful," continued the Liberator, tossing his large head like an amiable giraffe. "Archdeacon Wilderness has done much to inspire my thinking about the destiny of mankind. And I always enjoyed my little chats with Mr Carr-Baxendale about our cultural heritage. Please send them both my best wishes. As for you, Mr Bellingham,

I will be quite frank. We never met when you were Ambassador here before. No doubt you had your teeth examined by a superior dentist in London. And you never invited me to your Queen's Birthday Party, the culmination of the social season in Felicidad. I was not bitter about that, though I will admit that my wife and daughters were disappointed. I understood that you regarded me as a humble artisan. And then, after your time, I had to go into hiding."

"You will be most welcome at the Embassy," I said hastily, "whenever you care to come."

"No doubt," he said sardonically. "I seem to have become strangely popular these days. But let me continue. I have made enquiries about you from my old friend Hector Garcia, our ambassador in London. I am retaining him there, by the way. Throughout the horrors of the Raro regime he took discreet steps to assure me of his personal loyalty. We were at school together with the Jesuits, you know. Hector says you are a good friend of Concordia. So we will be happy to deal with you. Mr Haverstock-Jones had to go. I never cared for him. He was a patient briefly before I took to the jungle, and I remember that he was extremely remiss about flossing his teeth."

"I can see, Sir, that you are still a dentist at heart."

"There is truth in that, Mr Bellingham. A man's character can readily be deduced by the way he looks after his molars."

"But you will have no time now to exercise your old profession?"

"I am afraid that is the case. But in common humanity, I may have to help my compatriots when there is an emergency. The Raros specialised in causing pain. My policy is the reverse. I shall try to encourage some younger dental surgeons from my old college in the States to set up practice here, so as to relieve me of the load. But I cannot be too optimistic on that score. It was a modest school with only moderate standards, not like one of your great universities in England. And now, my dear sir, let us get down to business. Kindly make yourself comfortable in my dentist's chair. It is a joy to resume this kind of work after years as a hunted fugitive. I am a little out of practice but I hope that my hand has not lost its cunning."

So did I. Visits to the dentist have never appealed to me but at least I knew he would give me a prick to deaden the gum and, the existing pain being so great, I was prepared to suffer anything to make an end of it.

"There is only one problem," continued Fernandez cheerfully. "We have run out of anaesthetics, so I shall have to drill without a preliminary injection. I hope you do not mind."

"I do mind," I almost shrieked. "I mind very much."

"Come, come, Mr Bellingham, you are an English gentleman of the old school. You have been brought up in the great tradition of the stiff upper lip, much admired by us spineless Latins."

"I am not at all brave, Your Excellency," I bellowed. "Let me dispel that illusion at once. My pain threshold is unusually low."

"It won't take long." The ghastly drill descended and I shuddered in agony.

"Do keep still, Mr Bellingham," said the head of state. "If you jump like that, the drill might well go through your tongue. That's better. Now do have a good rinse."

It was a deep cavity and it hurt a lot.

"Keep still now, while I put in the filling."

Suddenly there came a frenzied knocking at the door. Fernandez invited the duty guard to enter and he clearly brought in an urgent message. It apparently required an answer, and my tormentor left me in the torture chair while he gave instructions to the guard.

"Stay where you are," he commanded me on his return. "That was from our advance detachment in the interior. Golosina is still making trouble among the Tozudo tribes in the swamps. We shall have to deal with that man."

It was impossible for me to make any kind of response. A dentist who is holding your mouth open with his implements, while he operates inside it, is inevitably at a considerable conversational advantage.

"I should like you to understand my aims," continued the head of state, as he compacted my filling. "I intend to run an entirely new form of government: a wholly peaceful state without any enemies, and with its citizens dedicated to the love of one another. A sort of Utopia, you might say, as envisaged by the great philosophers. We shall have no need for armed forces or any form of military equipment. The police and the prisons will be reduced to the absolute minimum. People like Golosina will be overcome simply by the power of rational argument. What do you think?"

I gave a groan of assent. It was all I could do.

"It's all over now," said Victor. "You shouldn't have any more pain. Do have another rinse. My word, I did enjoy that."

"You enjoyed it?" I echoed in astonishment. Was this man some kind of crazed sadist?

"I meant, it was a joy to practise my craft once again. Happiness has been defined as the proper exercise of function. How are you feeling now?"

"Rather wonky."

"Wonky! What a picturesque English phase. Do come and sit down in this comfortable chair, my dear sir. I hope you will join me in a glass of whisky. It is exciting, is it not, to be in at the birth of a daring experiment. I refer to my Utopia."

"It is a noble ambition," I agreed. "But whether it would work in practice remains to be seen. Plato, I seem to remember, tried to train some young tyrant in Sicily, and it was all a ghastly flop."

"One has to take the risk, Mr Bellingham. The world cannot be allowed to continue in its present aggressive way, or it will tear itself apart. Concordia must be a pilot project for a universal change of heart. You see, I believe that human nature is fundamentally good. Even the worst men can be argued with and calmed. Encouragement will be my watchword, not repression. They shall not hurt, nor shall they kill, in all my holy mountain."

Enlightenment struck. "You've got all this from Harry Wilderness," I said.

"He has certainly been a strong influence on me. You could call him my guru." I mentally cursed the Archdeacon for filling the Liberator's head with these ludicrously other-world ideas. No wonder the Church of England had never made him a bishop: a cleric who took the Sermon on the Mount so literally would indeed be an embarrassment.

"Is it your intention," I asked, "to call elections and then install a democratic government and parliament?"

"I am not so sure about that," replied the Liberator. "Mr Fairchild is encouraging me to proceed in that direction. But Archdeacon Wilderness is inclined to think that a benevolent dictatorship, with myself at the helm, would suit this country best. From what I can see of this world, politicians are not a very attractive category of human beings. Hitler, you know, was democratically elected by the German people. Government by dental surgeons could be a better bet."

"In England," I said, "we attach a lot of importance to democracy, even though we have ghastly politicians. Without that, our present ministers in the Foreign Office in London might find it hard to recognise your government."

"I shall bear that with equanimity, Mr Bellingham. I have already received charming messages from the presidents of both France and the United States. Though admittedly they both want to sell me arms."

"We want to sell you arms too. In fact, we have already offered a highly attractive package."

"I am aware of that. And I know that the Raros were about to sign a contract with your British firm. It is all very difficult for me, Mr Bellingham. As I have just told you, I should much prefer not to devote any of our scarce resources to the purchase of the weapons of death. But I am not a complete ostrich with my head in the sand. I know that we have to live in the real world. I have yet to take my final decision in the light of the advice I receive from various quarters. Do we have any other matters to discuss?"

"There is the question of the emerald mines, Excellency. As you know, these were developed by British capital and skill. The monstrous Raros nationalised them in their own interest. We should be very pleased to have them back. Or, at least, full compensation."

"That is another tricky issue. I shall have to think carefully. Our people were paid very poorly when they worked in your mines. And they often died young as a result of diseases acquired in the deep tunnels. There are arguments on both sides."

"I realise that, Mr President. But I am sure you will understand that your decision over the mines could affect relations between our two great nations."

"Oh dear, you're starting to threaten me, Mr Bellingham. Don't you see, I'm trying to run a completely different kind of country, where everything is settled with love and peaceful discussion. But now I can hear my principal adviser arriving. I would like you to meet him."

The door opened and another man entered. I gasped in astonishment. It was none other than Sylvester Marsala. The fellow gave me a toothy grin.

"Well met, Mr Bellingham," he chortled.

"I thought you were on the other side," I said, bewildered.

"So did the other side," retorted Marsala with a sinister chuckle. "But my organisation was with the Liberator all along."

"Mr Marsala has been a great help," said the new head of state. "He is so much a man of the world, whereas it is all new to me."

"I last heard of you leaving Calderbeck Abbey in rather a hurry," I said, "with that hateful boy, Dominic Raro. Where is he now?"

"We parted company," replied the American. "I believe he has gone to look for his parents. The kid was always fond of his mother. She'll be able to continue his training as a criminal lunatic."

"I thought the Raros were going to be arrested in London," I said. "Trevor Pilkington QC was mobilising an action against them for violation of human rights."

"An excellent idea," said the Liberator. "They must pay for their crimes by a lengthy period of re-education."

"So far as I know," said Marsala, "the Raros have never been found. Don't the Foreign Office tell you anything?"

"I haven't had time to study the telegrams," I said. "It's been a full-time job, nursing my tooth."

"You must both excuse me now," said the President. "I'm going to have my Zen meditation session."

"I'll be in touch," murmured Marsala to me, as we went out together. "We need to talk."

***

"I hope you didn't mind meeting here," said Marsala, as we sat together in the baroque Chapel of the Assumption of Our Lady, in the Cathedral of Divine Compassion. "It's a pity we can't smoke. But we both have enemies in this city. Nobody would expect to find us here. May I call you Ambrose?"

"Certainly, Sylvester." He gave me a conspiratorial grin which I found quite attractive. I had disliked the man intensely at first, but now I was beginning to warm to his robust personality. There was something frank and open about his patent villainy which I found a refreshing change from the sanctimonious piety of the Raros and the misty idealism of their successor.

"I'm going to level with you, Ambrose. You and I are two of a kind, and we ought to co-operate. Neither of us cares a monkey's tit for Concordia or, for that matter, Britain or the States. We're working for our own interests, aren't we? You represent that crook Molnar. I operate on behalf of an extremely powerful organisation. I don't need to mention its name but you know how strong we are in the States, Italy and other countries, including, nowadays, the former Soviet Union. You want to sell arms to Concordia and get your emeralds back. I don't care about that, but we *are* interested in maintaining a certain trade route linking Latin America and the States. I don't have to spell it out but you know it's all about money. We don't mind who rules this fucking country, so long as nobody louses up our strategic interest in this piece of real estate. Do I make myself clear?"

"Refreshingly so, Sylvester."

"Now let's look at the present situation. We got rid of that damn fool Raro. But now we're landed with this nutter who thinks he's going to live in a perfect world. You know what will happen? He will reduce Concordia to chaos within six months. If you ask me, Fernandez should have stuck to dentistry."

"He's all we've got," I pointed out. "The people are mad about him. They are longing for an honest, humane ruler."

"Then we have to stiffen his resolution. There's only one way to do that. He must learn two sharp lessons very quickly – one: that he cannot do without me and my people; two: that he has to buy arms and re-equip his forces. Fortunately we have the very thing for that: General Tiberio Golosina and his merry men in the interior. We have to encourage them to make their threat to Fernandez a very real one."

"Easier said than done," I pointed out.

"We have a piece of luck. Fernandez is worried about Golosina. I encouraged him to keep worrying. And I suggested that he ask some friendly diplomat to pay a secret visit to Golosina's headquarters and try to find out what he is up to, offering him safe conduct out of the country if he will renounce the struggle."

"But how to get to Golosina?" I asked. "There is a whole region of malarial swamps in the way. Inhabited, I understand, by man-eating crocodiles."

"Fernandez is willing to make available a helicopter from the Concordian Air Force. Regularly serviced in Miami. He has tried to persuade your American and French colleagues to take on this little mission, but both have refused. Homer Fairchild is frightened of the headshrinkers, and the Marquis de Marigny-Marmande has an allergy to killer bees. So the choice has alighted on you, Ambrose."

"What makes you think that I would be any more enthusiastic? I am an urban intellectual, not some madcap he-man. I have only one head, and I don't want to have it shrunken. Nor do I fancy those killer bees. I have always been frightened of wasps."

"You have something that will stiffen your resolution, Ambrose. A very strong, secret motive. Lots of money. When you reach Tiberio, instead of encouraging him to throw in the towel, you will do just the opposite. Persuade him to intensify the struggle and promise him help. I'll give you a nice big bag of gold to offer him. Don't even think of stealing it – my people would find you out, wherever in the world you tried to hide. You have heard of the Alice Springs Massacre and the Toulouse Hatchet-Killing. With the increase of threat from the interior, Fernandez will come to his senses. He will give up his damn-fool pacifist theories, and we will both get what we want."

"Very ingenious, Sylvester," I conceded. "But I don't think the Foreign Office in London would approve. They have a very conventional approach."

"They don't need to know. Just tell them you're going on tour within your own parish, to obtain evidence for analysing the situation on their behalf."

"You would have made a fine diplomat yourself, Sylvester."

"I was in the CIA once. But they found my methods ... too unorthodox. Well now, Ambrose, we can't waste more time. They'll be gathering here soon for High Mass. Will you do it?"

"All right," I answered, with modified rapture. "But I'm not at all keen on helicopters."

"Good man. I'll tell the Liberator you accept the assignment."

"What happens if I can't energise Golosina?"

"Then we'll bring the Raros back. Start a bit of a civil war."

"You know where they are, don't you?" I said.

"Shall we say ... they are being looked after by one of our allies. We'd better not leave here together."

He gave me a cheery wave. There was something delightfully straightforward about this truly wicked man. As I passed through the great cathedral, I saw him slumped, apparently deep in prayer, before the brightly garlanded statue of Saint Eulalia, the child saint of colonial Concordia, poleaxed by her barbarian stepfather for refusing to eat meat on a Friday.

***

"Are you all right, Darling? I can't hear you very well. It's not a good line."

"I'm perfectly well," said Susan. She sounded quite cheerful, which I found a bit disconcerting. I didn't want her to repine during my absence but she wasn't meant to enjoy it either. "What are you up to, Dear?" she asked.

"I'm going on tour in the interior."

"How nice for you, Ambrose."

"Nice?! It will be perfectly ghastly. I'm doing it all for you, Susan. To finance your new greenhouse."

"Thank you, Dear," she responded casually, oblivious to the horrible hazards.

"What news of Little Bigney?"

"Lady Moggeridge is getting up a petition to save that fine old oak tree at the back of the sports pavilion. And the O'Callaghans are emigrating to Canada."

"Oh, good."

"I'm not sure it is. The new tenant for their half of our house is said to be a keen amateur trumpet player."

"Oh, hell! What about your great chums, the Harrison Bedfords? Any dates yet for putting on my plays?"

"Not exactly. There's been a slight upheaval there. Griselda has gone off to Padstow to pay Mother a long visit. By the way, I hope you got my letter about my attempt to visit poor Neville."

"It hasn't arrived yet. What about Neville? Another his silly pranks?"

"He has disappeared again. He abandoned the hermitage somewhat abruptly, leaving a note for Father Abbot to say that, on reflection, the monastic life was not quite right for him."

"That boy will be the death of us, Susan."

***

I felt decidedly queasy in the elderly helicopter, swaying above the intense green of the Concordian jungle. One could imagine only too well what voracious, flesh-eating creatures were waiting down there beneath the tops of the trees. Our prospects, if we were forced to make an emergency landing, were too awful to contemplate. Was the machine sound? Was the pilot sober? I tried in vain to concentrate on my pocket edition of *The Last Chronicle of Barset*.

At last we were descending into a small clearing in the jungle. Khaki-coloured figures were waving us down. I only wished that the resourceful Potiphar could have been with me. At least we had crossed the dreaded swamps and seemed to be on dry, slightly more elevated land, presumably the remote Tozudo highlands, noted in zoological circles for their profusion of poisonous snakes, killer bees, and carnivorous spiders.

I was politely welcomed, and ushered unto a large tent, which seemed to be quite adequately furnished. A huge, shambling figure came forward to greet me.

"Welcome, my dear Ambrose," said General Golosina in his hearty bass-baritone. "I was told you were coming. Have you got the money with you?"

I handed over my box of cash, being careful to obtain a receipt. Golosina waved me to an armchair and gave me a stiff whisky.

"You see me in greatly reduced circumstances," he said, "but we have done our best to make ourselves comfortable." I looked around. Rich carpets decorated the floor, and there were fine tapestries against the sides of the tent. And there, surely, was the sinister Caravaggio, which Golosina had pinched from the National Gallery in Felicidad.

"I had long been prepared with a contingency plan for use in emergencies," explained Tiberio. "So we were not caught entirely unawares. You already know my house guests, I think."

Two figures had entered the tent. I looked at them in astonishment. One of them was Ludovic Molnar; the other none other than the duplicitous Casilda, reputedly the Condesa de la Rosas. They greeted me with an ironic show of warmth.

"Sorry to confuse you, Ambrose," said Ludovic, "but this is a highly fluid situation."

"I have to apologise too," said Casilda, pulling a mock penitent face. "I have the happiest memories of you, dear Ambrose. But I was distressed to learn that our meeting had caused you subsequent embarrassment. Not my fault, you know. Let us be friends."

I gave her one of my chilly glances but the cheeky hussy seemed quite unabashed.

"I didn't expect to find you here, Ludovic," I said.

"Tiberio and I are old acquaintances," explained Molnar. "Among other things, we share an enthusiasm for baroque music played on authentic instruments."

"Fortunately I was able to bring my record player," said the former Chief of Police. "And the generator is working. So we are not without culture as we sit in the firelight after dinner. Casilda, as you will have realised, is my life's companion and has been so for some years. She has nobly followed me into exile."

Casilda had paraded herself to me as fancy-free and readily available. I fixed her with a steady, reproving gaze which she pretended not to notice.

"Ludovic has come here for a special purpose," added Tiberio. "He has kindly agreed to take my Caravaggio to London to sell it at one of your great auction houses."

"I hardly think that will be possible," objected Ludovic. "Even Christies or Sothebys would not touch it. But I do know a reclusive Russian millionaire who could be interested. His *dacha* in the forest is full of missing masterpieces. That would provide further funds for you to continue the national struggle."

"The national struggle?!" echoed Golosina. "That's rather rich. I am a poor, pathetic refugee, skulking in the most unattractive corner of this God-forsaken country."

"Nonsense, Tiberio," protested Casilda. "You have here a body of trained men who would die for you."

"Only because they have no alternative. Most of them are my old comrades in the Secret Police. They would be torn to pieces if they ever dared to appear again in Felicidad."

"You must fight on," I said, "and even intensify the struggle.

That is what I have come to tell you. It is why Marsala has sent you money."

"You bewilder me, Ambrose. Are you talking on behalf of Her Majesty's Government?"

"Not exactly," I replied, in some confusion.

"He speaks for Wedmore and Bassenthwaite," chipped in Ludovic resourcefully. "You know about their special interest."

"It's all very well trying to hearten me," protested Golosina. "But please consider my position. I have had years of acting as a bogyman. I am human rights violator number one. My tortures and executions are legendary. We did have to be tough occasionally, of course. But my excesses were greatly exaggerated. The main requirement was to terrify the opposition, and I succeeded in that for a long time. Until that damned Liberator came along with his posture of simple goodness and brotherly love. I've lost the will to fight against that. I'm only here because there's nowhere else to go." The great brute hung his head into huge calloused hands. It was a pathetic sight.

"Now come on, Tiberio," said Ludovic in soothing tones, "you know how you love a good fight. Don't tell me you're losing your testosterone."

"He's still got plenty of that," said the false *condesa*, with a lewd giggle betraying her modest social origins.

"I am misunderstood," wailed Golosina. "Even by you, my closest friends. Because I am well built, I am seen as nothing more than a fighting machine. Or, even worse, as a sadistic chief of police in the Baron Scarpia mould. But that's not really me at all. Deep down, I am a sensitive soul with a longing for artistic beauty. I am sorely tempted to accept the offer of amnesty made to me by this insane dentist. Casilda and I will go quietly abroad. We will visit the hill towns of Italy, the Alhambra in Granada, the châteaux of the Loire."

"That would be lovely," said Casilda. "We must go to Rome and Florence too. For the shopping. They sell lovely leather bags and exquisite shoes there. The First Lady used to tell me."

"That option is hardly open to you, Tiberio," I pointed out. "You have many enemies, scattered throughout the world. Widows, parents, orphans. They would get you before long. The dreaded Trevor Pilkington QC, a veritable hammer of wrongdoers, would be on your track to the bitter end."

"And there's another thing," added Ludovic. "As a patriotic citizen of Concordia you should bear in mind how you would be leaving your nation: in the grip of a mad idealist; a declared pacifist who would abolish the armed forces, leaving the country open to invasion. He would serve vegetarian food at state banquets, and make smoking illegal. Prisoners would be let off with a caution, the gaols having been demolished. It would all end in disaster. We have a duty to prevent that."

"I take your point," retorted Golosina. "A man of infinite goodness would indeed be ill-equipped to run this country. But perhaps there is a better way to sabotage Fernandez. We might persuade the Cardinal Archbishop to preach against him in the cathedral. Pacifism is against the teachings of the Church Militant, which has traditionally been enthusiastic about the doctrine of the just war."

"That won't be enough," said Casilda. "The Cardinal is against birth control, but you can buy condoms in every bar."

"You must announce the reopening of the national struggle," said Ludovic. "I'll handle the announcement in the world press, and Ambrose will contact governments. The prospect of some juicy massacres should bring out the television reporters by Jacquaranda class. There's that splendid English woman Imogen Sheldrake, who never misses an opportunity to work the viewers up into a lather of excitement."

We argued for an hour and drank a great deal of whisky. But at last Golosina began to realise that his gentle giant posture was hardly viable, and that his best defence lay in carrying the war firmly into his enemy's camp.

"Very well," he said at last, with a slight groan. "You want me to be another Genghis Khan, and I will. Go back to Felicidad and tell them I am mobilising my Mongol hordes."

"I could come to you later," the *condesa* whispered in my ear as we sat at dinner. "You big strong man, you!"

"Your lover is big and strong," I said nastily.

"He is not very inventive. And he tires after a couple of hours."

"Casilda," I said firmly, "there is an old English saying which applies to this situation. Once bitten, twice shy."

"And now for a little music," said General Golosina, as we sat around after dinner with balloons of brandy hastily smuggled out of the presidential palace. "We can offer you a choice, Ambrose. A few delicious madrigals by Monteverdi? Or perhaps a cantata by Vivaldi?"

From outside, in the snake-filled forest, we heard the shriek of some jungle creature meeting a noisy death.

***

"I cannot give you much time, Mr Carr-Baxendale," I said. "I am due to leave the office shortly for an important meeting with the Liberator in person."

"It won't take long, Ambassador. I suppose we should call you that again now."

"Please don't fuss me. And I'm only Chargé d'Affaires. I wish you well in your researches into ancient Nevera funerary customs, but I cannot pretend that they rate very high in my scheme of things."

"Look, Sir, let's be practical. I know you need certain decisions out of the Liberator. You're competing against the French and the Yanks, who are also trying to hush him up. Now I've got something here which might just do the trick. Victor Fernandez is no politician. He remains a dentist at heart. And what secretly distresses him is that he went to a second-rate school in the States. He's got that on the brain. To give him a real thrill, we have to do something about that rather touching neurosis."

He opened a packet, and showed me a highly illuminated scroll.

"What on earth's that?" I snapped.

"A certificate stating that Doctor Victor Fernandez, President of Concordia, has been elected an Honorary Fellow of the Royal College of Surgeons in London. He'll be tickled pink."

"A nice try, Adrian. I am sure you mean to help, though I can't think what it's all got to do with you. But surely it should be the Royal College of Dentists?"

"There's no such a thing," said Carr-Baxendale. "Dentists like to think of themselves as dental surgeons. So they get their qualifications from the Royal College of Surgeons. Take it at once, Sir, and give it to the Liberator. You can't lose."

"All right." I was mystified by his initiative but the man was obviously trying to make himself useful. "I'm afraid I can't bring you with me to present the scroll. Our talk is to be private."

"No problem, Sir. I'll simply fade away." He was just the type, I thought, to withdraw into the shadows. Carr-Baxendale had always been a bit of a puzzle.

The Liberator hailed me warmly, instructing his aides that we were not to be disturbed. He had now moved into a large office in the presidential palace, where he looked singularly out of his depth. Rather incongruously for a head of state, he was dressed in a purple tracksuit and white trainers.

"I was worried for you, Ambassador," he began in his gentle voice. "You made a very dangerous trip on my behalf."

"I'll admit, Sir, that I wasn't keen on the wildlife. I encountered a homicidal spider on my breakfast plate on my last morning."

"I was really thinking of the former Chief of Police. A man with an appalling reputation for brutality. I never liked putting my fingers into his huge mouth."

"It was all a bit scary," I said, "but I had to bring you an answer. And now I have."

"Oh, good," said the President. "He's leaving? That is splendid news. We will have a non-denominational *Te Deum*."

"It's the opposite, Sir. He's not leaving at all. I urged that course upon him with all the eloquence at my command. But he asked me to tell you that he had declared war on you and will shortly be leading his troops to attack you here in Felicidad. These include a strike force from the Amazon Warriors recruited by the former First Lady. He intends to treat you as a war criminal, and hang you publicly on the terrace of the National Museum."

"How ghastly!" said the Liberator, growing pale. "This is terrible news. What on earth am I to do?"

"You must act at once. Strengthen your armed forces. Prepare for war."

"A civil war! How dreadful for my poor suffering people. After all they endured under the Raro dictatorship. What is the alternative?"

"You could bring General Golosina into your government as Minister of National Regeneration."

"Never! The man is an appalling brute. I should lose all credibility."

"Or you could flee yourself."

"Where would I go? What would I do?"

"You could continue your career as a dental surgeon. In England perhaps, or the States."

"That is a more tempting prospect, though my modest qualifications would not get me very far. I've always enjoyed working on an interesting set of teeth. But it would be a betrayal, wouldn't it, after all that has been done to get me where I am now. The people of Concordia have trusted me. I cannot desert them at this critical moment. Besides, my dear wife and daughters have now got used to an elevated standard of living."

"Then, Sir, you must do as I have suggested. Get your forces ready for battle."

"I had so longed to found a new society where brotherly love would reign supreme. I saw myself as another Sarastro from *The Magic Flute*."

"That could still be your ideal, Mr President. But you must postpone it. Until you have hanged Golosina."

"I do not want to hang anyone. I am strongly opposed to capital punishment. But I agree that he must be put out of action. A few years in a re-education camp would tame his savage spirit.

Unfortunately, as you know, my army and police are sadly lacking in the most modern equipment. If I am to fight a war, I shall have to buy arms very quickly."

"I am aware of that. And I am happy to advise you about your choice."

"The trouble is, dear Mr Ambassador, that your advice may not be entirely disinterested. As you have told me before, you want me to buy defence equipment from this British firm Wedmore and Bassenthwaite. But they were deeply involved with the Raro regime. Perhaps I should turn elsewhere. Your French and American colleagues have presented some interesting possibilities. The French offer a swagger stick which turns into a sabre. And the Americans have a self-exploding football to kick into unruly mobs."

"These gimmicks are greatly inferior to ours," I said stoutly. "We have much experience of quelling native peoples. We have fleshed our teeth on the Irish for centuries."

"Oh dear, oh dear," wailed the Liberator. "It is all very difficult. I am only a child in these things. You mention teeth. Now, if I were choosing a mouthwash or a dentist's drill, my long experience would be relevant and I should feel competent to make a choice. But how am I to select these horrible armaments when, as you rightly point out, a decision is urgently required? How on earth to choose between the French bayonet, the American howitzer and the British bazooka? There is only one thing for it. I must immediately summon my chief of staff, who now has an office in this building. Excuse me a moment."

He went out to give orders to an aide. I took the opportunity to unwrap the scroll given me by Adrian Carr-Baxendale.

"What is that, Mr Ambassador?" asked the President on his return. "It hardly looks like an instrument of death."

"See for yourself, Sir," I suggested.

Victor Fernandez examined the parchment, and then gave out an almost childlike whoop of delight.

"The Royal College of Surgeons of England!" he exclaimed. "Honorary Fellow! My dear sir, no gift could have given me more pleasure. FRCS! Just wait till I tell them in South Bend!" He gave me a beaming smile, and I mentally blessed the astute judgement of the Nevera scholar.

"The British have always been kind to me," continued the President warmly. "The British Council used to invite me to some delightful manifestations before I took to the jungle. I remember so well their highly realistic production of *Titus Andronicus*, with Dame Pippa Clinch. How I should love to go to London and attend a dinner at the Royal College in Lincoln's Inn Fields. It would be the apotheosis of my career."

The door opened abruptly, and Marsala bounced into the room.

"Sylvester, come here," said the President. "Look what our British friends have given me. I am a Fellow of the Royal College of Surgeons."

"Very pretty," commented Marsala abruptly.

"Mr Bellingham has brought us terrible news from the interior," continued the somewhat timorous head of state. "General Golosina has declared war on us. He intends to lead his army to Felicidad, with murderous intentions towards myself."

"I'm not at all surprised," said Marsala, barely suppressing a wink in my direction. "That man is a killer."

"We have only one option now," said the President, with uncharacteristic decisiveness. "We must buy new military equipment straight away, and prepare the army urgently for war against the forces of darkness."

"That's what I have been telling you all along, Sir," said Marsala.

"But which of the three packages to buy?" said Fernandez. "That is the question. When perplexed like this, Mr Ambassador, I usually have recourse to my exercise bicycle. May I ask you, gentlemen, to accompany me to my personal fitness facility. It is one of the new perks of my present position."

He led us into the gymnasium next door and motioned to us to sit on a piece of cork matting as he mounted a gleaming, stationary bicycle. My heart pounded. I knew it was the moment of decision.

"I quite like the French," said the President, pedalling merrily away. "Voltaire and Monet and crêpes suzette. The Americans too are a mighty people, with wonderful plumbing. Their baths, their toilets, their spittoons." Marsala and I exchanged apprehensive glances. "But my chosen nation," continued Fernandez, "are the English. Shakespeare, Sherlock Holmes, the Royal College of Surgeons. As a benevolent dictator, I can take the decision entirely on my own. And I have now decided. We will buy from Wedmore and Bassenthwaite."

He got off his bicycle and gave me a somewhat sweaty embrace.

"Congratulations, Mr President," I said warmly. "You have made the right decision."

"What do you think, Sylvester?" asked his nominal superior nervously.

"That's all right by me, Mr President."

"What about the emerald mines?" I asked, striking while the iron was hot.

"You can't have them back," said Fernandez. "They are worked by my people, and the profits must remain in this country in the future. But I'll tell you what: we will pay immediate and full compensation to the British shareholders, the amount to be fixed by independent arbitration."

"A wise course, Mr President," I said. "You will have made a good friend of Britain. That will help to negate the peevish squeaks of the disappointed French and the frustrated howl of the Americans."

"I am glad you are satisfied," said the Liberator, leading us back into his study. "Our business was transacted very pleasantly, wasn't it? That shows the advantage of not having a parliament or an elected government. I am beginning at last to appreciate the exhilarating experience of being a benevolent dictator."

"That's the trouble with dictatorship," commented Marsala dourly. "After a time, dictators do begin to enjoy it."

"There's another problem," I pointed out. "You must forgive me for speaking frankly, Sir. You may have decided to buy arms from Britain, but we still have to obtain an export permit from the British

Government."

"I thought that was all agreed under the Raro regime."

"It almost was," I said, "but a new decision will be needed now that there has been a change of government here in Concordia."

"There can surely be no difficulty about that," said the President. "I have shown that I am a friend of your country. Don't forget, I am a Fellow of your Royal College of Surgeons."

"Yes, but we have to bear in mind that these decisions are taken by a highly opinionated woman minister in the British Foreign Office. In her simplistic way, she likes to divide nations into Bad Countries and Good Countries. You have to be a Good Country if you want to buy defence equipment from us."

"How am I to achieve that, Ambassador?"

"You must organise popular elections and set up a fully democratic government. Then you will be Good."

"What do you advise, Sylvester?"

"I should go along with that, Mr President."

"But we have such terrible politicians. They will never care about the welfare of the nation."

"Of course they won't," agreed Marsala cynically. "But I'll help you make a list of the docile ones who can be bribed into keeping quiet."

"Very well. We have become a democracy, Ambassador, from this moment. You can report that to your lady in the Foreign Office. Is there anything else?"

"There was the little matter of the Foundation," prompted Marsala.

"Oh yes," said the head of state, slightly embarrassed. "You explain, Sylvester."

"The Liberator has set up a foundation," said the Mafia boss. "It is to care for impoverished intellectuals who need support for their higher studies into philosophy and cosmology. A noble aim, if I might say. But they are badly in need of funds. It would set the seal on our bargain today if the interests connected with Wedmore and Bassenthwaite could see their way to making a substantial donation. You and I can discuss the amount together."

"Very well," I said, without enthusiasm.

"The cheque should be made out to S. Marsala," pointed out the President briskly. "I will say goodbye to you now, gentlemen. I shall give the necessary instructions to our ambassador in London to go ahead urgently with the arms purchase. It has been a good meeting, hasn't it? I feel we have taken the first steps towards creating a better world."

***

"Why are you slowing down, Potiphar?" I snapped, as we drove down the frangipani-fringed Grand Boulevard of Felicidad.

"Man is waving to you, Sir." There was indeed a fellow trying to accost us. He was an unattractive sight, stained with travel, dirty and dishevelled, and dramatically muffled in a kind of peasant blanket.

"He's only a beggar," I said. "Drive on."

Potiphar seemed curiously unwilling to do so. The strange figure succeeded in reaching us and shouting into my open window.

"Ambrose," shrieked the apparition. "Stop the car, you fool." With shocked horror, I realised that it was none other than Ludovic Molnar. I swept him into the limousine and instructed Potiphar to drive us immediately to the embassy residence.

"What on earth have you been doing, Ludovic?" I asked.

"I'll tell you all," he gasped, "after a long, hot bath and a long, cold gin."

Later, when he had recovered somewhat, we sat on the terrace, gazing down on the tropical city as its lights began to twinkle. I had carefully rubbed my ankles with mosquito repellent but Molnar did not seem to need any. No doubt his blood was toxic, even to mosquitos.

"I have had the most ghastly time," said the Hungarian. "It was all right for you, flying back here by Air Force helicopter. I had to choose a less obtrusive method. I arranged with one of the Tozudo headmen to guide me through the swamps. But one night, as we bivouacked by the camp fire, I saw them staring at me in the most sinister way. It dawned on me that they were mentally measuring my skull to work out how much they could get for me as a shrunken head. After that, I wasn't taking any chances. In the middle of the night, I struck out on my own. It wasn't a pleasant experience. A log I was eating my sandwiches on the next day turned out to be a crocodile. I'm lucky to be alive at all."

"You should have come straight here," I said.

"I had to phone Marsala first. He told me how you got on with the President. Well done, Ambrose. It looks as if I shall be paying you your bonus quite soon." He gave me a seraphic beam. "But we can't afford to dawdle. The President, as you may have noticed, is not quite right in the head. He could easily change his mind about the arms purchase. If the French got to him again. Or if he found out that poor old Golosina is really a busted flush. So we're got to go back to London straight away, to persuade Dame Rosy to approve the sale before it's too late."

"You're right, Ludovic. But I can't just march out. I've taken over the Embassy again. I am a representative of Her Britannic Majesty."

"Ring up the Foreign Office first thing tomorrow. Tell them your wife is dangerously ill and you have to come home for a week on compassionate grounds."

"Isn't that tempting providence? To tell a fib like that?"

Nevertheless, when we met at breakfast the next morning I was able to give him an answer. With the time difference, it was much later in the day in London.

"They have appointed a new ambassador. He is coming directly from the Holy See. As you know, I was only here as a stopgap. I can leave straight away, and I don't have to come back here."

"Good. I'll book us on the first available flight."

"Not in the tourist class," I insisted. "It's too dangerous with this new syndrome."

"If you had ever been smuggled across the former Iron Curtain in the boot of a very small car," said Ludovic dismissively, "you would take a more relaxed view about physical comfort."

I went that morning to say goodbye to the Archdeacon, and found that Adrian Carr-Baxendale was also visiting him.

"That was a good wheeze of yours about the Surgeons," I said to Adrian. "Thank you."

"Glad to help," said the scholar graciously. "I'm leaving too, you know. My job here is done."

"Your job?" I asked.

"I mean, my work on the Nevera monuments." Had he really meant that? Carr-Baxendale had always struck me as a curious academic.

"What about you, Harry?"

"I am staying on, Ambrose. This has been my real home for years. My sister has been obliged to move into sheltered housing, so Saffron Walden is out for me. They offered me the Bishopric of Frinton but I'd rather try to help the dear Liberator by acting as a shoulder for him to cry on. He is so lonely. Isn't it nice? They are giving me the Order of Saint Eulalia, Second Class. I can't think why."

"Well, dear Harry," I said, "I beg you just one thing. Never lose your wonderful faith in the essential goodness of human nature. I know I'm a dreadful old cynic, but people like me need people like you."

"What about the new ambassador?" asked the Archdeacon. "It's most interesting that he's coming from the Vatican. I look forward to meeting him."

"Between ourselves, he's leaving Rome in rather a hurry. Some trouble with a defrocked nun. Quite in the great tradition of ambassadors in Felicidad."

This time at least, I gave reasonably generous tips to the residence staff. Felipe bowed low and old Teresita burst into tears, perhaps of surprise.

"Goodbye, Potiphar," I said. "I suppose you will now be going back to Cairo."

"Oh no, Sir," he replied, with a suggestive leer. "I go to Bournemouth to live with Mr and Mrs Haverstock-Jones." That made me wonder, though I am not a man for idle gossip. I could not help imaging their frolics.

At last I was ensconced in Jacquaranda class in the national airline en route to Miami. The stocky figure of Ludovic Molnar beside me overflowed onto the arm between our comfortable seats. Attentive young hostesses brought us drinks and cool towels to wipe the tropical grime off our faces. The aircraft wheeled over the city and then turned towards the blue sea far below. I detected a few familiar landmarks: the green lawn of the presidential palace, the grim walls of the central prison, and the municipal abattoir so beloved of the rapacious local vultures. For a brief moment I felt almost nostalgic for this strange little town with its gorgeous girls, beautiful flowers and permissive ambience. Something told me that I should never see Felicidad again.

5

"Susan darling, I'm back."

"Oh good, Dear."

"I'm in London at the Voyagers again."

"That's nice for you. I hope you'll be able to take in a few shows."

"My mission to Concordia was a fantastic success. Their new president is going to buy from Britain."

"Does that mean we will be rich at last?"

"Up to a point, Susan. But the richer you are, the more you have to think about investing your money, not spending it. No more of your silly splurges, please."

"I'm being a good little girl."

"What news of Little Bigney, Dear?"

"The man next door with the trumpet is quite decent. He's practising a piece by Purcell. But he has agreed not to play before seven in the morning."

"And the Harrison Bedfords? Any news of my plays?"

"They are slightly in disarray. Griselda's mother has very bad arthritis, and she has had to stay on in Cornwall to look after her."

"Look, Susan dear, I'm sorry to have to break this to you. But I can't get back to Norfolk straight away."

"Oh, really? Why is that?"

"I have a very urgent job here. Molnar wants me to see Dame Rosy Clumber immediately at the Foreign Office, in order to secure British Government approval for this arms order. If we delay, it could all collapse. So I've put in for an interview, and I have to wait in London until I can see her."

"Never mind, Dear."

"You do understand, don't you?"

"Of course."

"You won't be lonely without me?"

"I'll try not to be, Ambrose. There's always plenty to do in the garden. And Neville may come home. He has resurfaced, you know. He sent me a postcard from Seville. He's visiting the family of Jaime Damiel, that nice Spanish boy he knew at school."

"Without Sharon?"

"I suppose so. Jaime is the one with the charming female cousin called Isabella."

"I expect he'll be back," I said glumly. "When they chuck him out."

It had, on the surface, been a satisfactory talk. My dear Susan had acquiesced without fuss in my remaining in town. That was typical of her brave spirit. What a trouper the woman was! And yet a nagging doubt insinuated itself, for the first time, into my mind. Could it be that Susan actually rather enjoyed my absences?

***

"Come and sit beside me on the sofa, Selby," cooed Dame Rosy as usual. "And you, Mr Bellingham, could take that chair over there." It was never the other way round.

"You know what we have come about, Minister," said Selby Tritton. "The new president of Concordia wants to buy defence equipment from Britain. All the details have been agreed. But, as a formality, we need you to approve the export licence."

Molnar, our group mastermind, had instructed Selby and me to go in without him. There were times when he preferred to keep a back seat. I had agreed with Selby that he should take the lead, since the Minister of State was so obviously charmed by him.

"I have told you before, Selby, that in principle I am opposed to the sale of weapons of death. But I accept that there can occasionally be justification for supplying purely defensive equipment to friendly governments. The question is, does this application fall within that category?"

"Most certainly," replied Selby glibly. "Victor Fernandez, the new president of Concordia, nationally known as the Liberator, is a convinced democrat and supporter of the free market. He has declared publicly that it is his intention to organise elections as soon as possible, with a view to a popularly mandated government taking over immediately after that."

"He is closing the concentration camps, opening the prisons?"

"Of course."

"That is excellent news," said Dame Rosy. "But he is friendly to Britain?"

"Oh yes," I said. "He is an Honorary Fellow of the Royal College of Surgeons."

"Trevor will be pleased. You know how strongly we both feel about human rights. But why does he need defence equipment? Concordia has no external enemies."

"The dreadful General Golosina is still holding out against him in the interior, and is threatening to march on Felicidad. His forces include a much-dreaded combat group of Amazon Warriors. Fernandez badly needs our help."

"Are you sure we are sending the right things?" asked Dame Rosy. "This seems an extensive list of truly horrible armaments. I hope he will not go the same way as the Raros."

"Oh no, Minister," I said. "Fernandez is a kind-hearted idealist, dedicated to the relief of suffering. He has assured me that he will deploy only the minimum of force, in sheer self-defence."

"That does seem satisfactory," agreed Dame Rosy. "Foreign countries are always so complicated. It is not easy to spot which governments are on the right side and which are not. Our policy is perfectly straightforward. We support the good ones and oppose the bad. This Mr Fernandez would appear to be morally respectable, as I am sure Trevor would agree. I am prepared to recommend acceptance of this application."

"Excellent. But it is very urgent, Rosy," said Selby. "Wedmore and Bassenthwaite have aircraft standing by. Every day counts. Are you going to have to refer this decision upwards? The Department of

Trade are already enthusiastic."

"I take your point," said the Minister. "But I really ought to consult the Foreign Secretary. Unfortunately it is almost impossible to obtain his attention these days. He could not even attend the Anglo-Estonian summit this week. The entire Cabinet are wholly preoccupied with the dreadful question of the Ziggurat. The Kings Cross site has been cleared, as you know, and whole streets of poor families have been forcibly ejected. There is quite a bad feeling in the resettlement camps on what we are instructed to call the Foulness Riviera. But now the financing for the new construction has collapsed, ever since the Chancellor's brother got sent to prison. And all so near the election too!"

"It sounds like a major cock-up," agreed Selby cheerfully.

"It is a substantial problem," said Dame Rosy, more cautiously. "So we ministers outside the Cabinet are having to take a lot of decisions on our own. All right, I will approve the application. My private secretary has the paperwork, and will let you have it today."

"Splendid," said Selby warmly. "I'm sure you will not regret it."

"Fernandez did a fine job on my tooth only last week," I added. "He's keeping his hand in at dental surgery. Doesn't that show that he would bow gracefully to the people's will if they ever decided to dispense with his services?"

"One should always accept the people's will," opined Dame Rosy sententiously. "It's the essence of democracy, as I said to the Prime Minister the other day at his reception for show business stars."

"And what was his reaction?" asked Selby.

"He shuddered. Do you have any news of that dreadful General Raro and his unspeakable wife?" continued Dame Rosy. "Their visit to this country was a most unpleasant experience for me. But it did give the opposition in Concordia a chance to strike in their absence. And it should have had the extra advantage of trapping them here when the revolution came. Trevor did his level best, you know. He persuaded the Metropolitan Police to go and arrest them. They understood that the tyrants were sleeping peacefully in their suite in Claridges. One of the elite squads from Scotland

Yard went in with their breakfast tray in full combat uniform, but they had disappeared. Trevor is most awfully disappointed. He was so looking forward to conducting the case against them in the courts."

"I have no information at all," said Selby.

"Nor I," I said hurriedly.

"A pity. Trevor is convinced that they were spirited away by some vile person and are now being protected by a neo-fascist group. It is becoming a bit of an obsession with him. He thinks Britain should take the leading role in policing the world against the forces of darkness. I only wish I could persuade some of these idle diplomats here in the Foreign Office to make more effort. They have never recovered from Talleyrand's advice not to show too much zeal. I know they don't like me. But Joan of Arc was not universally popular either."

"It was wonderful about the revolution," remarked Selby unctuously as we bowed out of the room. "But it couldn't have happened, Minister, if you hadn't agreed at last to let the Raros come here. What made you change your mind?"

"That would be telling," replied Dame Rosy Clumber. Her smile was curiously enigmatic.

As we passed through the Minister's private office on the way out, we encountered a woman in a kind of khaki battledress, waiting to be received. I recognised her as Imogen Sheldrake, the distinguished foreign correspondent so well known on peak-hour news bulletins on British television. Her uncanny nose for death and disaster was understood to be the key to her success. It appeared that she was shortly off to Felicidad to report the expected shenanigans in war-torn Concordia. Dame Rosy Clumber must be giving her the benefits of a personal briefing. They would both have made good material, I whispered to Selby, for General Golosina's redoubtable corps of Amazon Warriors.

***

"I hope you didn't mind coming down to Kew Gardens," said Ludovic Molnar. "One of my favourite places. Don't you love that ridiculous pagoda? The truth is, my dear Ambrose, that I have a touch of paranoia. I am terrified of being bugged. One knows too much about these neat little electronic devices. Here at least, among the giant azaleas, one can speak freely. You said there were things you wanted to know. Can I help you?"

"Well, for some time now, I have felt myself to be in the grip of mysterious subterranean forces. All, I think, was not as it seemed."

"I owe you an explanation, Ambrose. We are all most grateful to you for the spirited part you have played in the successful conclusion of our operation. You will be receiving a nice fat cheque. We shall both have money now, and I recommend you to use yours to your personal advantage, as I shall do mine."

"It all came too easily. The revolution, I mean, and the complete change of regime in Concordia. How on earth did that happen?"

"It was brilliant coup by MI6 – the British Secret Service, aided by the CIA. The Raros had been useful in their earlier years but they had become too much involved with the drugs traffic. The time had come for them to go. The opposition were going to win some day, so it made sense to cosy up to them. Carr-Baxendale, as you should have spotted, was working for MI6."

"You mean all that Nevera heritage stuff was a fraud?"

"Not exactly. Carr-Baxendale is a genuine scholar. He knows Concordia well. That is why he was recruited for this particular assignment, under deep cover. They asked Lord Cumberland to employ him as a guest lecturer, so as to give him an excuse to penetrate Nevera territory. Cumberland, you know, like many of the aristocracy, is not such a fool as he looks. It was he who got Harry Wilderness back to Concordia, also with the Connoisseur Travel group. The timing of their second visit may have seemed unfortunate, but it was actually very carefully planned. Likewise, that trip by the British parliamentary group. They were sent there deliberately, so as to lull the Raros into a false sense of security."

"But surely they might have been killed?"

"It was decided to take that risk. Backbench Members of Parliament are considered expendable. Peers even more so."

"Surely Harry Wilderness is not a secret agent."

"He couldn't be told too much. You know what a holy innocent he is. But he has his uses. He's an old friend of Victor Fernandez, and we wanted him as a patently honest contact."

"Are you seriously telling me that Carr-Baxendale organised the revolution?"

"You could say that, Ambrose. At least, he set it off. It had been boiling up for a long time, of course. Fernandez had done a lot to mobilise the tribes. He had a great deal of popular support. But everything depended on the timing. Carr-Baxendale used the Archdeacon to establish his good faith with Fernandez. Then he was able to persuade him that the time to strike had come when the Raros were stupid enough to leave Concordia. By that time, the rebels had a network across the country. Potiphar was on the MI6 payroll too."

"What about my successor? Was he in the know?"

"Certainly not. MI6 have the greatest contempt for the general run of professional diplomats."

"All this is fascinating," I said. "But it doesn't explain the behaviour of Dame Rosy Clumber. First, she strongly opposed the idea of a visit to Britain by the Raros. Then she veered completely round and allowed the visit to go ahead. I found that most mystifying. She seemed confused about it too, almost as if she were playing a part."

"She was. Carr-Baxendale, who is a very able operator, managed to convince the silly woman that if she could get the Raros out of the way, he would be free to start the revolution in their absence. But she isn't much of an actress, and she found the whole thing somewhat embarrassing. Especially as they wouldn't let her tell the truth to her barmy husband and he kept giving her hell over the human rights issue."

"That's all very interesting, Ludovic," I said with massive dignity. "I suppose I had guessed most of it all along."

"No, you didn't. You can't fool me, Ambrose. You are another of nature's innocents. I find that rather charming."

"I still don't see how you come in, Ludovic. Weren't you supposed to be selling arms?"

"Of course I was selling arms. But I was also on the payroll of MI6. Just as Marsala works for the Mafia but is also happy to do little jobs for the CIA. It's only the mugs of this world who have just one paymaster. The two of us had helped Fernandez to set up the secret rebel cadres. Carr-Baxendale then gave him courage at the critical moment."

"And that bomb outside the cathedral?" I enquired sharply.

"Better not to ask," replied Molnar with a broad wink. "Shall we just say that the rebels received ... a little technical assistance?"

"Very neat," I said. "I never had much of an opinion of MI6 but this time they seem to have done pretty well. Did they have anything to do with the escape of the Raros?"

"No. That was a little initiative of my own. It turned out to be quite profitable, as the First Lady was persuaded to give me all her jewels for safekeeping. I got into their suite disguised as a well-built chambermaid, taking their early morning coffee before breakfast. I had them down that fire escape while Scotland Yard were still fastening their bulletproof vests. They were actually in my house when you called on me unexpectedly that morning."

"I thought you looked a bit secretive, Ludovic."

"I hid the President in my airing cupboard, and the First Lady in the Jacuzzi."

"And where are they now?"

"I don't think you ought to know that, Ambrose. In case you are captured and tortured by Trevor Pilkington." He gave me a broad wink. One could hardly help warming to the rogue, as one had done even to Sylvester Marsala.

"The real coup," he continued smugly, "was to persuade Fernandez to promise full compensation for the emeralds. That will be even bigger, you know, than the profits from the arms deal. It's going to make somebody very happy."

"Who will that be, Ludovic?"

"How should I know? Maybe you're on to something there. Why

don't you spend some time trying to work out who will be the real beneficiaries?"

"I don't even know how to start."

"Oh yes, you do, Ambrose. You heard Greg Atkinson up at Greyburn telling us that a certain lady named Amanda Beachcroft had left a lot of shares in Wedmore and Bassenthwaite to some unknown party. I mentioned at the time that you had the right to examine that will. You might find it interesting."

"Very well, I'll have a go. I have a legitimate concern, now that I'm a director for the company."

"I shan't be going back to Concordia," said Ludovic. "It won't be my sort of country now."

"You mean, there will be honest government?"

"I wouldn't say that. Fernandez may mean well but ruling other human beings is a terribly corrupting experience. He won't be very effective at it either. He should have stuck to teeth."

"Dame Rosy thinks he's going to be a Goody."

"Goodies and Baddies! What a delightfully simplistic view of this wicked world. Would you care to accompany me to the tearooms? They do some nice sticky buns."

"Why did you tell me all this, Ludovic? You didn't have to."

"I don't know, Ambrose. I suppose the truth is that I rather like you. You wasted your time in the Diplomatic Service. You could have had a great career on the shady side."

"Thank you, kind sir," I replied ironically.

"We would have made a fine partnership," said Molnar pensively. "You with your dignified manner and me with my brains."

***

The ear-splitting tones of a trumpet's higher register spliced through the thin walls which inadequately partitioned our Old Rectory in Little Bigney.

"I can't stand it a moment longer," I shouted, springing up from my armchair. "I am going to biff that man on the nose."

"Don't be silly, Dear. They are quite pleasant young people. He's already volunteered to mow our joint front lawn, which is more than the O'Callaghans did. Besides, he might hit you back, and he looks awfully strong."

"My dear Susan, I find your last argument the most compelling."

"Why don't you sit still and read your post?" suggested my peaceful partner. "There might be something interesting."

"Hardly likely," I retorted. "An appeal from the home for stray cats in Kings Lynn. And news of a production of *Charlie's Aunt* at the theatre in Norwich."

There was, however, one slightly mysterious envelope with an official flavour. I opened it and found that it contained something for which I had written a few days before: a copy, available to all citizens, of the last will and testament of the late Amanda Beachcroft. I read it with mounting excitement.

For some reason best known to herself, the wealthy Miss Beachcroft of Cheltenham had invested heavily in Wedmore and Bassenthwaite shares. Those had been left to a trust managed by a firm of solicitors for the benefit of a named individual, Miss Beachcroft's beloved nephew. While the trust was to hold the shares, the income was to be paid to the nephew.

Then I saw the name of the favoured relative. A name well known to me. It made me chuckle with glee. I realised that Ludovic Molnar's timely hint had presented me with a magnificent opportunity.

"I'll have to go straight back to town," I told Susan.

"Oh dear!" she said. "You'll not be here for Lady Moggeridge's *fête champêtre*. I promised that you would dress up as a gypsy princess and do fortune telling."

"I can bear to miss that," I countered drily.

"Is this business or pleasure?"

"Business. But pleasure too."

***

213

"Trevor and I try to keep our Sundays free," said Dame Rosy Clumber in somewhat acid tones, as we sat in the drawing room of their comfortable Hampstead home. "It is the day we walk Nelson Mandela on the Heath."

"Mandela?"

"Our Labrador," explained Trevor Pilkington QC.

"But I thought you had better come here at once, Mr Bellingham, as you said it was most awfully urgent and important."

"I am very sorry to disturb you," I said, "but I have just stumbled on some extremely delicate information. I have come as a friend, if I may call myself that, to try to save you both acute embarrassment. We have to act very quickly to prevent the story breaking in the media, with catastrophic results."

"For you too?" asked Trevor, in his best cross-examining manner.

"Oh no, Mr Pilkington," I replied, doing my best to suppress a grin of ineffable smugness. "For you and Dame Rosy."

"I can't think what all this is about," said the Minister. "You seem to imply that we have something to hide. I cannot think what you mean. There are no skeletons in our cupboard. In fact, we don't have a cupboard at all."

"Out with it, Bellingham," said Trevor briskly. "I can see you're enjoying this but we are not. It would have been a lovely afternoon in the Vale of Health, with tea at Kenwood."

"All right," I began, warming to the task. "The truth is that, quite by chance, I have learned something very surprising about the ownership of Wedmore and Bassenthwaite."

Trevor Pilkington QC would have made a good poker player but even he was unable to control the faint spasm of apprehension which crossed his distinguished face at that moment. I knew that I had scored a hit, a palpable hit. It was a delicious moment, which I intended to savour.

"If I might remind you, that is a firm who make a wide variety of defence equipment," I continued. "Dame Rosy has recently announced the approval of the Government of a very large order from that company for the Government of Concordia."

"That was well received by the House of Commons," commented the Minister happily. "The Conservatives are all for selling arms, and the Labour party and the Lib Dems were glad that these were going to a country which cares about human rights."

"As you say, the matter has been very much in the public mind. Perhaps the Government hyped it to counteract public interest in the problems of the Ziggurat." I gave a gentle smile.

"The Prime Minister was certainly pleased," admitted Dame Rosy. "You will have seen the pictures of him and me with the Wedmore and Bassenthwaite team outside Number Ten, Downing Street. I am shortly to receive a civic welcome in Greyburn. They are making me an honorary councillor."

"I am afraid all this makes it much worse," I said grimly.

"I don't know what on earth you are talking about, Mr Bellingham. Do you, Trevor?"

Her husband remained uncharacteristically silent. "Come to the point, Bellingham," he gulped at last.

"It relates," I said solemnly, "to the will of the late Miss Amanda Beachcroft of Cheltenham. On her death, her share portfolio included a considerable number of shares in Wedmore and Bassenthwaite."

"Beachcroft!" said Dame Rosy in astonishment. "That must be your old Aunt Amanda – the one with all the cats. I always thought she was quite dotty."

"She may have been dotty," I said, "but she was also very rich. In our society, the two are by no means incompatible. Her Wedmore and Bassenthwaite shares were left to, guess who? Her much-loved nephew. That, of course, was you, Mr Pilkington."

"Is this true, Trevor?" asked the Minister of State, in the authentic voice of Victorian melodrama.

"Up to a point," replied her husband cautiously. I could almost see the wheels of his massive brain turning, as he mobilised his huge legal experience to extricate himself from a moral quagmire.

"I knew that Aunt Amanda had left you money," conceded Dame Rosy. "Don't you remember, you insisted that we should go to the funeral, for that very reason? All those dreary people from the

Cotswolds. But I had no idea that you were in armaments."

"I can explain all," said Trevor, darting me a hostile look. "God knows why Aunt Amanda bought all those shares. I suppose her broker thought they were a smart thing. Anyhow, she left them to a trust run by a solicitor friend of hers, a rather silly old buzzard with whom she used to play bridge. He and his younger partner are supposed to administer the trust on my behalf and I receive the income. But I don't control a penny of the capital."

"Why didn't you transfer the shares into something more reputable?" asked Dame Rosy. "After all, we are both publicly opposed to the foul trade in armaments. Except in rare cases to fully democratic governments."

"I wanted to. I begged the trust to do so. But they refused, and I had no power to make them. The income kept coming in, and I couldn't stop it."

"I don't think that will play very well with the House of Commons," said Dame Rosy nervously. "After I have just approved the Concordia contract and you have made such a name in human rights cases. Malevolent persons might think we were humbugs, at best."

"People are so malicious," I agreed helpfully. "Especially about politicians. The media love to believe the worst."

"I can't think why Aunt Amanda didn't just bequeath me the wretched money outright," moaned the eminent QC. "It's usually a mistake to set up a trust, because it leaves the heirs at the mercy of some damned solicitor."

"Perhaps she didn't have confidence in you," suggested his wife nastily. "She may have thought that you would blow the inheritance on wine, women and song."

"She was as mean as sin herself," said Trevor unkindly. "Staying with her was never very pleasant. She used to go round the house turning out the lights in the corridors when one was still in the bath. I could never stomach more than the odd weekend. But Mother insisted that I cultivate the old creature."

"Which you seem to have done with considerable success,"

snapped Dame Rosy.

"I cannot deny that the income has made a difference to our standard of living," said Trevor. "Those continental holidays which you so enjoy, with all that wine, and rooms with lakeside views."

"She seems to have spotted your extravagant ways, Trevor."

"She thought I must be some madcap spendthrift because I once arrived from the station in a taxi. She always treated me, you know, as if I were still a child. Her eyes weren't too good by the end, and I don't think she spotted that I had grown up. She was referring to me as Master Trevor when I was already a QC."

"I think it might have been more complicated than that," opined Dame Rosy. "Your Aunt Amanda was a very peculiar old lady with a strong, though malicious, sense of humour. She was very much on the right wing of the Right, as you will remember, with all those semi-fascist friends in riding boots. Our work for human rights never appealed to her at all. In fact, she used to make fun of your efforts. It's possible that she bought those shares on purpose, as a last derisive gesture, and left them to you in such a way you couldn't get rid of them."

"Do you really think so?" said Trevor. "That had not occurred to me. Anyhow, it's academic now. What are we to do?"

"That depends," said his wife, "on how many people know about her will. Not many, I suppose. The solicitor wouldn't tell, and most people have better things to do than looking up the bequests of deceased persons they never met."

"Perhaps you can enlighten us on that point, Mr Bellingham?" asked the QC.

"There is only one human being who knows," I said.

"Apart from you."

"No. I am the only one."

"Thank God," said Trevor. "That's a huge relief. I should hate this to get out. So would you, Rosy."

"You were quite right to come and tell us what you had discovered, Mr Bellingham," said his wife. "But now let us forget the whole silly business. It is only a technicality, after all. Trevor has no effective control over the firm."

"That's the point, Bellingham. Put the matter out of your mind. Would you care to stay to tea?"

The time had come to strike. I braced myself for the kill.

"I would love to forget this conversation," I said. "But unfortunately, as one grows older, memory becomes rather quirky. Sometimes things mist over completely, while other recollections remain crystal clear for years."

"In which category will this subject fall?" asked the eminent barrister sharply.

"That depends," I replied darkly.

"Depends on what?"

"Whether we can come to some arrangements."

I smiled nastily. There was a sinister silence and a sharp intake of breath. Then Trevor put his hands out and I spotted him snapping on a concealed tape recorder. No doubt he was used to interviewing some pretty dicey customers.

"This is absolutely disgusting," burst out Dame Rosy. "I never had much of an opinion of you, Mr Bellingham, and I know all about why you never got higher than Felicidad. I thought you were a silly ass but I never thought you would stop as low as this. Blackmail is a crime, you know. Trevor can get you put away. Don't you realise what is at stake? If this got out, my career would be at an end and Trevor would lose all credibility in human rights circles. We would be reduced to walking Mandela all day and every day. I never cared all that much for the dog."

"Say no more, Rosy," commanded her husband. "You are not helping. I should prefer to come to some civilised accommodation with Mr Bellingham, who has us by the short and curlies, as he well knows."

I smiled, reflecting on how much I had learned from Ludovic Molnar. This was an exciting new career, for which I seemed to have a marked talent.

"Shall we open the negotiations?" suggested Trevor, adopting a slightly unconvincing attitude of perfect calm.

"Not until you turn that tape recorder off," I said. He did so, with a look of grudging admiration.

"How much money do you want?" he asked.

"I do not want money," I replied. "Thanks to my contribution to British exports, I have suddenly become quite rich. What I require is a small service from Dame Rosy which would cost her very little trouble and would never become publicly known."

"And then you would forget?"

"Then I would forget."

"What on earth do you want, Mr Bellingham?" she asked. "You're not having my body, you know. Is it something else?"

I told them.

"You could manage that, Rosy," prompted her husband nervously.

"I could try," said the Minister, barely concealing her contempt and loathing.

"Then I would try too," I said. "But I mustn't keep you longer from your walk. You should still be in time for tea in the delightful old coach house at Kenwood."

"You are an unmitigated scoundrel, Bellingham," opined Trevor Pilkington QC as he showed me out. "But I must admit, I rather admire your nerve."

***

"Why do you have that look on your face, Ambrose?" asked Susan.

"What look, Dear?"

"You seem to have developed a permanent smirk."

"It is simply an expression of placid contentment, my dear. I am thinking of all the malicious people who will have to revise their opinion of me."

"What do you mean?"

"I have received some good news. The Honours Section of Protocol Department in the Foreign and Commonwealth Office have just written to me. The Queen, God bless her, has informally approved a proposal by the Foreign Secretary that I should receive an honour. They wish to be sure that I will accept before the Queen takes her final decision and the award appears in the next honours list."

"How extraordinary," said Susan. "There must be some mistake."

"Why should I not receive an honour?"

"Everyone knows that you don't get an award after you have retired."

"I am being honoured for my services to British exports."

"Oh, how funny!" I found Susan's reaction decidedly unflattering. "Haven't you got an MBE already?"

"This is far superior to the MBE," I retorted with a tingle of asperity. "I am to receive the KCMG."

"What on earth is that?"

"Knight Commander of the Order of Saint Michael and Saint George. Informally known as Kindly Call Me God."

"Do you mean that you are actually going to get a knighthood? You will be Sir Ambrose? Not just knighted by the Raros?"

"Indeed." It was a proud moment.

"So I will be Lady Bellingham!"

"Indeed you will, my dear." I got up and kissed her lightly on the nape of the neck.

"How lovely!" Susan almost screamed, jumping from her chair and kissing me with enthusiasm on the lips. "I never knew you had it in you."

"Nor did I."

"Neville will be so pleased."

"I thought he despised the baubles of this world," I replied.

"Don't be too sure," said Susan. "This will be one in the eye for snooty old Lady Moggeridge. It will go round the village like wildfire."

"Not till after the next honours list, please. Her Majesty has asked me to keep it confidential until then."

When the list did come out my award received, as I had expected, an astonished reaction in British diplomatic circles. The chagrin, nay jealous fury, of my contemporaries was deliciously enjoyable. They simply could not understand it. Of course you retired with a knight-hood from Washington or Paris, or even Rome or Madrid. But the idea of a knighthood for an ex-ambassador to Concordia was not just against the pecking order – it was simply ludicrous. I was being inexplicably promoted from the ranks of the failed Misters to those of the successful Sirs. What would happen next? It was as if, one morning, the sun had failed to rise. Diplomats have tidy minds and do not care for shocks to the system.

My appearances in public rooms at the Voyagers were now doubly enjoyable. I heard whispers as I entered the coffee room, and saw eyes levelled discreetly in my direction. Once, I even heard myself being directly discussed. I had retired to a large armchair for a postprandial nap. I was just nodding off when, behind me, I heard the familiar voices of two of my old sparring partners: Sir Toby Carruthers, formerly our ambassador of Washington; and Sir Launcelot Unsworth, who had just retired from Paris.

"Have you heard about old Ambrose?" asked Toby in his stran-gulated Etonian tenor.

"Yes, indeed," replied Launcelot in his gruff Wykehamist baritone. "Quite extraordinary, isn't it? There must surely be some mistake. Confusion, perhaps, with a more worthy person."

"There could only be one Ambrose Bellingham," pointed out Toby. "He's not exactly like anyone else."

"No, indeed," agreed Launcelot with relish. "What a perfect ass that man was. Do you remember the time he solicited Lady Finkelstein for a hefty donation to the Palestine Liberation Fund?"

"And that telegram he sent from Paraguay suggesting the Prime Minister might call in there for a Burns Night supper on the way to the Falklands. For Ambrose, with his absurd lack of judgement, everywhere he went was the centre of the world."

"It sounds like a dreadful cock-up. I don't know what has happened to the Office since we left."

"Ambrose was quite good fun."

"Do you really think so? He was never in the least witty."

"No, but he was a source of wit in others. Like Malvolio, though

I never actually saw him cross-gartered."

"Where is the silly old chap these days?"

"I neither know nor care."

"He is here, gentlemen," I said suddenly, rising from my chair and making them a low bow. The anguished look on their malicious faces rather made my day.

It was even more fun in Little Bigney. The impertinent juvenile at the garage looked at me with increased respect, even volunteering to check my tyres, perhaps in the hope of a substantial tip. The man with the trumpet next door took to playing 'The Arrival of the Queen of Sheba' when he saw me coming up the front drive. Lady Moggeridge was quick to invite me to open the next church fête, Tracy Snodgrass, with her adenoidal delivery, not having been quite the success anticipated. It was a pleasure to reply that I would be too busy with my international commitments.

The Harrison Bedfords turned up in person to proffer their salutations. My dear Susan received them with her usual warmth but with a certain tinge of embarrassment. I could see that her unexpected title of My Lady would take some getting used to, whereas I had taken to my knighthood like a duck to water.

"Hearty congratulations, Ambrose," boomed the Admiral, crushing my paw in a vice-like grip. "I always knew that Susan was a lady."

"Congratulations from me too," said the submissive Griselda. I thought she looked sad. Living with Rowley would not be all beer and skittles, though Susan seemed to be able to get on with him.

"We've decided to do one of your plays at the amateur dramatic," said the Admiral in his usual quarterdeck manner. "We picked on the shorter one, *The Tame Pigeon*. I liked the scene where the henpecked hero turns on his bossy wife. Not quite the situation around here!"

"Ibsen in reverse," I pointed out, feeling secretly rather delighted. I would invite the Ambassador of Concordia down for the opening night.

I decided to resign from the Voyagers. One had endured enough of the sustained hostility of my old colleagues. But I still needed a

London club. Fortunately at this moment I received the welcome news that I had been elected to membership of the Sheridan. It was a thrilling moment when I found myself standing in the bar next to Sir Emrys Merioneth, the elderly thespian.

"Good evening, Sir," I said. "I remember you so well as Macbeth at the Old Vic. You quite made my hair stand on end."

"In the theatre," replied the old trouper, "we don't refer to that drama by name. It is considered unlucky. We call it the Scottish play."

"I'm sorry. You were wonderful as King Lear too at the National."

"That production was an immense strain. One has to carry on the hanged Cordelia in the last act. A marvellously poignant moment. Not a dry eye in the house. Unfortunately Cordelia was a tall, stocky girl with a highly developed bone structure. I nearly ruptured my back at one of the matinees."

"May I have the honour of buying you a drink, Sir?"

"You may indeed," replied Sir Emrys promptly. "A pint of the best champagne please, my dear boy." There would be many such exciting moments at the Sheridan.

Father Manfred wrote to congratulate me, inviting me to come and stay at Calderbeck for a weekend as a matter of some urgency. I felt obliged to accept.

"It's good to see you here again," said the headmaster, as we sat in his study after High Mass on Sunday. "One likes to keep in touch with the more eminent parents. How is Neville, by the way?"

"He is still in the south of Spain, I believe," I said. "No news is good news."

"A remarkable young man," said Father Manfred pensively, "but unfortunately with a totally over-optimistic assessment of his own abilities in the realm of theology. Now let me tell you about our trouble here. As you know, construction was started on the Raro Business Centre. But it has had to be stopped because no money is now available. You will see for yourself how awful the uncompleted shell looks, so near to the Abbey church. What are we to do? I would even be prepared to take Dominic back as a day-boy, if the Raros could resume the flow of their generosity."

"That will be quite impossible," I said. "The Raros are hunted fugitives. Nobody knows where they are."

"A pity. They may have had faults but they also had funds. Do you know any other very rich people?"

"Only one," I answered thoughtfully. "If you are so desperate, I'll have a go."

"Thank you, Ambrose. We will pray for you."

***

"Come in, Sir Ambrose," said Ludovic Molnar in his usual hearty way. "Please forgive my state of undress. As you see, my darling Ilona is giving me one of her wonderful massages."

How hairy his back was, I thought. I had a mental picture of a younger Ludo running in moonlight with the wolves on the endless plains of the Hungarian *puszta*.

"That's enough, angel," he said to his voluptuous paramour. "Ambrose and I have got to talk secrets now." Blowing me a kiss, Ilona withdrew and Ludo put on a silk dressing-gown. We sat by the window with its incomparably expensive view over the Green Park towards the Palace.

"Sensational news this morning about Dame Rosy Clumber," he said with satisfaction.

"I haven't heard," I said. "I was in the train from Lancaster."

"The woman has been moved from the Foreign Office. She is being succeeded by Joyce Adekunle, the Member for Mile End."

"And what about Dame Rosy?"

"She is becoming Minister for the Ziggurat!"

"The Ziggurat! That will be the kiss of death," I said. "Number Ten must be trying to wreck her career."

"That would be my reading too. I suppose they considered her expendable." Molnar gave one of his nasty grins.

"She seemed to be enjoying herself in the Foreign Office, throwing her weight around," I said. "I got the impression that the Foreign

Secretary allowed her to reign supreme over large areas of foreign policy. Including, of course, Concordia."

"That was the trouble, I gather," said Ludovic. "My spies within the Foreign Office tell me that she overreached herself in the end. Something about a highly unsuitable recommendation for a senior honour which she managed to slip through when the Foreign Secretary thought he was approving something quite different. When it came out, the permanent officials were wild with rage and demanded her blood. What makes you smirk like that, my dear Sir Ambrose?"

We raised our morning glasses of champagne in a silent toast. There was no need for words. We understood each other only too well.

"What brings you here so early?" continued Ludovic. "Presumably you want something else out of me."

"Don't you think," I said reproachfully, "that I might enjoy the pleasure of your company for its own sake."

"Nobody ever has." There was pathos in his tone.

"Well, it's about Calderbeck Abbey." I briefly explained Father Manfred's dilemma over the incomplete and now unfunded Business Centre. I named the alarming figure still to be found.

"You want me to donate this money?" he asked.

"That was my hope. I know nobody else rich enough to do so."

"I will think about it," conceded Ludovic. "I might be able to help, if asked very nicely. I could promote the abbey choir in a CD of angelic music. They might well make the Top Ten. But the Business Centre would then have to be called after me."

"I feel sure that would be acceptable."

"The Molnar Business Centre, ceremonially opened by the Cardinal after High Mass at the Abbey. Made possible by the amazing generosity of Count Ludovic Molnar, so called because the Holy See have just made him a Papal Count. Not bad for a poor boy from the back of beyond. One of my first jobs, you know, at the age of twelve, was to launder and darn the priestly robes in the Benedictine monastery at Pannonhalma. It was conveniently near the Austrian border."

"You are very generous," I murmured.

"Not really. I just believe in using my money to promote my ambitions. I'll let you into another of my little confidences. That arms deal wasn't my only interest in Concordia. Oh no, I had much bigger fish to fry. The really huge scoop was getting Fernandez to promise full compensation to the British investors for his country's takeover of the emerald mines. At that time, the shares were at rock bottom. Nobody wanted to buy them because no compensation was in prospect. So I acquired them all for a song. I became the legal proprietor of those damned mines. The compensation is now coming to me. The shares are worth a fortune."

He scratched his chin and grinned, looking more than ever like some overgrown gnome.

"Congratulations," I said coldly, remembering that it was I who had extracted that valuable concession from the Liberator.

"You sound a bit sour, Ambrose," said Ludo. "Don't worry. Your helpful services will be recognised. I intend to make you a present of some highly attractive shares in my new timeshare project. Imagine the adverts on the Internet: Enjoy the adventure holidays of a lifetime. Book for a fortnight every year in the unspoiled and tranquil woodland wonderland of inner Concordia. Enjoy its teeming insect and animal life, and the opportunity to study at close quarters the exotic habits of rural tribes unsullied by civilisation. That could be quite a winner, I think."

"A superb opportunity to get your tiresome wife eaten by the headhunters, and your noisy brats devoured by basking crocodiles," I suggested.

"They won't know that, will they, until they have paid the money. That's the beauty of a timeshare. You have to shell out for all those delightful holidays in advance."

What on earth had induced me, I wondered, to go into business with this appalling crook? It was hardly the usual way for a British diplomat of the old school to employ his well-earned retirement.

"Now I'll confide to you anther of my little schemes," continued

Molnar, inspired perhaps by the excellent champagne. "I have decided to sell some of my emerald shares and use the proceeds to make a huge donation to party funds."

"Which party?"

"That really doesn't matter, does it? The point is that the party chairman has been most obliging. I am shortly to become a peer. I have decided to take the title of Lord Molnar of Esterhazy. You know how I love music. Prince Esterhazy was the great patron of Haydn, and his huge palace is still to be seen in western Hungary."

"You, a peer of the realm?" I gasped.

"Why not? I have had British citizenship for years, you know. They think I will be very useful in the House of Lords with my business flair. Besides, they are committed to greater representation for the immigrant minorities."

"So, my dear Ludo, you are becoming one of the vermin in ermine."

"It is a beautiful success story, is it not? You must lunch with me in the House some day. They have an excellent restaurant, subsidised by the kind-hearted British taxpayer, and they will pay me an allowance every day I go there. As the Bible points out: To him that hath, more shall be given."

"Could I become a peer too?" I suggested. "Lord Bellingham of Little Bigney?"

"Don't push your luck, Ambrose."

"They don't know that you helped the Raros to avoid arrest, do they, Ludovic?"

"No, they don't. And you are unlikely to tell them because you yourself have so much to hide."

"All the same," I said, "for sheer curiosity I should love to know where the Raros are now."

"Marsala's American associates arranged with their Russian partners to spirit them off to Siberia. There's a town there near Novosibirsk, which was specially built by Kruschev in the Golden Valley on the Ob River to house forty thousand scientists. They weren't sent there as prisoners, but to enjoy special facilities for research. They had a university, an artificial beach, illuminated ski runs. Quite a pleasant spot, I gather, though nowadays somewhat run down. The boy has joined them there, and they should be safe. I'm thinking of using that venue if I do develop my idea of establishing a secure haven for retired tyrants. That could be a real money-spinner."

"You are truly a universal man, Lord Molnar. I don't know why you bother to live in this overtaxed little island."

"Why not? I love Britain. I feel very much at home here. Other nations are equally corrupt, but there is something quite wonderful about the coating of hypocrisy with which you cover your immoral behaviour. The French know they are wicked, but you delicious British actually believe that you are good."

"There is something to be said for hypocrisy," I replied. "It has been called the tribute that vice pays to virtue."

"That is delightfully English. My point exactly."

"You have become cynical, Ludovic, through mixing with evil people. But there are good people also in this world."

"I will take your word for that, Sir Ambrose. All I can say is, I have yet to encounter them in any great number. You may come back, Ilona. There is time for a romp before luncheon."

***

Now that Ludovic had fixed me up with a lease on a handy bachelor pad in Curzon Street for use during the week, I was free to devote myself to my new career of freelance fixer and man-about-town. Susan was behaving very sensibly – happy enough to see me for the weekends and, during the week, to devote her time to gardening and blameless village pursuits. Except on the occasions when I was being taken out to fancy restaurants by members of Molnar's business circle, who hoped to get something out of me, I tended to eat most of my meals at the Sheridan club. In fact, I was becoming quite an institution there, well known among the congenial group who propped up the bar every morning, tottering down to luncheon all together just before last orders at two o'clock. I had been obliged to avoid Sir Emrys Merioneth, who kept hailing me in the expectation of receiving more pints of champagne at my expense, but there were other show business stars to whom I had now become well known. It was a glamorous existence after the rustic solitude of Little Bigney.

I was seated at lunch one day at the centre table, toying with a juicy steak washed down by the club's incomparable claret, and exchanging badinage with my neighbours on my right and left: a vivacious High Court judge, and a senior member of the Royal Shakespeare Company, who had just scored a hit as Polonius – a role in which he hardly needed to act. To my slight annoyance, the head porter appeared and tapped me on the shoulder in the middle of an anecdote.

"Excuse me, Sir Ambrose," he murmured. They were strong on names and I had made sure they registered my knighthood. "There is a gentlemen at the door who wants to see you. He says he's your son."

"Ask him to wait, please," I said with a sinking heart. The prospect of Neville appearing in person at the Sheridan was the stuff of nightmare. I could imagine his appearance only too well; the haggard, unwashed countenance; the lank, greasy hair; the pauper's overcoat; the ragged-collared shirt; the scuffed old shoes. It really was a shame that he should embarrass me so in front of my high-profile new friends, who thought of me as a dapper diplomat with, like the late Sir Noel, a talent to amuse. But I dared not send the boy away. He might make a scene or send me an offensive message just when the director-general of the BBC was entering his chauffeur-driven limousine.

With a heavy heart, I descended the steps to the main door, where my visitor was waiting. To my surprise, there was no sign of Neville. The only person there to be welcomed was a beautifully dressed young man wearing a dark overcoat with astrakhan collar, under which could be glimpsed a stiff white collar and a smart grey tie kept in place by a pearl-studded tiepin. A tasteful black hat, leather gloves, a stick with a lovely handle of glistening amber, and a pair of neat, handmade black shoes completed his ensemble. The total effect was perhaps a trifle old-fashioned but it was encouraging to see a young person who had bothered to tog himself up correctly to visit a gentlemen's club. The promising son of some more fortunate Member, I thought with bitterness and jealousy, thinking of the unkempt appearance of my lone offspring. I smiled approvingly at the young Adonis, whose features seemed vaguely familiar.

But where on earth was my own son? There was no sign of those long, greasy locks or that dreadful overcoat picked up (perhaps only too literally) at an Oxfam shop in the Holloway Road. I was about to round on the porter and demand an explanation, when the young Beau Brummell addressed me.

"Hello, Dad," he said.

"Neville!" I exclaimed. "I hardly recognised you."

"Thought it would give you a shock, Dad. Hope I'm not disturbing you."

"Have you had lunch?" I asked.

"Yes, thank you. They gave me a bite at Boodles."

"Come and have coffee and a brandy then." This was a child of whom one could be legitimately proud.

"And now tell me," I said, as we ensconced ourselves in a comfortable corner of the Smoking Room, "what on earth has come over you? Whence this dramatic sea change? Very much for the better, I must say."

"All the world's a stage, Dad. You must have noticed that for yourself. One has to dress for the part."

"I gather that you are now moving in more affluent circles?"

"You could say that. The truth is that I am now a Grandee of Spain. I'm so glad you made me learn a bit of Spanish in Concordia."

"You are a what?"

"A member of the Grandeza, one of the highest aristocracy. You will find us in the Almanach de Gotha."

"My dear boy, this is quite beyond your old father. I am Sir Ambrose now, by the way, and your mother is a Lady. You will have to explain."

"Well, you remember my Spanish school-friend Jaime Damiel,

with whom I have been staying in Seville? He had this sexy little cousin Isabella, whom we boys used to lust after. She's still sexy and, what is more, she is now a duchess."

"You mean, she is married to a duke."

"No. Her father was a Spanish duke. He died and Isabella was his only child. So, under Spanish law, she became a duchess in her own right. The Duchess of Miraflores-Santiponce, though she has seventeen other titles."

"Good heavens! But I still do not understand why this has had such a dramatic effect on your wardrobe and personal grooming."

"Everyone wanted to marry Isabella after that, because whoever did would become a duke himself. There were carloads of sharp-faced lads arriving from Amsterdam and Stockholm. But Isabella's a sensible lass. She didn't bother with any of those. She decided to marry me. I think she was fascinated with the idea of going to bed with an ex-hermit. Anyway, we were married quite quietly in the family chapel to avoid a lot of fuss. Sorry we hadn't got time to alert you and Mum. I'm going to see Mum this afternoon. She always wanted me to make something of myself, and I have. I am the Duke of Miraflores-Santiponce, usually addressed as 'Excelentissimo'."

"You astonish me. I will admit, you certainly look the part. But where is Isabella?"

"She went to Madrid to try to calm her numerous grand relations. They won't really mind when they know I am at least a nominal Roman Catholic. By the way, I have the other seventeen titles too, but you can't really use them all at once."

"Is there any chance that you could spare one for your mother and myself? I should like to be a Spanish marquess."

"Sorry, Dad. It doesn't work like that. But Sir Ambrose is pretty cool."

"I suppose," I said hopefully, "that you are terribly rich."

"Isabella is theoretically. In land, palaces, pictures by Goya and El Greco and all that. But," he added hastily, "there's only a limited amount of actual cash. Isabella gives me a monthly allowance, and I've been spending most of it on clothes. *La bella figura*, as they say.

You taught us about that in your embassy days."

"You are a great credit to us, Neville," I said, "but how are you going to employ your time from now on?"

"I'm taking flamenco lessons. And I shall be running the palaces. Her uncle offered to train me as a gentleman matador, but I think that could be dangerous."

"My head is still whirling," I said. It would be delightful to be able to refer to 'my son, the Duke of Miraflores-Santiponce'. That would surely do much for one's social cachet.

"But what about Sharon?" I continued. "Surely this is going to be a terrific blow for her? She was so much against titles and all that."

"Sharon?" asked the young Duke. I could see that he had momentarily forgotten her. "We are a bit out of touch. I understand that she is in Concordia. You know they're having a sort of mini war there now. General Golosina is deploying his squad of Amazon Women. They are believed to be the most effective part of his army. So the Liberator formed a counter-squad called the Fighting Females, and Sharon went to join them. Damned risky, I should think, but you know how strongly she felt about the future of the world."

"Good luck to Sharon, but Isabella sounds a better bet for you. Are you making each other happy?"

"Delirious, Dad. That celibacy lark is much overrated."

"My dear boy," I said warmly, as the young duke lolled beside me in a huge club armchair. "You are a chip off the old block."

Neville smiled saucily. "I should prefer to call myself, Dad, a block off the old chip."

***

"It's lovely to get away from the ship," said Susan, "if only for the afternoon."

"An afternoon in Venice!" I exclaimed. "Isn't it wonderful here on the Grand Canal?" We sat taking our coffee in the sunshine. It was a Canaletto day. Nearly opposite us rose the baroque splendour of the Salute and upstream we could see the beautiful arch of the

Accademia Bridge.

We were enjoying a Mediterranean cruise on the magnificent liner *Paradise* owned by Dreamscape Cruises. This was a top-of-the-market enterprise, and the prices charged to paying passengers were phenomenal. Fortunately we were travelling at the expense of the company. I had been enrolled as a guest lecturer and was giving a series of informative talks on 'Memories of a Diplomatic Career.' We had been slightly disappointed on embarking at Barcelona not to be allotted one of the luxurious suites on the promenade deck with their own helicopter pad. But, as Susan pointed out, one must not be greedy, and we did not really need a helicopter pad. We had made ourselves quite happy in our own capacious state room, somewhat nearer the waterline, where room service provided an unending flow of free food and drink.

There had been a splendidly large and eager audience, nearly all American, for my opening talk, which dealt with my early youth and first posting – to Montevideo. After that, the audience figures had declined abruptly for some reason, which the cruise director politely ascribed to competition with the sunshine on deck and water volleyball in the pool. As many of the prosperous passengers seemed to belong to the criminal fringe, I felt that it was salutary for them to be exposed to the old-world manners of an English knight of the realm and his gracious lady. Susan alleged that we had only been invited because I had a knighthood, and certainly there had been a marked shortage of such offers when I was only a humble Mister. It was good now to be away from England at a time when the Ziggurat riots were tearing the nation in half.

Suddenly I noticed the couple at the next table. Could it possibly be? Yes, it really was. I hastily averted my gaze but it was too late. The massive man, who looked like a tug-of-war champion gone badly to seed, waved breezily in my direction. So did his companion, a glamorously dressed female, not perhaps in the first flush of youth but still provocatively nubile. The very sight of her at that moment filled me with horror.

"Hi, Ambrose baby," shouted General Golosina.

"Hello, Darling," yelled Casilda, reputed Condesa de las Rosas.

"Who are those extraordinary people?" whispered Susan.

We exchanged greetings, Susan at length remembering that she had met Tiberio in our old days at Felicidad. I explained the reason for our being in Venice.

"I heard you got a knighthood," said Tiberio cordially. "Well done, Sir Bellingham."

"It is a pity that our son is not with us," I said casually. "He has to be in Seville for the fiesta, now that he is the Duke of Miraflores-Santiponce." Casilda eyed me with new respect.

"What are you doing here?" I asked.

General Golosina lowered his voice to a decibel level not much higher than a normal bellow.

"We are here incognito," he tried to whisper. "You may have heard that I threw in the sponge, leaving the ring to Fernandez. I'd had enough mayhem, Ambrose. I'm a peaceable guy at heart, and that killing stuff is not really my scene. So we left Concordia and disbanded the Amazon Women. Now I'm on the run. Trevor Pilkington has been empowered by Interpol to organise a massive search for me. We're only safe here because Sylvester Marsala sent him a bum steer to the effect that I was up in Alaska, so he's in Anchorage with his team at the moment. I hope he gets frostbite. I believe that boldness is the best disguise. That's why we are staying at the Daniele."

"What happens next?"

"We are boarding a Russian ship here tomorrow. I have been offered a fascinating new job. Head of Security for the City of Novosibirsk with special responsibility for the Ob River Riviera. And, best of all, my darling Casilda is coming with me."

"I couldn't leave you alone, Gorgeous," said Casilda in that low, husky voice which had once worked me up to paroxysms of lustful rapture. "Some other designing hussy would have got her mits on my lovely strong man."

"Casilda is taking over the Ballet Company of Western Siberia in the opera house of Novosibirsk. It seats eight thousand. You know she has a terpsichorean past." Golosina gave her a look of almost avuncular pride.

"I am so happy to see you, Ambrose," the woman cooed. "And to meet your lovely wife. She is so beautiful," she added unconvincingly.

"Thank you," replied Susan in a rather frosty voice.

"We shall not be alone in Novosibirsk," continued Golosina. "Other friends are there already."

"So I understand," I said cautiously.

"From there we shall organise our fightback, to show the world that we never meant any harm. I shall write my memoirs. Marsala has found a publisher already in Palermo, Sicily. As you know, the world is his oyster."

"We have to get back to our ship now," I said. "She is berthed across there, on the Zattere."

"What a pity," said the former Chief of Police. "I was going to invite you to join us this evening for a concert. They are doing one of my favourites, the *Magnificat* of Vivaldi, in Saint Mark's. I adore that church. Dark and devious, like me."

"We could have done some shopping together," said Casilda to Susan. "Venice is glorious for leather and glass. I am sure we should have had much to talk about."

"Susan and I don't think much about Concordia," I said hastily. "We live for the future."

"Don't forget the past though, my dear Ambrose," retorted the false *condesa*. "Yours is so very interesting."

"Yours too, I have no doubt," I retorted sharply. One could see that beneath the surface bonhomie, the woman was full of bile.

"Needless to say," said General Golosina, "we would beg you not to tell anyone that you have seen us here. We have still to reach our promised haven in Novosibirsk."

"Your secrets are safe with me," I said.

"And yours with us," added Casilda provocatively, with a pointed look in the direction of my poor Susan.

Later that day, we sat sipping our complimentary champagne in the comfort of our state room while the great ship slipped through the lagoon on its way to Dubrovnik. Susan was staring at me in a slightly disturbing manner, indicating that her mental processes were unusually active.

"Is there something wrong, Dear?" I asked at last.

"Not really, Ambrose. I was intrigued to meet that woman. She had a curious attitude towards you. Almost proprietorial."

"What on earth do you mean, Susan?"

"Well, it was obvious that you had been to bed with her."

"How could you possibly know?"

"One always knows. I don't understand how. Come on, Darling, let's have it out. You had an affair with her in Felicidad, didn't you?"

"Hardly an affair," I retorted, aghast. "I believe they call it a one-night stand. I was awfully sorry about it afterwards. I thought how I had let you down."

"Yes, you did."

"Will you ever forgive me? I'm not going to follow her to Siberia, you know."

"Of course I'll forgive you," said Susan, with a smile. "I have to, don't I, considering what I got up to while you were away."

"What can you possibly mean, Susan?"

"Surely you must have spotted that I had a tremendous fling with Rowley when you left me so much alone? I thought it was so decent of you not to say anything about it."

"Rowley! That abominable admiral?"

"Do you really mean that you hadn't realised? Oh, you poor innocent sweetie! Why did you think that Griselda went away to her mother's?"

"But he's old and fat!"

"I'm used to that, Ambrose. He's still very keen in bed."

"Are you planning to continue this affair?" I asked coldly.

"Certainly not, Dear. We broke off weeks ago."

"You're not leaving me then?"

"How could I, when you are so hopeless at managing on your own? You will forgive me, won't you, Darling?"

"I'm not at all sure," I riposted. "I'm absolutely disgusted."

"But it's only what you did, Ambrose."

"That was different," I said, giving my faithless partner a long, cool, glance of shocked reproach.

***

It was the great day of the investiture. I had come to the Palace to receive my knighthood. I had brought with me my dear Susan, now restored to favour, together with our photogenic offspring Neville accompanied by his wife Isabella. We were all beautifully turned out and afterwards would be adjourning to the Sheridan for a celebratory lunch. Susan and the children, as we playfully called them, had been directed with the other family members and friends to the investiture chamber itself, where a military band was entertaining with selections from *The Merry Widow*. I and the other recipients of honours were established next door in a large anteroom, waiting for the signal to come forward and present ourselves to the Queen. We were a motley bunch, ranging upwards from humble people scheduled to receive minor honours for meritorious service, right up to major players, like myself, who were to be dubbed with the award of a knighthood. I am by nature a modest man, but on this special occasion one did feel inclined to indulge in a little mild preening. In Japan one would have been designated as a living national treasure.

Looking round for someone worth meeting, I was surprised to see the small dapper form of Archdeacon Harry Wilderness.

"What are you doing here?" I asked.

"I have come to receive an MBE, Sir Ambrose. I can't think why I got one, but I did."

"Congratulations," I said urbanely. "Are you still living in Concordia?"

"Oh yes. It is a wonderful place now. Imagine a country ruled by a completely honest and good man, dedicated only to the welfare of his people. You should see for yourself, Sir Ambrose. It might restore your faith in human nature."

"It sounds like a most unusual experiment," I commented drily. "Just the kind of Utopia where you could risk thrusting your hand into the den of the basilisk."

"Well, the war is over now," added the Archdeacon happily. "They shall not hurt, nor shall they kill in all my holy mountain. I am very close to the Liberator, you know. I report every day to the presidential palace to advise him on ethical problems. Sylvester Marsala acts as a sort of prime minister. He's tremendously useful because of his international business contacts, and he's making the economy quite prosperous in various ways, which have not been explained to me. But I have direct access to the Liberator on all moral issues. He wants me to become Cardinal Archbishop at Felicidad. You will remember that the present prince of the Church is well advanced in years."

"But surely you are an Anglican?"

"I have always been very ecumenical. The President is negotiating a new concordat with the Holy See whereby there will be a system of fast-track promotions for outstanding clergy converting to the Catholic Church, on the precedent of Cardinal Newman."

"Good Heavens! What a farrago of improbabilities that place always was. Sometimes I think of it as a dreamland. But I am glad you are doing so well, Harry. I think you may be the only good man I have ever met."

"You should get to know the Liberator better, Sir Ambrose. Do you know what he is doing now? He has decided to use his Fellowship of the Royal College of Surgeons for the benefit of the nation. He gives public masterclasses in root canal filling and wisdom tooth extraction. These have attracted many young dental surgeons, especially from Mexico and even the United States. They are encouraged to combine the course with white-water rafting adventures in the Tozudo heartlands. Concordia is fast becoming a world leader in dental tourism."

"You amaze me," I said.

"The regime has a heroine too," continued Harry with his usual unfocussed enthusiasm. "She is called La Purificadora and she played a vital part in the Battle Against Evil, as we call the recent confrontation with General Golosina."

"What exactly did she do?"

"She led the international brigade of the Fighting Females, and they did a wonderful job in hand-to-hand combat and burning down enemy property. She does a lot of public speaking now, addressing the masses. Admittedly her Spanish is still a bit halting but she *was* born in England. That stage name is perhaps unfortunate. So easily confused with the Concordian Spanish word for laxative. Come to think of it, you know her, Ambrose. She is a girl called Sharon, who was once engaged to your son, I understand."

"Neville has moved into a totally new sphere," I said with dignity. "He is here today with his young wife. They are the Duke and Duchess of Miraflores-Santiponce."

"How odd," said the little Archdeacon. "But then human creatures are strangely constituted, aren't they?"

"Fifty per cent of the human gene is shared with the banana," I remarked. "We have only one thousand genes more than the humble mouse."

"Could that really be true of the great saints?"

"I find it hard to believe in great saints," I said. "Or even in a sharp distinction between goodies and baddies, as silly Dame Rosy used to do. I see myself as the only serious central character moving through a vast comic novel, peopled with a wealth of absurd eccentrics designed to make one laugh."

"Oh, I don't know, Ambrose," said Archdeacon Wilderness. "You're quite funny too."

I was about to meet this rare flash of spirit with one of my thunderous put-downs, when we were interrupted by the cultivated voice of our attendant courtier.

"Ladies and gentlemen, please prepare to move forward," he said. "Her Majesty is ready to begin."

6

"Wake up, Ambrose," said Susan. "You've been asleep for hours. You know what happens when you nap after lunch. You will be up half the night, complaining of indigestion."

"I have been recharging my batteries," I countered coldly.

"There's an envelope for you, my dear," continued my over-attentive wife. "It comes from that horrible place Concordia."

It certainly looked decorative, bearing the presidential palace arms and an elaborate picture of the presidential palace in Felicidad. Inside was a personal letter to me from the Liberator himself. He was enthusiastic about this dental masterclasses, now attracting so many young disciples. This called for an expansion of the University of Felicidad.

He had been advised by La Purificadora, who remembered me well, to invite me to come at once and take over the prestigious position of chancellor of the university. In that capacity he hoped I would give a series of lectures on great warrior dentists. I might start with the Czar Peter the Great, who had adopted dentistry as one of his principal diversions. He had delighted in publicly extracting the teeth of his most prominent courtiers, with or without their prior permission.

Was the Liberator moving in the same direction? I realised with a thrill of horror that his regime could well become quite as dictatorial and malevolent as that of his predecessor. So much for his idealistic pretensions of running a new Utopia! It could all develop into a version of Animal Farm.

"They want me to go back," I gasped.

"And what have you decided?" asked my loyal wife, with one

of her pained looks.

"I think I shall stay here," I replied, "with you, my darling. It is all so pleasantly uneventful."

Susan looked pleased but somewhat surprised, as she escorted me indoors for a substantial afternoon tea.

"Did you see *The Times* today?" I asked. "Sir Gregory Capulet has died at ninety-two. We shall have to go to the memorial service."

He had once been so majestic a figure in my young life. Thank God, I thought, I at least was still alive.

About the Author

Born in 1928, the son of a doctor in Saint John's Wood, London. Educated at Arnold House School in London and Bembridge School, a progressive independent school evacuated to the Lake District during the war. From there he won an Open Scholarship to Brasenose College, Oxford. There he took part in amateur shows with people like Sandy Wilson, Donald Swann, John Schlesinger and Ken Tynan who achieved fame in the theatre. He left Oxford in 1949 with an Honours Degree in Modern History.

The next two years were spent in the Army on military service. Having begun in the Rifle Brigade, he ended up as a commissioned officer in the Royal Army Educational Corps and then as an Intelligence Officer at a Brigade Headquarters on Salisbury Plain. He also directed a production of *Arsenic and Old Lace* which toured widely, being especially successful at the Porton Down Germ Warfare Centre!

In 1951 he passed the exam for the Senior Branch of the Foreign Service where he worked until retiring at the age of sixty in 1988. He served in a variety of posts throughout the world; such as Washington, Laos in Indo-China, Argentina, Turkey and Nigeria. In the Foreign Office itself he also had a number of interesting positions such as Private Secretary to the Secretary of State (the temperamental George Brown) and later Head of the Personnel Department sending people round the world, which gave him a further opportunity to explore from Chile to south Africa and then Japan.

He married in 1960 Jenifer Mathews, the daughter of a Hatton Garden expert in precious stones. She tragically died in 1981. They had three sons and two grandchildren. He is now happy again with a civil partnership.

In 1976 he was promoted to the rank of Ambassador. From then until retirement he served as Ambassador to Hungary, Spain and Sweden, passing the Foreign Office language exams in Hungarian and Turkish. He was awarded the honour of Knight Commander of St Michael and St George in 1982. He also served as Leader of the UK Delegation to the European Security Conference in Belgrade in 1978, which involved publicly debating with the Russians and their Allies on the subject of human rights. Never a dull moment.

On retirement he has served in several honorary positions such as Governor of the Sadler's Wells Trust and later the Hospital Trust in King's Lynn, and also the Chairmanship of the Ruskin Foundation and now of the West Norfolk Musical Society. He has also travelled widely as a lecturer on Swan Hellenic and other cruise ships including four visits to Australia where he was nearly eaten by a crocodile.

In addition he has pursued a literary career. Apart from his first story, published in *The Nursery World* when he was seven years old, his second career really began in 1967 when his first novel *None of Us Cared For Kate* was published by Cassell (and Dutton in New York) under the pseudonym of John Haythorne to avoid giving his superiors the impression of frivolity! Four more novels have since been published and so the new venture by the Melrose Press will be his sixth novel. During this time he received support from his agents in both Curtis Brown and Peters, Fraser and Dunlop until they sadly retired and died respectively.

He has also written for the stage, his plays having been produced professionally at the King's Head Theatre in Islington and a dozen other fringe theatres in London, Brighton and Edinburgh. His plays have been published by Samuel French, earning royalties from some unlikely spots. He is particularly big in Bangalore! Finally, the periodical *Poetry Today* has published several of his poems. So it has been a full life and still goes on!